PASSAGEWAY

STEVEN A. COULTER

BOOK 2

HOMO SAPIENS FUTURIS

JUBILATION MEDIA

San Francisco

Published by Jubilation 2024

ISBN: 979-8-9854814-8-8 (Paperback)
ISBN: 979-8-9854814-7-1 (ebook)

Cover design by Jeff Brown
Chapter illustrations by Billy Bacsko, OwlGhost Studios
Interior book design and formatting by Erin Stocco, modernbookdesign.com
Content editing by Katherine V. Forrest

Other books by this author:

Copperhead (published 2023)
Copperhead 2 (published 2024)
Rising Son, The Chronicles of Spartak (Book 1) (published 2017)
Freedom's Hope, The Chronicles of Spartak (Book 2) (published 2018)

*"In an infinite multiverse,
there is no such thing as fiction."*

—Scott Adsit, American actor

GLOSSARY OF TERMS

The Multiverse. The theory that the expanding universe around us is but one in an unimaginably massive ocean of universes.

The Three Earths. Nearly identical, each is approximately five hundred years apart in history.

E1: Earth 1, the 26th century.
E2: Earth 2, the 21st century
E3: Earth 3, the 17th century.

Passageway. An underground access point set in 21st century Earth allowing travel to either of the other Earths, origin unknown.

Buena Vista Park. An urban forest in approximately the center of San Francisco.

The Cabin. Where Uncle His lives in a side niche in Buena Vista Park. A small, inconspicuous single-story building purchased around the time of the Gold Rush with secret hallways leading down into the Passageway.

The Guardians. Twelve indigenous warriors from the 17th century with 26th century equipment and mental enhancements. Protectors of the indigenous New World (North, Central and South America) from interference from Europe or any other continent. Here, America does not exist.

Homo Sapiens Futuris. The term for how humans may evolve over the centuries.

Canoe. A 26th century hydrogen-driven, invisible two-seat aircraft. Stored under the cabin in BV Park.

Warbird. Also called **Mars.** A 26th century all-purpose fighter plane and science laboratory.

MAJOR CHARACTERS

Uncle His. Also known as **Katnu Hisman**. The first Guardian, the leader. Two hundred years old. Has known personally many of the U.S. Presidents.

Darwin McQuaid. A seventeen-year-old senior at Beckman High School in the Haight-Ashbury neighborhood in San Francisco. First encountered Daruk while being pursued by bullies.

Daruk. Also seventeen, from Earth 3. Darwin's lover. Adopted by Katnu Hisman, he is a skilled warrior who has lived periodically in the Buena Vista cabin.

Miguel Medina. Darwin's sassy, best friend since boyhood.

1.

Maia stepped with precision through the forest, moving as a ghost, not daring to risk waking the boy and having him cry out, alerting the killers. The raven-haired teen inched between the shoulder high ferns, moving every frond so as to leave each Huckleberry branch, laden with dark berries, intact. As always there must be no sign she was ever here. She and her people had lived this way beyond memory, sometimes near the humans but always invisible. Until now.

Legend said the mountain had been ripped by glaciers thousands of years before, carving the granite into deep valleys, leaving scores of streams and small lakes glistening like jewels, endless meadows full of wildflowers and deer, boundless stands of rock, forests thick with redwoods, pines, maple, red alder, Douglas fir, western hemlock. But she had no time to enjoy the beauty. She glanced at the dramatic rock formation above, carved like a howling wolf.

Ahead, to the right, a redwood had long ago collapsed against some rock, its bark covered in moss and small ferns, leaving a small hollow where she might hide. She inched through open grass and squeezed into the hidden space. Settling down and comforting her newborn, she reminded herself that carelessness had allowed the strangers to find them. She stood, stepping out and, noticing some indentations in the forest floor, held a knife in her hand and raised her arm, closed her eyes and chanted in a whisper. Slowly, the soil shifted and leveled; her scent evaporated. Satisfied, she slipped back into the dark crevice. The child started to whimper. She opened her robe and lifted out a breast. The boy giggled happily and grabbed hold.

She heard shouting, coming closer. A group of killers. When they came across her campsite just days ago, their language made no sense but they'd gestured that they came in peace. But the strangers took out their weapons, different than any they had seen before.

She watched their images on the medallion around her neck as four humans came within a dozen feet and looked around, searching for a trail. Finding none, they cursed and split up, by-passing her position. She looked at the knife in her hand, the carved bone handle, the brilliant silver blade covered in sigils and glyphs. It was powerful if she had a chance to use it, knowing that she was less skilled than others.

Her people were dead. It was her fault because she was careless and let the humans find them. She and her son were the last.

Then the baby giggled again, his lips swollen and red.

2.

"The Russian Wilderness? You want to take me to Siberia? That's a terrible idea." Stretching out and fluffing my pillow, still sleepy, I was surprised at the suggestion from Daruk.

He rolled onto his side and reached over, effortlessly pulling me tight to him on the bed. I loved it when he took charge. Sometimes I did, although with a lot more effort. He kissed me lightly on the lips, a forearm under my head, a hand dancing over my chest and down lower.

I laughed. He was such an optimist. "I don't think anything is alive down there after all we did this morning. And last night. And earlier last night. And yesterday afternoon, and…."

"Is it my fault that you are irresistible?" he interrupted. "I love you, Darwin McQuaid, my handsome boyfriend. The Russian Wilderness is in Northern California, not Russia. It is adjacent to two other major wilderness areas and is beautiful to visit, relaxing. It is all roadless and serves as a major habitat for wildlife in the region with very few people passing through. It is not as magnificent as some of the forests in my world, but it is close. I think you will find it regenerative. We both need that after what we have been through."

"My handsome travel guide. At least it's still on my earth." As opposed to his, five hundred years in the past through the Passageway, a time portal to a world we called E3; mine was E2, earth in the 21st century. "Just so you know, I'm waiting for you to use a contraction at least once when you talk."

"It is not in my programming, my genius high school senior. You are on summer vacation and so we have time for the trip. If I promise to use a contraction sometime, will you show excitement and go with me?"

"Like that's gonna happen. Is this another clothing optional adventure or can I be fully dressed?"

His hand got frisky and I giggled.

"If I agree," I said, "my parents must be cool with it. Our previous adventure still has 'em spooked. Remember I'm seventeen, in high school and live with them most of the time. They're my legal guardians for another year. I love them and my brothers and they all worry about me."

He nodded. "You are also admired by the other Guardians. How many could have done what you did, my pyrokinetic boyfriend?"

He was referring to the prevention of an apocalyptic Aztec war where we both had become major participants. "I don't know of any other than me."

I asked, trying to look sexy although not sure how to do it, "Would you go with me as my date for the senior prom?" I tried to look hopeful and adorable, blinking at him.

"Do you have something in your eye?" He put his hand on my forehead and lifted an eyelid with his thumb.

"Stop! I was trying to look sexy."

"You are naked and in bed. We have had sex multiple times of the last few hours. Do you really think you have to do more to be desirable?"

He was impossible. Impossibly sexy. "Senior prom is a big deal for a graduating senior; I don't want to go alone."

"I think I understand the concept. I do not dance as do twenty-first century teenagers. Remember I was born five hundred years in the past, on a parallel earth, and my first years were in an indigenous village. The music and loud volume give me a headache. We had no electric guitars and trumpets, nor would we want them. I also do not have a dinner jacket or whatever I would have to wear. I would look silly."

I ran a finger over his chest and kissed a nipple.

Faster than I could react, he flipped me on my stomach, straddled my legs and started tickling. Damn he was strong. "Okay! Okay! I give up! We'll ask my parents tonight if you ever let me out of bed. And…please think about the prom."

He stretched out on top of me, wrapping his arms around my chest, holding mine tight to my sides, licking behind my ear, biting an earlobe, rubbing his body on mine. "Maybe we can just stay like this until they get off work."

"No! We get up now and have breakfast."

3.

The slim cigar shaped aircraft floated silently above the knife-point peaks of the remote mountain wilderness. Seemingly endless forest, meadows, lakes, rock outcroppings. Daruk had offered to teleport us into the area but since teleportation made me nauseous, we'd taken this craft, much like the one we took to Renaissance Rome a few weeks back. It did not pollute, was silent, invisible and would leave no footprint on the environment. Our aircraft for that romantic trip was on the other side of the Passageway, in the 17th century. If we did spend the night, it would be in a heated aircraft with doors that locked, not in a tent. That was not an argument to make with my outdoor loving lover.

We circled the area for an hour, quietly enjoying the beauty and watching wildlife. There were black bears romping through a wildflower meadow. Elsewhere, a dozen mule deer munched grass on a hillside. We hovered over a remote hiking path thankfully deserted. A cougar stalked something not in our view. I'd no idea mountains this magnificent were in my home state.

"I am not sensing any people." Minutes later, we floated over a mountain peak.

"What is this?" He sounded concerned and raced our craft deep into the valley, hovering over what looked like a camouflaged campsite. "There was violence here." He pointed to the screen. "Three bodies that I can detect. Recent kills, the corpses still warm. A structure, nearly invisible in the tree line, is like a yurt." On the viewer was a closeup of one woman and two men. Dressed in robes and trousers that blended perfectly into the rocks, trees and soil. There was also a lot of blood. The bodies looked like they'd been hit with major firepower, like a machine gun, almost ripping one of the bodies in half.

"How long ago, do you think?"

"I am testing now and making a recording. It happened less than an hour ago." The scanner swept the ground. Daruk pointed. "There, near the rock outcrop, there are footprints, like boots. Maybe four or five people," he said. "Look at the soft coverings on the feet of the dead, like mukluks, a soft boot made of reindeer skin often worn by Arctic aboriginals. No heels. The footprints are from outside this group."

"Over there." I pointed to a corner of my own screen. "The boots seem to be moving out of the camp, likely running based on the spacing, deeper into the valley."

"Yes. Good observation, my beautiful Darwin. Notice the trampled plants." Daruk performed another test. "There is a trace of gunshot residue."

Our craft rose higher. "We shall follow the trail. I will scan for human lifeforms within a five-mile circumference." The killers were moving fast through the forest, their trail easy to follow. "There is someone ahead of them leaving no physical trail. The person is moving with caution, perhaps familiar with the terrain."

There was a flash of light a mile ahead. We closed on the site in seconds. A woman, cradling an object, was being chased by two men. There was a gunshot. She kept moving. The pistol perhaps a warning to stop.

"Look! She's being flanked by two others coming up from that hillside. There's a cliff."

"Grab your bow. We will engage. These people are killers."

The craft hovered just a foot off the highest point in the uneven forest floor. Daruk jumped out and I followed, running the hundred yards to the site.

The men were together, talking to her in English with a few words in various languages, as if seeking to be understood.

She held up a long knife and was chanting. A bright flash shot toward the men but flew overhead. She growled in frustration and turned to run toward the cliff. One of them fired, hitting her in the back. She fell, screaming, clutching what now appeared to be a newborn.

Daruk pulled out his sling. Seconds later the skull of the shooter exploded.

"Kill as you must," he instructed.

Two men turned to us and raised weapons, one a pistol and the other what looked like an AR15. I pulled back the string of my bow and sent an arrow through the neck of the man with the rifle. A rock crushed the larynx on the one with the pistol. They squirmed on the ground, dying rough.

"Stop! Stop! I can explain!" the remaining man shouted, turning to us as he held up his hands. He had a pistol on his hip.

"If she dies, your corpse will be left for the coyotes," Daruk said in controlled fury, the Serpent's Tongue in his fist, my new name for his wavy blade short sword. He ran to the man and slashed his belt, drawing blood, the pistol falling into the dirt.

"Please, please, don't kill me!" he begged dropping to his knees, lifting his arms.

I kicked away his holster and drew an arrow, aiming at his head.

"Kill him if he moves," Daruk said. "I will check on the woman."

As he passed the two dying gunmen, he swiped a hand over each of their temples, the two instantly unconscious to die with greater dignity. Beside her, he dropped to his knees.

"Who are you?" I asked my prisoner. He was an older man, Caucasian, well-tanned, short white hair and a white goatee. I would guess in his sixties.

"I...I'm Professor Arnold Whitacre of Brentwell University near San Francisco. I'm an anthropologist. We believe she's... she's the last of a mysterious group of people we've been studying from afar for weeks."

"Who are the dead men?" I wanted as much information as I could gather in case he was killed. In case I had to kill him. I couldn't think about that.

"Two are ex-military I hired to help me track. The third, the one who fired the gun, is a graduate student at my school. His name is Otto Heinrich."

"Why did he shoot her?"

"She flashed some sort of energy charge toward us... and... we thought she was going to jump off the cliff. To kill her baby."

"She detested you that much?"

I could see Daruk trying to save her, using his medical kit.

"She is dead!" he shouted, his tone both angry and frustrated.

While I was momentarily distracted, the professor dove for his gun. I put an arrow into his chest. He shouted, rolled on his back, his eyes pleading, and died.

Daruk walked up to me, holding a baby wrapped in a soft bundle. "You did what you had to do, Darwin. Feel no guilt. These men are murderers. This was justice."

I was shaking. Two dead because of me. In my world, not his. The downloads within me gave me the capacity to do this, to dispense frontier justice, otherwise I would be just another helpless, frightened teenager likely peeing in my pants.

"We have six dead men, two dead women and a baby that is unlike any child I have ever seen." He opened the cloth and let me have a look.

"What...what is he?" The naked, squirming boy was surprisingly thin but still robust looking. There were no nipples on his tiny chest. His eyes were extraordinarily large, his ears more animal than human.

"Whatever he is, the boy must be protected. I will contact Katnu."

4.

The triangular war machine was theoretically invisible but when it moved over us and blocked the sun, it was in all its 26th century glory. Thirty minutes after Daruk made the call, the aircraft dropped silently and hovered just off the ground. There were two such identical aircraft, one called *Puma*, kept in the 17th century, and this one which we called *Mars*, for the Roman god of war. Each was an isosceles triangle in shape, two long sides and a narrower base. Each could seat six or the seats could fold down for added cargo space. In the back were storage units, a chemical lab, manufacturing center, a sleeping area, bathrooms and a range of other services. Mars had been brought through the Passageway to this world in small sections and re-assembled by a team of engineers. Its fusion power source was endless and the craft was capable of traveling many times the speed of sound and, as part of its stealth design, did not create sonic booms. It dwarfed the size of our little craft which we called *Canoe*, because we were being silly when we named it. It was shaped like a cigar but cigars didn't float on a river, but canoes did, at least theoretically. *Canoe's* operational manual said it could travel underwater, not that we tried. Comparing the two, *Canoe* worked in practical ways. Mars was like a battleship in comparison and its firepower exceeded anything in this century.

Katnu Hisman, the man I called Uncle His, and loved as a grandfather, hurried down the steps. His long black hair, streaked with silver, was braided down his back; his brown skin contrasted with his tan cargo pants and blue hoodie. Given his speed and steady moves, you would never guess he was over two hundred years old.

"Let me see the child."

Daruk held the squirming crying baby cradled in both arms. Katnu placed a palm on the boy's forehead; he quieted immediately. Pulling back the blanket, Uncle His held up a small silver tube over him. A bluish light flashed; the tiny body was scanned in a few seconds. He studied the results on a small screen that projected above it. Frowning, he held up the tube again for a second lengthier examination.

"Remarkable. Give him to me."

Daruk covered the child with the cloth and gently handed him to Katnu, who held him close to his chest, head high.

"Both of you, bring the mother to the medical lab. I am concerned about feeding the child and given what I have found, we may need a special milk formula. Even if we had a cow or a pregnant human female, it might not be enough. Hurry. Pull out a table in the back near the lab."

Daruk and I looked at each other, our eyes wide, and ran to the body.

Katnu stepped up into the ship, pulled a blanket from storage on a platform between seats, and set the child on top as he gave orders to the search engine. He ran the back of his hand over the side of the boy's and smiled. The child smiled back. He gave quiet commands and flipped through numerous entries on the screen. Behind him, Daruk pulled out a table from a storage wall and secured the end to stabilize it. I pulled out a blanket and covered the area. The mother was placed on top, behind the seats.

"Apologies, my dear," Katnu murmured, "for the awkward

space and what I must do to save your baby. This is a ship of war not a medical transport."

"Her blood is still warm," I said, wiping my hand on a damp cloth and trying to think about anything but that I had just carried a body.

"Darwin, gather as much of her blood as you can. She is no longer bleeding out because her heart has stopped. I will stimulate the heart into working again for a few minutes. This procedure will make blood easier to extract and help with our main purpose. Use the sterile tubes in the drawer on the left behind you. Also, there are sterile needles in the same space. Draw several vials if you can. This is tricky on a corpse but still valuable if we can succeed. The more we know about her the more we can protect the child. Your medical care enhancement should give you adequate phlebotomist skills."

I did my best to focus on the task, not thinking about what just happened. More blood was pooling on the table, the blanket sodden and red. I had just killed two men. Drawing blood at least gave me something else to focus on even if it made me queasy. Even if it was drawing blood from a corpse.

"Daruk, work on making a version of the manual breast pump I have pulled up on the screen," Katnu ordered. "I will need at least two sterile collection jars with lids. I hope we have the time and equipment to retrieve some of her mother's milk," he added, pulling back the sheet covering her body. "Darwin, more work for you when you finish with the blood. I have pulled up details on creating a natural hormone that plays an important role in lactation. It is called oxytocin and the chemical ingredients are listed on the second screen. Work verbally with Wizard, the ship operating unit, to manufacture a small vial. Mother's milk is a complicated process in the body; it may help."

I felt overwhelmed. A woman's body was to my right, her chest totally exposed. I felt embarrassed for her and enormously sad. And the men I killed seemed to be screaming at me in my head. The screen led me through a series of questions which I answered as best I could. My brain enhancements, gifts accorded to me by Daruk and Uncle His, included a wide range of medical information. I squeezed around the body to the back of the ship, placed a vial under a blinking light. It filled with the hormone.

"I have the chemical," I announced.

"Bring it to me."

"I am assembling the suction device." Daruk turned from the machine and twisted the clear unit together, taking a moment to spray it with disinfectant and then dry it. I was amazed what the ship could accomplish and how masterfully my friends could command it.

Uncle His scanned one breast and smiled. "There is still viable milk." He slipped on a pair of rubber gloves, took the vial and rubbed the hormone over each nipple. He waited a minute before attaching the pump. He squeezed the handle. Several moments later milk flowed into the storage jar underneath. He filled one container then pulled it off and added a second as he moved to her second breast. "Even in death the mother is saving her baby. What could be more noble or beautiful?"

"Or more precious?" I added. The full power of his words and what he was doing to save a life hit me with a slap. Tears ran from my eyes. How could a high school kid from a lower middle-class family be here, doing this? The woman looked a bit elfin to me, tall and thin, high cheekbones and a small, narrow and slightly turned up nose. Maybe I'd read too many books about magical people.

When finished, he closed her robe for privacy, nodded as if offering a silent prayer, then took the two jars to a work bench to examine the contents. "Darwin, find the design of a baby bottle and have it made. No, make two. Boil some water to warm them."

Minutes later, Daruk held the child in his arms, a baby bottle full of mother's milk in hand. My heart sped faster watching my warrior boyfriend doing this most basic act with love in his face. He said "goo-goo" a few times, a perfect term in any language, rocking the child as he ate hungrily.

"The bad guys are dead," Katnu said. "The baby is saved. Now we must get the ingredients for more milk. The analysis says it is different in important ways from cows' milk or traditional human milk. He is good for a few hours so we can finish here and then go get what I need to make the new baby formula."

"May I hold him?" I asked Daruk. He smiled, his face so soft and loving, and handed me the sleeping child. I rocked him slowly and did my own cooing like I had for my two young brothers years ago.

The woman's blood continued to pool but the flow was slowing. "Daruk, help me turn her over. I want to examine and cauterize the wound and stop her heart. It is already slowing." Carefully she was turned face down. The back of her garment was ripped by the gunfire. He opened the wound with a probe and a small bottle for samples. "She was shot in the lower back, snapping her tailbone and ripping her ovaries, among other things. I will take samples of each."

I had to look away.

When I glanced back up, he was placing two items, one in a sterile bottle, the other in a ceramic like box.

"These need to be held in stasis," he said, putting the box inside a chamber about the size of a microwave. He adjusted a dial and typed in instructions. A light came on and there was a barely audible hum.

"Darwin, hand me the blue container just above where you got the blood equipment. I have stopped stimulating her heart and will spray her wound to seal it. Find me some clean sheeting to cover the body."

Uncle His and Daruk held her off the table in the new sheet while I mopped up the blood and tossed away the soiled robe and blanket. Then they set her down. Seeing her wrapped in a clean cloth, her modesty returned, she seemed more at peace. Daruk lifted a corner of the sheet and reverently covered her face.

Katnu went over to the chem lab and worked on his new samples, pulling blood and bone from the woman's back into a small analyzer attached to the main computer. His concentration was intense, eyebrows pulled tight in a squint. The occasional grunt and "no, it can't be" riveted us on what he was doing. Twenty minutes later he put away his tools, deep in thought.

He turned to us. "Gentlemen—I believe you said the bodies of the other three tribal or family members were about a mile away. We should secure them. There are wolves and coyotes aplenty in this mountain range. Their bodies should be respected and interred here. I also need to examine them to see if she and the baby are an aberration or if we have indeed come across an advanced race of humans."

"What?" I shouted, not sure I heard him right.

"I believe the technical term would be *Homo Futuris*, or *Homo sapiens Futuris*. If the others are similar, then this is an astounding discovery. If confirmed, how do we handle it? There is no precedent for this that I know of."

"How can you make such a statement?" I found his conclusions incredible.

"I could not if I only had twenty-first century technology to work with. This is a twenty-sixth century lab. In the mid twenty-third century, scientists perfected a way to use aDNA—the "a" stands for ancient—to reconstruct the genetic code and from that the genome of long-gone ancestors and relatives. The big breakthrough came a few years back when experts were able to use it to reconstruct the genome of *Neanderthals*, *Homo neanderthalensis*. Now I have used a more accurate technology to determine where this young woman sits within our own family tree."

He was quiet, looking ahead, pondering his own statement. Daruk and I stared at each other. Yet we had more to consider, something also urgent. "That is stunning. But isn't this also a crime scene?" I asked. "Do we need to contact police or forest rangers? And what do we do with the bodies of those we killed?"

"How would we explain our presence? Two twenty-sixth century warships."

Uncle His removed his gloves and dropped them in a receptacle. He then rubbed his chin as he often did before reaching a major decision. "I will call President O'Connor now. And look after the child. Go retrieve the bodies."

5.

C*anoe* hovered three feet off the ground and ten yards from where we first saw the bodies. The forest floor was thick with ferns and other brush. After landing, we walked to the open site. It was clear, pristine.

"This is where they were," Daruk said, stooping down and examining the soil. "There is blood, a lot of it but no bodies."

"The tent's gone." I ran to the place where it had been. The ferns looked healthy and upright. Why weren't they flatted by the tent? "I know this is where it was."

Daruk stood and took out a small slim box attached to his belt. He did some calibration and slowly turned in a circle. There was a low beep every few seconds as it did its work. "I find no other human presence, just two bears over that ridge and a few deer. If wolves came, there would be more blood and scattered body parts. No, the bodies were lifted and carried away. The tent was taken down even though plants where it stood seem undisturbed. There are no footprints. The site has been intentionally cleared of any evidence."

"Other than the blood."

"Perhaps we interrupted whoever cleaned the area."

"There might be other tribal members."

"My search parameters should find the bodies just as it did when we flew over the mountain peak. Now, nothing. I was out two miles on this search. No single person could carry three bodies and a tent over that distance in this rugged terrain while hiding any trace of their presence at this site. As you suggest, perhaps there is a group. If that is so, surely they would be easier to locate." He rubbed his palms over his eyes. "I am baffled. You are the recognized high school genius. Give me more ideas."

"Could they be in some subterrain hiding place? Maybe a cave?"

"Not only are you handsome with a large musical penis, but your suggestion is good."

"I thought you weren't going to ever again mention that dreadful rumor you helped create in your home village?"

"The legend is too rich and precious to quash. The white boy with the giant singing penis. It does sing to me but not with the kind of music suggested in the gossip." He stood and started walking back to *Canoe*. "There are more sophisticated scanners on board."

He lifted the ship over the site and worked some equipment. "I am looking for human lifeforms within five miles. I am also looking for anomalies in the geology in the area. Things like caves or unusual formations of rock."

I sat beside him at the controls. He reached over and pulled me tight then he slipped a hand under my knees and lifted me onto his lap. He kissed my cheek. "I know today has been torturous for you. I deal with death. You do not. You saw it in my world. But this is your Earth, in your century. Please realize you did what you needed to do. The men would have killed us, just as they killed the mother and the others who were here. Somehow, we will figure all this out. Katnu is brilliant at this sort of thing." We kissed, slow and warm. He pushed his tongue into my mouth, a welcome distraction.

There was a clacking sound from the scanner. We broke apart

but I remained in his lap. He turned to the screen and his fingers bounced over a keyboard. He scanned the findings.

"No humans detected. Hmmmm. There is a large cave with what might be a small opening in the backside of this peak." He maneuvered the craft over the mountain and stopped a few dozen yards from the entrance.

"I don't see any cave."

"Nor do I, my handsome Darwin. But it is there. The shrubs conceal the site and the downed redwood that is half rotted marks the entrance. Look, there is a kind of rugged path in the rock leading up the mountainside."

"You've quite the imagination thinking those rock fragments are a path. But no humans, dead or alive, right?"

"If they are deep enough inside it might obscure their presence. We know little about the rock composition deep into the mountain, only what is on the surface."

"Should we go inside?"

"It should not be a 'we.' There are limited options inside a cave. It would be strategic if you stayed here so you could contact Katnu if I do not return."

"No! Nada. Not gonna happen. I want to be next to you if there's trouble. I can fight."

"You are my special teenage warrior boyfriend." He grinned and I snorted.

The craft drifted lower, stopping just two feet from the ground with the door next to a rock stand for easy dismount.

We moved silently to the pathway in the stone, using hand signals for communication. Walking behind the huge rotting redwood, we saw an opening about six feet up from the trail. It was not generous in size. Daruk crouched down, moving his fingers to his temples. He looked deep in thought. A minute later he took out a small com device and silently typed in a message and showed it to me.

"I sense a power from inside pressing against my consciousness."

6.

Daruk shifted his thoughts, trying different ways to listen and communicate, working with different comm downloads. The message seemed to be both a camouflaging and a warning to stay away. There was something almost magical about it, not that he had ever encountered actual magic. Yet many in his world saw what he did as magical. Where did that thought come from? What did magic sound like?

These were not Native Americans. He didn't know what they were. There were witches in some Native American tribes. He thought of *Kâ'lanû Ahkyeli'ski,* an evil spirit and a feared Cherokee witch said to rob the sick and dying of their hearts. This was nothing like that.

He tried reaching out like he did when he wanted to create problems for an attacking force but there was a barrier of some kind. He tried sending "friend" out in as many languages as he knew. He followed with images of two people hugging, two people shaking hands, two people eating, two people kissing, two people making love. Of babies playing.

He sensed something shift in his brain. Was he being invited inside? He would take a chance. "Darwin, we are going inside. Leave all your weapons on the ground before we hop inside. Make a big show of it. Think about it as you do it, using exaggerated gestures."

Daruk stood before the entrance. Placed his bow and quiver on the ground. Dropped his sling. Took out his sword and held up his empty hands.

Darwin set down his bow, quiver, and knife. Held up his hands.

Then they both jumped to the opening, slowly swinging their feet inside and entered the darkness. They both kept their hands up.

Daruk said, "My sense is we follow the light source straight ahead. I am also being pulled mentally in that direction." They walked carefully over the surprisingly smooth stone floor that was covered with what might be a form of area rugs. The light source was a small pit. Not a fire but light. Certainly not electrical. But it was soft and warm, filling the room in a kind of twilight. They could not see the walls or ceiling but there was a sense it was a big space. It was impossible to determine much in the semi-darkness but there appeared to be some kind of vertical supports. .

As they neared the light, a figure emerged from deeper in the cave. He was tall, wearing a tunic that came to his hips, slim trousers and flat leather boots. He gestured for us to come near and sit on some furs covering a curved sofa of sorts, perhaps made of stone. He walked within three feet of Daruk and spread his arms in greeting but not touching, lowering his head. Daruk responded in kind. He did the same with Darwin. They all smiled cautiously and sat.

The man was well over six feet and slender despite the clothing. He seemed to have no weapon. Looking deeper into the cave, Daruk saw what he presumed were the three bodies on platforms. So, there had been two survivors, this man and the child.

"Daruk," Daruk said, pointing to himself. "Dar-uk."

"Daruk," the figure stated in a male voice but softly and he tripped on the pronunciation and repeated it until it was correct.

Daruk nodded and pointed to Darwin. "Darwin, Dar-win."

"Darwin," the figure responded.

"Haldir," the figure added, pointing to himself. "Hal-deer."

They repeated his name. As he studied the figure, Daruk realized the man was actually a boy, likely on the cusp of puberty. His hair was combed low over his forehead and hung below his shoulders down his back, dark, but maybe there was a touch of red. His eyes were extraordinarily large, no whites that were apparent. His nose was thin, almost delicate, and slightly turned up, like that of the dead mother. His lips were full, the top one almost heart shaped. His ears were larger than expected and resembled the ears on the baby and the dead woman. They seemed to be folded, almost like they were hinged, so they could be moved, a bit like a cat's but all skin, no hair.

Daruk could feel the boy—or man, or whatever he was—exploring his brain, a kind of gentle presence. Maybe he was telepathic, but they couldn't yet connect.

The man/boy lowered his head and placed his fingertips together as if offering thanks. He pointed to each of them. With Daruk, he swung an arm around like he had a sling and flung it forward releasing an imaginary rock. For Darwin, he gestured as if he held a bow and released an arrow. He nodded again and spread his arms wide. He seemed to indicate he knew they had killed the attackers and was grateful.

He held out his left palm as if asking for a moment of quiet. They watched as he lifted a heavy bronze chain from around his neck and held out a raised green medallion for them to examine, urging them forward. It was about three inches in diameter. They moved, both of them dropping to one knee within an arm's length. The medallion looked weathered, perhaps ancient, the design resembling a plant motif, with various tendrils moving around some kind of animal head at the center. He turned it around and the back was smooth and reflective. He whispered,

"Tar ar an saol mo áilleacht."

The back of the medallion lit up. It was as if he had turned on a video, the fight scene when they killed the four men who had murdered his tribe member. It lasted less than a minute, the time it took to take the killers down and Daruk trying to save the woman and holding the baby.

He turned the medallion back around. He smiled and nodded as if asking our reaction.

Darwin glanced at Daruk, lifting his head, as if urging him to take the lead. The language clearly did not fit any of the data bases in his brain.

"Thank you," Daruk said. "We were too late to save her but there was justice." His grim look quickly morphed into a hopeful expression, and he reached out and touched the boy's shoulder.

Haldir looked at both of them and nodded, perhaps aware they did not understand his words but his expression suggested he was grateful for what they had done. After a moment of silence, he mimicked holding a baby and raised his eyebrows. He wanted to know if the child survived.

Darwin grinned, pretending as if he held the child, and nodded. He moved an arm, and raised his eyebrows, as if asking if he wanted to visit.

The young man smiled. It was a broad, satisfied grin, straight white teeth. Not what Daruk would expect of a secret race of people hiding in the wilderness. His breathing suggested he was joyful at the news, holding his hands together as if in prayer, lowering his head.

Daruk felt his mind being explored more intensely. At some point, maybe they could communicate. He hoped Katnu would have ideas on telepathy and maybe some insight on the medallion, more a functioning video comm tool than just a static piece of art. Who was this man? What was he?

The young man stood, his eyes seeming to examine his home and his options. With a bit of a grunt, he pointed toward the entrance. Daruk and Darwin scrambled to their feet. He started to walk gracefully to the exit, jumped up and bounced out of the cave. They followed.

On the stone ledge outside they got a better look at each other. Haldir was tall, maybe six foot four. His flawless skin was light brown and youthful. No facial hair. The hair on his head was thick and black but with a red hue. He must be in his early teens. His eyes were large; Daruk noticed the pupils going from full eyeball and dark green to tiny emerald dots surrounded by white in the sunlight. Did he have night predator eyes, like a fox or cougar, the ability to see in low light? His ears twitched and turned, listening for danger. They were humanlike but not exactly human, more pointed, and seemed to have the ability to move and fold. Again, perhaps a survival mechanism gained through centuries of natural selection if this really were an advanced race of humans cut off from the rest of humanity. His forehead seemed larger than an average human's, perhaps related to a larger brain.

Haldir gestured for them to lead. Daruk and Darwin picked up their weapons, attaching them onto their bodies, raising their hands to indicate they were not a threat before stepping off the path and down the hill to their aircraft. The boy followed but stopped when he realized it was there. It was only partly invisible. The sun reflected off the exterior. Daruk went down and slid back a door. He smiled and invited the boy inside. Darwin, looking his boyish best, nodded and grinned. The boy seemed to be considering his options then stepped to the craft and inside.

He whooped when *Canoe* rose silently up into the sky. He put his nose to the translucent wall of the ship, in total awe. He said some words they didn't understand but could assume referred to the landmarks of his world. Maybe also a *'Holy shit!'* Or two.

Daruk sent a message to Katnu explaining what had happened. He didn't want to speak aloud and spoil the sense of wonder spread across Haldir's face.

7.

Our ship set down next to the warbird moments later. Uncle His was standing outside the exit stairs holding the baby.

As soon as Daruk slid open our doorway, Haldir leaped out and ran toward the child held by Uncle His, his arms wide, repeatedly bending at the waist as he ran, apparently trying to show he was unarmed and meant no harm. Katnu signaled for him to come closer as he pulled back the blanket from the child's face.

Haldir said something joyous and leaped in the air and then dropped to his knees, openly crying. Katnu touched his shoulder and their eyes met. He offered the child and Haldir took him gently. He kissed the baby's forehead. The baby cooed and smiled, reaching out with both arms. He took a tiny hand and kissed it, tears running unchecked.

It was hard to fathom just what he had gone through this day. His family murdered. His emotions must be shredded.

"Maia?" he said hopefully, looking up at the three of us. *"Maia?"* he asked again. *"Càite a bheil mo cho-ogha?"* His voice was barely audible. Perhaps it was a request for something or maybe the dead woman's name. Uncle His seemed to understand his in-

tent and gestured toward the steps leading to his ship. The boy hesitated so I stepped forward and walked up the steps, encouraging him to follow as I smiled and tried to look as innocent as Daruk said I did. I thought we had a connection. He was hesitant but came inside.

He went straight to the body, uninterested on the inside of a warship. He pulled back the sheet covering her face and ran the back of his fingers over her cheek. He stood there, quiet, in thought, struggling with his breathing, then he bent down and kissed her lips. He looked at the baby he held in one arm and spoke quietly as if in prayer, before kissing the child's cheek. He dropped to his knees and handed me the child. His hands together as if in prayer, he began to softly chant. We stepped back to give him privacy.

Katnu worked the master control and quietly said: "I am recording everything he says to see if we can find any speech pattern or understand words to determine meaning. His voice is so soft it is hard to understand whatever language he is speaking."

The boy stood, his back to us and seemed to be trying to pull himself together. He wiped his eyes with his palms. Daruk was ready and stepped up, handing him a warm damp towel. Haldir took it in obvious surprise, as if trying to figure out what to do with it. Daruk pantomimed wiping his face. He boy nodded in gratitude and did just that. Then he looked at us, seeming desperate, lost, and likely very lonely. Daruk took the cloth from him and then Katnu stepped up to him and wrapped his arms around the boy. The young man stiffened and then leaned into him. I was next up, holding the two of them. Then Daruk joined us. A foursome. The boy looked at us and seemed to crumple. We held him tight.

Soon Daruk put four readymade dinners in the warmer and we went outside. As we ate, it was obvious he had never handled a fork but copied us. He looked dubiously at everything he was eating, smelling each bite, tasting with the tip his tongue, and only then putting it in his mouth. He spat out the meat, his face a grimace. He picked up a vegetable, tasted, smiled and chewed with enthusiasm. Beef no; broccoli yes. A new adventure for him, these new tastes. Maybe he was hungry. Had he ever tasted either, given where he lived?

Uncle His opened a screen on a mobile device, turned it to Haldir, and began calling up pictures of trees, rocks, the sky, pointing to the forest, deer, the baby and photos of hundreds of objects. Katnu would say our word for the item and Haldir gave his words. Slowly a vocabulary, a dictionary was being built. But it would be a long process unless there was a breakthrough in pairing his words against thousands of other languages. Easier still if Uncle His or Daruk had a breakthrough on telepathy.

. . .

A message pinked on Katnu's phone. He read it and smiled.

"It is from the FBI. Boys, take *Canoe* and go to these coordinates. Set down in a meadow 75 miles outside the city of Redding. Two agents will meet you. Also an academic who works with the FBI on forensic anthropology. The conversation with the President and the head of Homeland Security was great. The agents and scientist are sworn to secrecy and are to answer to me; I report to the President. We don't want anybody else messing this up or going public. They're bringing cow's milk and the additives we need for the baby. Plus groceries, baby clothes and clothes for Haldir including a knit cap to cover his ears."

"You wanted to inspect the bodies," I said to Uncle His. "Can you do it with law enforcement and being sensitive to Haldir's faith or customs?"

Uncle His smiled at me. "Thank you for being empathetic to the boy's needs. He has faced enough trauma without seeing us doing anything disrespectful and that he might find horrifying. I am thankful I pulled samples from the girl's body before his arrival. Every society is different in how it deals with the dead. I will continue working with him on vocabulary and will experiment with ways to communicate on complex issues such as his customs and religious practices, should he have any. He can help me set up tents while you are gone."

Haldir watched us as we talked about him, lifting his head when he heard his name, curious about what we were saying and trying to hide the deep sadness reflected in his posture and eyes.

"Be careful on what you say to our new guests. They don't need to know about our worlds. You could just say you are not authorized to give details and they should talk with me. Not that I know what I will say."

"Let's go, Daruk." I nodded to the young teen, giving him a kind of soft salute, which made him smile, as we went to our ship. We hurried on board and were in the air almost immediately.

8.

"There's the meadow," I said, looking out the window and glancing back at our coordinates on the screen. A brook wound its way down one end of the space, maybe three football fields in size. Mostly weeds and a grassy area at one end. No people that I could detect. A variety of trees, lots of oaks and my sensors identified a particularly bright green tree as California buckeye.

We hung motionless in the sky for nearly an hour. Katnu had called and repeated a message from Homeland Security. A plane from Los Angeles had been delayed and it was arriving soon.

We kissed, held each other, watched the sensor devices for other planes headed our way that would not see us, and speculated about what Katnu had said about these people being humans of the future.

"Hold that thought," he said. "Here comes their helicopter, about two miles out, headed from the southwest."

Daruk and I were both wearing our E3 style clothing which wasn't all that outrageous for E2, my earth. Brown baggy pants that looked like leather but were an almost indestructible fabric with lots of pockets. I had on a blue sleeveless tee that Daruk had picked out saying it matched my eyes. It was also too tight which he said he also liked. He had on a green one, plus utility belts and moccasin-like boots. A knife was strapped against my calf and out of sight. Serpent's Tongue hung in a sheath from his belt in the back and his pouch with stones and sling were on a separate belt on his right hip. Standard crush the enemy dress for the wilds of the 17th century yet still working as costume in the 21st. My auburn hair was getting long; I wore it pulled back and tied at the base of my neck. Daruk's thick black hair was braided nearly all the way down his back.

We watched from above, invisible to them as the craft landed and three disembarked, two men and a woman. The pilot helped unload the luggage. The chopper took off almost immediately. We waited until it was five miles out.

We descended in silence just a few feet from their position. They looked around like they sensed something but were unsure what it was. Daruk pulled open the door and jumped out. The two men shrieked at the sudden emergence of an indigenous warrior seemingly out of the air.

Then they stared, hands on their holsters. *Canoe* and my hot boyfriend did have that impact on most people. Muscular, tall, a hard Raptor face when he wanted, and he did today. No one to mess with. Then I got out. Much less intimidating, the cute, innocent sidekick. But I did my best to look tough. At least I wasn't naked like I was in much of my time in Daruk's world where nudity was common, especially for men. Nothing makes you less intimidating than having your dick and butt exposed. At least for me.

He stood in front of them, letting them take it all in, the aircraft, the hardened warrior. "Agents Williams and Tomas, I presume," he said in a firm, no nonsense voice. The woman was a wiry and tough looking African American. He was a white Hollywood-style male beauty. "And you with the Indiana Jones hat must be the forensic anthologist, Wilkins Vardan."

They nodded. Vardan smiled and touched his sable-colored

fedora. I almost laughed but stopped myself. Was he the real thing or a poser?

"I am Daruk and this is Darwin. We work closely with Katnu Hisman who contacted President O'Connor. Perhaps on the way up to the Russian Wilderness you can tell us what you know. Or you can just enjoy the spectacular scenery."

He picked up one of the suitcases marked *FBI Lab* like it weighed nothing, plus a second one marked *Supplies* then turned and stepped to the craft. I picked up another, it must have weighed 150 pounds, and followed, pretending it was no big lift, hoping my back wouldn't spasm. The others carried their individual duffels and entered *Canoe* warily, touching the outside and doorway, eyes wide. I likely had had the same look the first time I saw this machine.

With that we lifted the suitcases into the craft and helped them inside. We ascended at high speed to a thousand feet, the only sounds gasps from our passengers. I suspected Daruk was showing off what the ship could do so they knew they weren't in Kansas anymore.

I set the course on the screen; we surged forward toward the mountains. "To answer the question you are all thinking," Daruk said. "Yes, we are invisible to the eye and radar." We were over the highest peaks of the Sierras in minutes, everyone staring out the side walls. There were no windows, it was all clear, even part of the floor, which could make you queasy if you looked.

"Holy shit!" someone behind us said. He probably did.

We were at least two thousand feet above our landing site when the craft slowed, swiveled around three times—again Daruk having fun—and dropped like a rock, hovering three feet off the ground in a way that the passengers' bodies were lifted and plopped down. Daruk looked at me and winked. *Canoe* inched lower, stopping a foot above the ground; I slid back part of the exterior and jumped out, reaching inside for one of the suitcases and the supply duffle and setting them outside.

While we were gone, Uncle His and Haldir had set up three beige thermal-walled tent like structures. Katnu was standing near the front of his craft, arms crossed, stern-faced, unquestionably the man in charge. Behind him stood Haldir, holding the baby.

"Welcome to our camp, madam, gentlemen," Uncle His said, almost smiling. His voice was not unfriendly but carried a hint of steel.

Each of them stepped forward and identified themselves, hands out but still lacking the confidence I would expect for FBI agents. Uncle His shook each outstretched palm, looking somber and in charge.

Katnu turned and pointed to Haldir and the baby. "Here are the two survivors of an attack by anthropologists seeking to take control of the child. They brought a pair of military veterans for security. Four members of Haldir's family were killed. We made certain that he and the child were safe. The killers' remains are lying as they fell about a mile east. So far, the cougars and wolves have left them alone. Time is of the essence if it is to be a useful crime scene."

The three talked quietly among themselves and Katnu gave them the time to adjust to our reality. "I am not sure what the President and the head of Homeland Security told you. I am still working on finding a common vocabulary to converse with Haldir. He speaks a language not in sync with any database including IA. But we have made progress. A breakthrough is no longer inconceivable." He paused. "Which is not to say it is imminent."

There was one larger tent and two smaller ones. Katnu pointed to one and Daruk and I carried the suitcases there.

"We have supplies in these duffels," Agent Gabriel Tomas said. He stooped down and opened one, took out two large plastic containers of food. He also lifted out a cotton bag with clothes. I tried to keep from staring at the man. How could someone be this gorgeous? He reminded me of the super-hot guy on the Netflix *Night Agent* series. Maybe late twenties, short brown hair, clean-shaven, square jaw, All-American football quarterback sexy with a dimple on his chin, a boy next door vulnerability. Maybe it was simpler to just say he was hot.

"Thank you for the supplies. The baby is hungry and needs a

unique formula." Uncle His looked at the head agent, the woman. "What you brought will allow me to mix the kind of formula necessary to keep this child alive." He offered his famous grand-fatherly smile. Then continued: "I enjoy studying the meaning of certain words. I believe your given name, *Amare*, has two origins, one Ethiopian meaning 'handsome.' The other is Indian, meaning 'immortal,' if I am correct. You are well named on the first and hopefully so on the second."

She smiled, clearly surprised and pleased. "I'm both African American and Indian. No one ever made that connection before. Impressive, sir." She nodded. Katnu grinned.

"Please put your things in the tent where Daruk has taken your work implements. A note on housekeeping—at this point, we have no bathrooms but considering this is a wilderness area, we have two compostable toilets set up behind those rocks." He pointed to the left. "We dropped a ten-foot hole in the dirt for each, still well above the groundwater level and constructed a simple box with a traditional toilet lid out of plastic covering each opening. Amazing what a warbird can make in a pinch. To avoid surprises, you may want to call out or cough when going over there to avoid any embarrassment in case they are in use. There is toilet paper in a box by each site; also, a stack of smooth rocks if we run low on the paper. Not as soft but strategic and can work. Toss them in the hole when you are finished. We will disinfect and seal the holes when we leave.

"There is a container outside the main tent," he continued, "which provides endless water, instantly adjustable to any tempera-ture you need. It is refilled by a suction device that pulls ground-water about five hundred feet below us and transports it to the surface. Sorry, no showers. Please note that the water is pristine and delicious." They all looked at him, blank-faced. "Any questions?"

"You're serious?" The woman was staring.

"I am always serious, madam. With more advance warning I might have been able to bring some additional materials."

"How did you dig such a deep hole?" the beautiful male agent asked.

"Agent Tomas, I believe?"

"Special Agent, yes."

I watched the conversation wanting to hear his voice and see how he moved.

"How did you dig those kinds of holes in this kind of hard rocky soil? Ten feet?" he continued. "Certainly not with a shovel? I don't understand how you can transport water from so deep in the ground. What does transport mean? Is this some new technology?"

"All fair questions, Special Agent Tomas," Uncle His responded. "You have experienced my smaller aircraft and behind me is a much larger warbird. Both, I assume, are well beyond your experience. These are among the reasons you all signed non-disclosure agreements. We have access to technologies you have not seen before nor been briefed about. Given that this is an active crime scene with multiple bodies and hungry wildlife, we need to focus on that task. I suggest you go there immediately. Afterward, I may be able to answer more questions. My apologies if this seems brusque. Right now, if you will excuse me, I need to spend time with Haldir to continue efforts to decipher his language. What he knows is crucial."

He indicated Daruk and me. "They will be happy to help and transport you to the site where she was murdered. They are however not authorized to give you details on what happened beyond what I discussed with the Director of Homeland Security and the President, and whatever they used to brief you when assigned to this task. See me if you have questions after working the sites. This is what your leadership insisted on to control information flow." He turned and entered the warbird; Haldir and the baby a step behind.

The agents looked a bit miffed, probably used to controlling every crime scene, people intimidated by them and quick to answer questions. Uncle His was beyond their experience. It made me grin.

Agent Amere Washington came up to me and smiled. She was a tough beauty, wearing a red tank top that contrasted nicely with her black skin, and cargo pants with a pistol on her hip. I guessed she was in her forties. "Director described your take down of the men after the girl was killed. It's hard to imagine you killed two men with your bow. You look like such an innocent high school student, yet you're a warrior. I respect that and am delighted we're working together."

"I *am* a high school student."

Her jaw dropped before she laughed, then stepped forward, wrapping her arms around me, and hugged, lifting me off the ground.

"Wow. Thank you, ma'am. I take that as a compliment."

"Call me ma'am again and I'll show you a few new things about combat."

"I'd love to learn whatever you want to teach me."

The movie star gorgeous agent, Gabriel Tomas, observed the conversation and extended a hand. "We've not formally met and I want to shake your hand. Also, to stay on your good side." He grinned. His hand was almost hard, maybe calloused, his grip strong but not crushing. He wasn't a showoff. He was in stunning shape, obvious in a too small black T-shirt. But he didn't hug me. Too bad.

I found myself a bit flummoxed. He was so good looking it was distracting. How was it possible to look like him? In school, I was mostly ignored by the beautiful kids. He'd have been their leader. Even so, no comparison to my indigenous warrior. Daruk walked up and ran his hand down my back. I turned and tilted my head; he kissed me on the lips, making sure pretty boy knew we were a couple. I kind of liked that kind of possessiveness, not that he had anything to worry about.

The forensic anthropologist was maybe fifty, brown hair with a touch of grey at the temples, at least what I could see, and a day's growth of beard. He was about my height, had a slight paunch but carried himself well in cargo pants and shirt. . He had a knife and canteen on his utility belt. His blue eyes studied us closely. His hat was ridiculous for up here. But I needed to slow any judgements until I knew him better.

I guess we were well beyond their normal crime scene associates. At least Uncle His and Daruk, super tough exotics. I was just the pale skinned, auburn-haired wanna be warrior.

"Young men," said Amare. "We would like to visit the crime scene now, if possible. Can you give us ten minutes to drop off our stuff and then we exit?"

"No problem, ma'am," Daruk responded. "Bring what equipment you need; we will meet at the smaller ship when you are ready."

I noticed she didn't scold my boyfriend on calling her ma'am. Of course, calling out someone who looked like Daruk should be done carefully. It made me laugh. I was desperate to find anything to make me smile, lighten the tension of the situation.

While we waited, I inspected and used one of the special open-air toilets. Such a treat, looking at an eagle in the sky while I peed. This city boy could handle it. It was better than what we did in the wilds of Earth3 where you had to use a latrine while groups of children observed.

Agent Amare Williams was the first to join us at *Canoe*. She carried a backpack and a small suitcase. Beauty and Hat were close behind lugging their gear.

9.

We landed at the edge of the kill site. Four bodies were as we left them except for the grad student. His corpse had been dragged about ten feet by a cougar, Daruk announced after examining paw prints. Our arrival had apparently scared off the creature. I looked at the two men I'd killed. One with his AR15 strapped around his arm and lying across his chest. The other with a pistol in his outstretched hand.

Our three guests got to work. Agent Amare asked us to repeat what details we could, and we did so, how instruments on *Canoe* sensed bodies, alive and dead, when we passed over the ridge. We followed Uncle His's advice and didn't give any new details, only offering a timeline and locations. She thanked us and said it would take at least three hours to complete their analysis. She said she would call us on the satellite phone if they finished earlier.

Special Agent Heartthrob asked about the current location of the woman's body. Daruk explained that we were trying to figure out how Haldir's people handled the dead so we could be respectful. The young woman was someone important to him. Tomas asked when they could see the bodies of the other tribe members, before letting his irritation break through, his voice gruff: "You know, this is an active crime scene and we are the FBI."

"True," I responded, surprised by his tone, "yet this is also a unique, national security situation as dictated by the President of the United States." I looked right into his beautiful eyes, not wanting to let my team down. "That said, we believe Haldir moved the bodies and cleaned up the killing field before we found him, perhaps in accordance with his traditions or he just wanted to make sure his loved ones were not exposed to the climate and wildlife. We just don't know. Katnu is trying to find a way to understand those traditions, today if possible, so we don't add insult to his relatives on top of all the horror that happened today." I tried to sound reasonable, not wanting to complicate the situation.

"Thanks," Agent Tomas responded. "Sorry if I barked. Maybe by the time we're done here things will be clearer. We understand the sensitivity. Given all that's happened, the young man seems remarkably poised." He turned and started photographing the site.

"Let us return," Daruk said to me. We got back into *Canoe*, landing in minutes next to the warbird.

"Wait a moment, please," he said before I could exit. "I want to show you some photographs." I settled back into my seat behind him, and he pulled up some video of when we first found the murder site. I leaned forward and watched the screen: there were the three bodies of the tribe members. It was grim but likely useful in launching a discussion with Haldir.

"Can you take a single frame, maybe from a distance?" I asked. "It might be less horrific for him to see. We should also provide the originals to the agents."

"Agreed. Let me try to do a single print." He made some adjustments I couldn't see and then I heard a buzz and a photo printed out. He looked at it and handed it to me.

"Still tough to see but it gives us a way to ask where they are now. Do we indicate we know where they were?"

"Let Katnu make that determination. He has been working with him."

Inside the warbird, the two were continuing to build vocabulary and talking in rudimentary ways. Without the verbs it made for confusing conversation. A language did not survive on nouns alone. Maybe I'd try that pious statement on my English teacher. Or not.

• • •

When Haldir seemed to falter, stumbling, and holding his head, Uncle His suggested he go to his tent and rest. The man had to be emotionally exhausted. Daruk went with him so that he was never alone.

We used his absence to continue our research. I helped Uncle His with his special equipment to further examine the body of the dead woman. We did not touch the body, trying to limit doing anything that might be against the religious practices of the young man's people. Before, Haldir was not in the picture; now he was, and his needs had to be part of our calculations.

Katnu wanted to confirm his earlier findings and go further with more powerful organ imaging equipment. They left her lying in place on the table in the warbird and held up two different machines overhead and from the side.

"Do you have what you need?" I asked as we set the equipment back in place.

"I believe so. I am anxious to examine Haldir as well as the bodies of his relatives in the cave, if he will permit it."

"Can I ask what you found?"

He leaned against a console. "Vestigial organs and body parts refer to those that have little or no purpose in humans. They are a vestige left over from our ancestors. Charles Darwin suggested that such organs serve as evidence for evolution. Various reports I have seen suggest we have more than a hundred vestigial anomalies, the most renowned of which are the appendix, wisdom teeth, coccyx, external ear, and male nipples."

"What's the coccyx?"

"A small triangular bone at the base of the spinal column.

That area of her spine was ripped by the bullet and where I collected my sample. It was not there in fact nor in the imaging."

"And this means what?"

"She has none of these useless organs and body parts that we still have. Somehow over the last centuries or millennia of her people, evolution leaped forward and eliminated them, or, perhaps they were never there to begin with, so early was their split from the mainstream homo sapiens. Evolution has been known to suddenly make giant leaps in some species. That her ears are radically different, like the baby's and Haldir's, is obvious. Their external ear acts like a satellite dish, amplifying the sound waves reaching the external auditory canal, middle ear, and inner ear. Our human ears are comparatively rudimentary, serving little biological function other than to be a place to rest our glasses. For them though, it may be important to their survival." He paused, looking again at the body.

"She has an area of the brain next to the cerebellum about the size of your thumb, that is not found in our brains. While many useless parts of the human body have been removed from her over time, something else has been added in. It must be useful for her survival. Our instruments have no idea what it is." He took a deep breath, looking up as he exhaled.

"Did you find it in the baby?"

"I did not. Perhaps it is something that develops in puberty or some other time. If I have the opportunity, I will check the baby's brain again, knowing what I am looking for."

"For this high school kid all this is hard to take in. What if it's larger in Haldir? Size means better in some organs."

He ruffled my hair, grinning.

"Something else is amazing. Most research suggests that in the distant future our bones will become lighter, thinner. That seems to be the case here already. Yet something seems a bit off on the readings on bone composition. I hope to study the small piece of her spine I collected earlier."

"I assume you won't cut into her body again without his permission?"

"Correct. Bodies across all lines of belief need to be buried or cremated soon after death. Our time is limited in making a breakthrough with the boy."

"Maybe you can use the need for burial as a way into his beliefs. His reaction will tell you how they do or don't do it."

"That might work."

"Your hypothesis that Haldir and his people are what humans might become in a thousand years, does this confirm it?"

He shrugged. "They are potentially a version of humanity in the future. Sometime in their distant past, something happened to make them leapfrog evolution, perhaps multiple leaps. Stress could be a reason caused by their environment. In what I have done so far, I am only looking at physical traits. I have no detailed knowledge about their mental advancements, only my own surveillance."

"Like you did when you met me in the dog park near my house and determined I had the wiring to handle the mental augmentation the twenty-sixth century had developed to fill up most of my brain."

"Yes. He possesses great intelligence and much of his brain is in use, unlike humans in general. He also has telepathic powers. He regularly reaches out to my brain touching, exploring, trying to connect. It is like a dance where we both hear different music."

"Daruk says he's had the same experience. The knife we found with her body was strange. A steel blade with markings, like the runes you see in stories about witches and warlocks. She shot some kind of energy force at her attackers. We should show it to Haldir, see his reaction."

"If they are stone age people which would be one possibility, however unlikely, where did they get the steel or steel-like knife? My impressions are a bit barren at this point. They appear to be evolutionary advanced humans living a life we do not yet comprehend."

I smiled at him. "Nothing is simple and easy with you Uncle His. That makes life so much more interesting."

...

Four body bags sat in one corner of the big tent. The agents had finished that part of the crime scene investigation. Now they wanted to examine the body of the murdered woman.

Darwin carried out a platter with seven pre-prepared meals in Pyrex dishes, steaming hot. Daruk followed with a salad made from what the agents brought up that morning. Uncle His and Haldir entered the main tent behind them; it had a table set up low to the floor so people could sit on the ground to eat. No chairs at this restaurants.

"Fork," Haldir said holding one up as he sat cross-legged across from Katnu. A long piece of cloth was slung over his shoulder and around his chest to hold the baby so it could sleep, kept warm and near a beating heart. He held a baby bottle with the new formula, and the child's lips gripped the nipple, sucking hungrily.

Uncle His smiled. He pointed to a plastic glass filled with water.

"Cup," Haldir said. "Water," he added.

"Excellent," three of us responded with grins. He blushed, which was perfect.

"How's he progressing?" asked Wilkins Vardan, the forensic anthropologist.

"He is doing very well," Katnu responded. "We have identified nearly a thousand words from his language and cross-checked them with ours. He understands some of what we are doing and is anxious to communicate."

"We're kind of his family now, aren't we Uncle His?" I knew it wasn't technically true, but I felt like we were all he had. I wanted us to give him as much comfort as we could.

"Yes, Darwin, in a sense. All his blood relatives are dead, except for the child, at least that is an assumption. There is very little that we know of him, his people, his life. Finding a way to communicate is critical."

"What do you think should happen to Haldir and the baby

once we leave this mountain?" Vardan asked.

"Should we call you professor, special agent or some other term, maybe just your name?" Katnu asked, turning to the bald, goateed man across from him.

Vardan put down his fork, staring at Haldir while he spoke. "I'm Associate Professor at California State University in Long Beach. I have a Ph.D. from UC Berkeley, so doctor works. I'm not a Special Agent with the FBI, I work with them on special projects. I'm here for a distinct reason that uniquely qualifies me. I was at the FBI office in Los Angeles when the call came in from Homeland Security that we were to leave immediately after the briefing. I keep a go bag in a locker." He smiled, making fun of himself. "So, Wilkins works, or doctor, or even 'goatee man.' How close do you think you are in being able to fully communicate with this remarkable young man?" He looked back at Katnu.

"We are running searches on dozens of language databases around the world. We can hope for a Rosetta Stone that helped break the code on Egyptian hieroglyphics, but that is not probable. It may be an archaic dialect. While we search our focus now is building a dictionary. Haldir is young but smart. He understands what we are trying to do and wants us to succeed. He is also in deep mourning for the loss of his loved ones. We need to remember that and treat him accordingly."

"Tell me doctor," I asked, "do you know anything about one of the dead attackers, Professor Arnold Whitacre of Brentwell University? Or his graduate student assistant, Otto Heinrich? They were both anthropologists."

"I'm afraid I don't but I'll try and reach the chairman of the department to see what they were studying."

"I assume you will not divulge the reason for your curiosity," Katnu stated, not a question.

"Of course not. The Director and President O'Connor made it clear. But a curious inquiry from one anthologist to another shouldn't be suspicious, calling to see what the department was doing that might be of interest. I know the chair, Dr. Melbourne Hummidy, from my days in grad school. He was one of my professors."

"At this point, "Agent Williams added, "we can't divulge our mission or the fact that those two are dead."

"Understood," Vardan responded. "Did he say anything of interest before you put an arrow in his chest?"

My mind flashed to when he lurched for his pistol when I was momentarily distracted by Daruk's efforts to save the woman, and I flinched at the memories. "Yeah, he said they'd been tracking a group of remarkable people. That his student shot the woman in the back because he believed, they believed, she was about to jump off a cliff to kill her and her baby rather than be taken—taken by this group that had already murdered three other members of her group. Easy to understand why she'd be skeptical of their good intentions. Why would anyone bring an AR15, a weapon of war, on a scholarly study of an unknown tribe? I hope this answers your question, I hope you learn something from the dead professor's school." Somehow his manner irked me. Not sure why, but I decided not to disclose the energy charge the dead man mentioned. We needed to understand it better.

Agent Tomas looked at me, measuring his words. "Remind me not to get on your bad side. Taking down a military veteran armed with an AR15 and you with a bow and arrow—*unreal*. Why were these anthropologists willing to murder? What were they hoping to find? For me, it's beyond comprehension."

"I hope my gentle sleuthing with the chairman will give a clue," Vardan added.

Katnu stood. "Gentlemen and madam, it has been a pleasure. Haldir and I will retreat to the warbird to continue our own sleuthing on language."

With that the meal broke up.

10.

Back inside the warship, Uncle His and I sat with Haldir. The woman's body lay next to us, not that there were many options in this tight space. I shared photos I'd pulled of people being buried, examples of graves being dug, bodies in caskets. I also included a series of photos on bodies being covered with various natural elements such as mulch, woodchips and wildflowers, until it decomposed, typically four to six weeks, then the bones crushed, the material returned to the earth, perhaps being scattered in a garden or forest. Finding something that would reflect cremation was more complicated. We settled on shots of bodies being burned on piles of wood. The hope was these photos and mentioning Maia and the others in the cave would lead to a discussion on burial practices.

Uncle His pointed to the body of the dead woman and back to the photos.

Haldir swallowed, rubbed his eyes, exhaled and looked down. We gave him time. He reached over for the pictures and selected the ones for human composting. It made sense to me that someone living in the wild and close to nature would choose to replenish the world that gave life.

I held out a photo of the other three bodies and shrugged and raised my eyebrows, hopefully a way to make it a question. He looked at it and cried out. I felt guilty throwing so much at him at once when he was so emotionally vulnerable. He closed his eyes and sat up straight, apparently to collect his thoughts and calm himself. He seemed to chant quietly. Then he opened his eyes, pointed at the bodies, then at himself and waved an arm perhaps indicating he would take us to somewhere off in the distance.

Uncle His touched his shoulder and the two looked at each other. I wondered if they were communicating telepathically. Haldir looked grim. So something had happened.

Katnu touched his temple. Daruk hollered from outside, "On my way."

Such an efficient way to communicate.

"We will alert the others," Katnu said and we went to the main tent, Haldir with the baby in his arms. We found both men in their underwear preparing for bed, startled to see us.

Katnu announced, "Haldir is going to guide us to the spot where he placed the other three bodies. If you want to join us, bring any gear you need. We will take the warbird." He gestured to Haldir. "I am not certain of how he will react since we are still not able to communicate beyond simple concepts."

• • •

Mars lifted in silence. Amazing that a machine this large could be totally stealth and maneuver like a race car. It was obvious from their expressions that our FBI friends were stunned, eyes wide and staring. Agent Beauty's mouth was open. Great teeth. Of course.

We set down on the other side of mountain and just below the peak where we'd stopped before with *Canoe*. There the massive craft simply hovered, its front entrance two feet off the ground. Uncle His flipped a switch and in the late evening the entire entrance was lit bright as a summer's day.

"Darwin, pick up the red and blue light box," Daruk said.

High intensity flashlights hung from our hip belts but the box would illuminate major areas of the cave. I had no idea about the power source for the box, but it really didn't matter to me. All I had to do was carry one and push the on button.

Haldir exited first, holding the baby, running to the opening, jumping up, grabbing the rock with one arm and slipping inside. Daruk was close behind and handed up various pieces of equipment.

"Bring that small suitcase in the corner," Uncle His ordered. With an equipment bag in each hand, he walked out the door and easily climbed over the rocky surface to the rough steps leading to the opening. In short order, everyone was in the cave.

It was still twilight inside; the bright lights from the ship didn't have much impact given the tiny entrance and this wide expanse inside. There was the softer light from deeper in the cave in the pit we saw before. Given what we observed about Haldir's pupils, they may not have needed much light, able to see in semi-darkness.

I turned on one of the small lamp boxes we carried in and it was like daylight.

"Níl! Múch an solas." Haldir shouted, sounding irritated. He pointed to the light box and it went dark. He lifted an arm, gesturing to the left and right. The walls instantly emitted a soft glow.

"What the fuck?" Agent Washington barked.

"Unbelievable!" Wilkins Vardan shouted, his mouth open. He reached for his camera.

Agent Tomas moved toward the nearest wall, his eyes a few inches away, starting to touch what he saw and then changing his mind, like a little boy discovered doing something naughty.

Daruk glanced at Katnu and exchanged reactions telepathically.

"This is not a cave," I said, struggling to remain calm. "It's a temple."

"This confirms my first hypothesis," Uncle His stated, his voice calm. "Haldir is part of an advanced race of humans. Perhaps a vanishing civilization."

...

Like everyone else, I just stared, too shocked to move. The room had to be the size of a football field. Along the walls, seemingly carved in stone, were scores of giant figures, some in robes, some in ancient military gear, some shirtless or nude. They were older but still had some of Haldir's features and most seemed to be half again as tall as he was, maybe ten or twelve feet. Mostly men but numerous women. They were remarkably three dimensional, many painted with such skill they seemed alive, about to step toward us and speak. Above them were patterns of vines, flowers and trees, snaking upward toward a barrel ceiling which must be nearly twenty feet tall with a dozen vaults. Across the room, in perfect symetry, were dozens of support columns, like stalagmites and stalactites melding together. One near me was covered in carved and painted symbols like a pentagram, an eye, shield knots and other figures once seen in old England.

Across the room and in front of us, deeper in the cavern, were a series of doorways. The floor was smooth and covered in dozens of large colorful rugs, all reflecting flowers, vines and nature. Wooden chairs and sofas were covered in brilliant fabrics, placed in conversational groupings like one might have for friends talking or maybe in a classroom. Some furniture looked very old, maybe European antiques, perhaps even medieval, others likely carved locally and upholstered in brilliant nature scenes that reflected the mountains we were in now.

It was both familiar and otherworldly. It reminded me of photos I'd seen of Egyptian tombs, only far more lifelike.

It was a pleasant temperature, maybe mid-60s, unlike the low 50s outside. This was early June, temperatures were cool but could get hot in the summer.

Uncle His walked deeper into the space, stopping where my boyfriend and I had first met Haldir. There was the curved stone seating draped with thick animal furs. Nearby were the three raised platforms holding the bodies. Except for our breathing, footsteps and exclamations of awe, all was silent.

"Let us gather here and make plans," Katnu finally said. Everyone came to him. "Our focus right now is dealing with the bodies."

"Are we permitted to examine them, photograph our work and record our findings?" Agent Williams asked. She was being deferential, showing her appreciation for the complex situation with the young man.

"As long as we are respectful," Uncle His replied. "We can work in tandem. I will go first, using a special scanning device to examine the bodies and create a record. We should move slow and deliberate, treat them as family. I believe Haldir is comfortable with what I and you need to do. We have made progress in our communications. It is still imprecise, but I believe he trusts us, or at least trusts Daruk and Darwin. He will not likely interfere if they observe and are agreeable."

"For a complete record we should capture how we found the bodies, how they are wrapped and their surroundings," suggested our forensic anthropologist, pushing his fedora to the back of his head.

The lead agent went to the first body, fingers exploring the covering. "It is like a type of wool." She looked at Haldir and gestured that she wanted to remove it.

He looked at me and I nodded. The young man whispered something: *"Feuch gum bi thu measail."*

"Go ahead," I urged. The fabric of the clothing was already new to me, like a combination of lamb's wool and silk. Very thick but also soft. I had no idea what it was. Uncle His had saved some of the clothing we took from the young mother earlier today. Was it still today? So much had happened in a few hours.

The first body was male with the same kind of features as Haldir, the young woman and baby. Uncle His ran his silver tube over each body. The agents slowly pulled away the covering and then the clothing, the trio lying there naked and cold.

Haldir let out a cry, handed me the baby and leaned into me. I held him as he bent down and pushed his face into my shoulder. I felt honored that he trusted me and was determined to respect that privilege.

There were two bullet holes in the chest and one in the forehead. I suddenly felt even less guilty for killing the two murderers.

Photographs were taken of the corpse and wounds. Agent Amare said, "It's obvious that this young man cleaned them up for burial. Katnu, I think you said that he indicated they did a natural internment."

"Correct. You should get what you need now in case such burial is necessary from his perspective. This is not a typical FBI murder investigation. We are writing our own rules."

"He is six foot seven," said the female agent.

I forced myself to look at the body. He was thin but with impressive musculature. The skin was the same light brown as the others, maybe a tad darker. I suspected they were not conducting all the tests they normally would because of limited equipment and, perhaps, not to upset the young man who was crucial in understanding what happened. He was the only witness.

The next body was female. She was bloodless but it was obvious that a fusillade of bullets had nearly cut her in half. It was gruesome. Hard to imagine what Haldir felt when he'd found the bodies and carried them inside, washing them in preparation for burial. I rubbed the back of Haldir's head, trying to comfort him.

"She is shorter, five feet-eleven, Agent Handsome announced.

The last body appeared to be an older man. More gray in the hair and some wrinkles around the eyes yet still very youthful looking. When they turned him over, there were six bullets in his back, including the base of his skull.

What would lead anthropologists to be such vicious executioners? It also dawned on me that none of deceased were wearing the raised green medallions carried by Haldir and on the mother's body. They must have been stolen and were perhaps in the killer's camp. I needed to talk to Katnu about finding it. It might hold answers to some of our questions.

As the bodies were rewrapped in their clothes, the two agents pulled body bags from a backpack to put the first body inside before I could protest that he should ask.

"NÍL!" Haldir shouted, stepping up and pulling away the bag. *"Fág iad ina n-aonar!*

He shook his head and looked almost angry at Agent Williams. She backed up, nodding her understanding, took the body bag and put it back in the pack.

"I guess we aren't going to take the bodies," she said.

"Apparently not," Uncle His confirmed. "Let us thank him with a nod and smile and return to *Mars*. Darwin, please stay and see what you can determine. He trusts you more than any of us, even Daruk. We will wait your return."

I put a hand over Haldir's shoulder, holding the baby in my other arm. As the team left, he turned to me and offered a wan smile along with an appreciative nod.

What did he want to do? I shrugged and raised my eyebrows. He nodded and turned toward the back of the cave. I followed. The deeper we went, the more the carvings on the walls changed. No more human figures. We came to a giant carved sun, painted in vivid colors. Next to it were double doors, likely wood carved with intricate scenes of a forest with flowers and sun rays shining through the leaves. We walked inside what was a very clean space maybe twenty feet deep and thirty feet long. The ceiling was flat, the walls painted in a faded scene of flowers on a grassy hillside. There were half a dozen stone containers, like bathtubs only larger. Each was empty.

From what appeared to be a cabinet, Haldir pulled out four tightly woven wicker-like mats, each about eight feet long and maybe four feet wide. He placed one in each of four tubs and pushed them down so they were curved into the interior. He went back to the cabinet and took out a large basket.

He placed it on a shelf and gestured for the baby which I handed it to him and the boy was placed inside, his blanket wrapped around him. From his robe Haldir pulled out a baby bottle we'd been using, held it close to his chest and said something then gestured I do the same. I did and he squirted milk some into my palm for testing. The milk was warm. I grinned and nodded approval. He took the bottle to the baby. The child opened his mouth and suckled with a contented groan.

We went back to the bodies. He carefully lifted one up and nodded for me to do the same with another. I swallowed, not real comfortable with handling dead bodies, but I did as he suggested, reverently bearing the weight. We carried both back to the room and placed them on the wicker mats. He smiled and pointed back to where we came—I should get the last one.

When I returned, he was covering each body with straw, alfalfa, I suspected, and wood chips. He also had a basket of flowers. Where had this come from in a cave? I'd read about natural organic reduction, also called terramation and human composting. There is no embalming with the use of carcinogenic chemicals. Microbes in our bodies are still alive after we die and the body will decay naturally, aided by the organic materials and a slightly warm environment. After about two months, everything converts to nutrient-rich soil. Any bones or teeth that remain can be crushed and returned to the soil. I remember a statistic I read about the amount of steel used each year in crypts and caskets being equivalent to all the steel in the Golden Gate Bridge. Natural burial had been common in America until the Civil War when embalming was used to preserve bodies for shipment. I thought it was beautiful, watching him reverently place flowers into the folded hands of each of the three family members.

He looked at the baby who was now sleeping quietly. He looked at me and waved for me to follow. We left the cave and returned to *Mars*. He walked immediately to the body of the young woman and lifted her in his arms.

I quietly informed everyone: "Haldir has started a natural burial process for the other three and this young woman will join them. I think it's magical and we need to respect his wishes."

No one spoke as we left the warbird. I helped him lift the body into the cave. She was placed in the fourth container. He arranged some pink flowers in her folded hands over her chest and then filled her with the organic material until she was covered.

He gestured for me to follow him to the back of the room. Six stone covers leaned against a wall like surfboards. He pulled one away and nodded for me to pick up the other end. We carried it carefully to the first container and placed it on top. Soon all were covered. He leaned against a wall and bent a knee against his chest, pulling up the pantleg to reveal a leather sheath, strapped to his calf, holding a silver knife, maybe ten inches long. I thanked him for allowing me to examine the knife which was similar to the one the woman had had, covered with several different symbols, the most prominent a seven-point star. Knife in hand, he walked to the first container, chanting in a whisper, moving it over the stone as he spoke. He then did the same with the other three.

I'd read that Jewish law forbids embalming for traditional burials, considering it desecration of the body. Islamic law orders the deceased be washed and buried with only a wrapping of white cloth. We could learn from them.

He gently picked up the baby, still sleeping, and held him close. Then he touched my arm for a moment, squeezing my biceps, watching me with his emerald eyes, perhaps confirming I was a friend, needing to connect, then nodded. He took my hand and led me out of the room, closing the doors behind us.

As we walked across the room, I stopped to examine a set of chairs and a table. The wooden frames were heavy and ornately carved. The fabric was colorful, like a flower garden captured in fabric, the material soft.

He moved toward an opening in the middle of the room. We walked through and to the right there was a door, likely wood; he opened it. Inside it was pitch dark. I touched his shoulder and he turned to me. His pupils covered the entire eye. Seeing in the dark was no problem for him. He said something and a soft glow immediately filled the room. He looked at me to see if I was satisfied.

"Thank you," I said and smiled.

The modest space held a bed, covered in thick blankets and pillows, a table with two chairs. There was also a shelf of what appeared to be—but no it couldn't be—books. Looking closer I saw they were leather bound. This mysterious man was full of secrets. I pointed to a volume and raised my eyebrows in a pantomime of asking permission.

He picked it up. The cover did indeed seem like old worn leather. He handed it to me and I held it reverently before opening to pages that were thick, maybe like the vellum used in medieval texts. The words were in a very neat script, looking handwritten but too perfect and consistent for that possibility. The language made no sense to me. My brain had been enhanced with about a dozen languages and none could interpret it.

He gestured for me to follow, indicating I could keep the book, which I tucked carefully away. We walked past several other rooms, probably also sleeping areas. We passed through another set of double doors into a dark space. At his command a low-level light filled the space. The walls here were covered by storage spaces and what looked like cooking equipment. Pots hung on hooks and there was a kind of flat cooking area with metal like strips across it. The heating source must be underneath. I noted a hole in the ceiling, similar to what I imagined a natural vent for a volcano would be, smooth, almost polished rock rising up and twisting to the surface. He gestured at a wall and a panel slid back revealing a half dozen small tables and chairs surrounded by baskets full of various vegetables and other items in small ceramic-like containers.

He took my hand and led me to an adjacent space where a door opened. From the elegant ceramic-like seats, each with a deep hole underneath, I guessed this was the bathroom, a communal one. Maybe privacy was not important to them but I didn't really want to investigate too closely. An open area with what appeared to be a large square hole in the rock, held a half dozen steps leading to the bottom where water flowed into a series of smaller holes. Likely a bathing area, kind of like a community Roman tub, but I had no idea where the water originated from.

We went deeper into the cave. He opened a door that forced me to shield my eyes from light as bright as sun lamps. There were rows upon rows of shelves with every kind of edible plant I'd ever seen. Obviously this was where their food came from and the flowers for the burial. His people were mostly vegetarians, I assumed, given his aversion to meat.

He led me back into the main room and from there we returned to the warbird.

Uncle His put away his instrument he was using as we neared and walked toward us with a smile, and Haldir returned it in kind. "Did you learn anything new?"

I described my tour, concluding, "As astounding as all that was, there was a shelf of books in his room." I held the book out toward him. "Can you believe it? This could be a breakthrough in understanding his language."

Uncle His looked at it with interest, holding it carefully, opening it and scanning several pages. "I have no idea what it says."

Agent Gorgeous, who was standing next to me and Katnu as we talked about the book, looked shocked. "A written language?" he said, both a question and statement. "That's stunning. Almost as shocking as the inside of the cave. Or your planes." His face looked like he'd just had a revelation. "One possibility, and the book makes it more probable, is that this is not just the last remnants of a mountain tribe; it's a vanishing civilization. My theory is that these anthropologists somehow found it and were willing to murder to gain the fame and glory to go with it.".

Uncle His looked up from the book. "I think you may have a point Agent Tomas. Seeking celebrity has led to many villainous acts. Darwin, I have an assignment for you." He drew me to a corner of the ship, away from the agents.

"Take *Canoe* and return to the Passageway. Travel to the chancellor and have his top linguist, her name is Wylinda Topaz, examine this book. Take a digitized memory card of my findings to date. I have my suspicions on the language but want more input. I need a translator that can be uploaded and used by the four of us."

He wanted me to go by myself? I felt overwhelmed but also proud he had such confidence in me. "It's late at night. I've never flown *Canoe* by myself, and I don't know how to land it. I don't know the codes to E1. Sorry if I sound panicked."

"I will give you what you need. With your enhancements, your skill level is far more than you think. Believe in yourself."

A half hour later, I lifted *Canoe* and headed home following my own coordinates. I was the pilot and only passenger and so I carefully studied all my notes, hoping I didn't pee. A recurring concern of mine given all that was happening. Not a good look for a Guardian.

11.

wished I'd paid more attention to how Uncle His had parked *Canoe*, unobserved and mysteriously silent, into a secret door on the side of the hill over the Passageway. As I approached, fog suddenly appeared around the hillside as if blown in from the ocean. Did *Canoe* do this automatically or were we going to crash? I punched in a code Katnu gave me and crossed my fingers. We moved forward in zero visibility.

I shrieked when *Canoe* started turning 180 degrees.

"No! No! This can't be right!"

Canoe ignored me and we started moving backward. I braced for a crash. Somehow, we slipped through, parking precisely and automatically in a tunnel. I'd only been in *Canoe* a couple of times on my earth. There was a similar craft on E3 in the 17th century. Three earths in the multiverse did complicate our options. Secrecy was less important there. Plus, Daruk was known to distract me when Katnu was piloting.

I went directly to the portal to take me to 26th century San Francisco, the elevator to the surface, at least what was left of it, just a half dozen hills surrounded by ocean. I stood for a moment, contemplating what had been lost here but was still alive in my world. Unless politics and human greed changed, my world was facing the same fate. I shook my head, no time for this now. I made my way down a short path and to the tall, half round teleporter covered in stone to hide the electronics. I pushed my back against the curved wall and said what Daruk instructed:

"I am Guardian in training Darwin, on a mission for Guardian Katnu Hisman. Take me to Yellowknife."

I really hated feeling like I was going to vomit, such was the special effect of this transport system on my gut. Two minutes later I was standing, wobbling being a more accurate term, inside a silver cylinder over a thousand miles away. I held onto the wall strap and took a deep breath.

My one time here before, the dashing Captain Phillips had opened the door. Now, no one, nothing. Was there a handle? I ran my fingers all over the door and around it. I found a slight indentation at the top and pressed. The silver curved door slid open. It was dark but I stepped out anyway. Where was Phillips?

"Hello," I said. I repeated it louder. And louder.

"Hold on!" a male voice responded.

Lights came on and a young soldier ran in my direction. He held a pistol and stopped a few yards from me. "Identify yourself! Why are you here unannounced in the middle of the night?" The man, likely a teenager, was pale with blond hair and his beret was pushed back on his head, as if he'd just pulled it on. He was nervous. His face showed the crease marks of sleep. "You're not a Guardian!"

I raised my arms. "I have no weapon. I'm on an urgent mission for Guardian Katnu Hisman. It's about a major discovery on E2. We need the help of a linguistics expert to solve the problem. My name is Darwin McQuaid, a high school student on my planet, lover of Daruk the Guardian and a Guardian in training. I was here before about a month ago. Can I ask your name?"

"You can ask. Let me contact the Chancellor. He won't be pleased." He adjusted a device on his sleeve, waving his pistol. "Look at me. I need a photo for ID."

I tried to look non-threatening which wasn't hard since everyone said I looked innocent. He spoke quietly, covering his mouth. "Keep your arms up!" he barked; I did as I was told. "What's in the backpack?"

"An ancient book that needs translation."

"Who do you need to see?"

"A linguist named Wylinda Topaz. Katnu gave me her name and specific instructions."

He pointed to the hallway. "The Chancellor wishes to talk with you in his residence. Walk in front of me. Keep your arms up. Higher! Don't try anything or I'll shoot." The soldier opened a door into a massive room.

Daruk had told me about it but seeing it was a stunner. One of the most awe-inspiring spaces I'd ever seen, it looked like a stylized version of a grand and exaggerated Gothic cathedral from the Middle Ages, high vaulted ceilings, sculptural moldings, statues not of saints but various historical figures and gargoyles. Most important, indeed the purpose of the design, rows of tall arched windows, stacked one above the other, looked much like stained glass, with scenes of Earth's former natural glories. Light shined through the windows and given the hour it must have been artificial. It created a feeling of supernatural beauty and awe, almost holy.

We walked past several tables and sofas. A guard under a giant circular stained glass window recalling glories of long ago suddenly jumped up from a chair and straightened her uniform. The building was a grand conceit, Uncle His had told me, built by the Chancellor, so rich and powerful he could indulge his whims, to remind people of his power and that of the Council. Religion was no longer well regarded in this age and on this Earth, given its role in wars, pogroms and human misery. The room was inspiring, almost shocking to enter if you were unprepared.

The guard stiffened as we neared. No salute in acknowledgment of my escort, so my unfriendly guard was not high ranking. But what big shot military person would be guarding empty rooms at two in the morning. Although I wasn't sure of the time. That was the hour on my world and it could be different here just like Daruk's world was a few hours off.

My guy said, "Keep going down this hallway." I did as he ordered, my arms still up. A few hundred feet was another grand doorway. "We are here," he said into whatever device he had.

We waited some more. "Can I put down my arms?"

"No!"

Several minutes later the door opened. A sleepy looking older man in a bathrobe and slippers answered the door.

"Bring him in," the brown skinned man said, sounding cranky. I would guess he was in his seventies and shuffled when he walked.

"Sit there," he said in an irritated voice, pointing to a chair in a small library. He went through another doorway and closed it behind him.

I sat, my arms still up, noticing the soldier's pistol was now aimed at my head. Worse, his hand was trembling. I guess someone arriving via teleporter unannounced in the middle of the night was a big deal. Not exactly the friendly reception I was hoping for. "Maybe you'd be more comfortable if you sat in the chair over there," I said, indicating one against the opposite wall. "It might steady your aim if you have to shoot me." As soon as it was out, I was sorry about being flippant.

"Don't talk," he growled. Slowly he stepped back and sat.

The door opened, the guard jumped up, and the Chancellor stepped into the room followed by his aide. He was a bit less imposing than when we had met before. But so was I in my casual work outfit. His long gray hair flowed over his shoulders, his goatee tightly trimmed, and his face held a snarl.

"Chancellor." I stood sort of at attention.

"Is it your custom to pay unannounced visits in the middle of the night?"

"Sorry about the hour. Katnu Hisman sent me."

"I remember you, young Darwin. Victor, you can leave us. Guard, wait outside." The other two stepped away and it was just the two of us. "Please sit. Apologies for not having tea ready but I suspect you don't need any," he said, sitting, straightening his robe and crossing his legs. "Katnu is a big fan of yours, convinced you'll make a brilliant Guardian. So, you need a linguist. Tell me about your mission. Come sit with me so we don't have to shout."

I moved over and sat next to him on the sofa. I gave him an overview.

"Stunning. May I see the book?"

I pulled it from my pack; he looked through it, reverently. "A potentially advanced form of Homo sapiens. We will help in any way we can."

"Thank you. Perhaps equally as surprising as the physical nature of the young man and baby is the architecture of his cave."

"Please explain."

I gave him details and showed video on my comm device and photos of Haldir.

"I will notify our linguist, and Private Dondle will take you to her. I look forward to a detailed report."

"Can you tell him I'm no threat and not to point a pistol at me?"

"His caution is understandable given the hour. He's a young soldier not much older than you." He smiled and walked me to the door, where he issued orders.

"Take him to the residence of Wylinda Topaz. I will contact her now. You can also put away the weapon. Thank you for your diligence. I will tell Captain Phillips you handled yourself well."

The private looked relieved, holstered his weapon and we walked down the hallway to an elevator. It was a half hour trip through an underground shuttle to her home.

It had been a quiet trip with the Private, and Ms. Topaz did not look happy either when she opened her door. She had a floral scarf over her head and was in a floor length blue plush robe and matching slippers. She looked maybe fifty with dark brown skin and even darker brown hair with streaks of red on her forehead. "I don't get many male callers at three in the morning. At least not ones this young. Do come inside," she said shaking her head. "Now what is the question? I assume it must be earth-shaking."

"Certainly, it could shake up E2, ma'am. Thank you for seeing me."

"When the Chancellor calls, no matter the hour or purpose,

we smile and do our part. Show me what you've got."

The soldier followed me inside. She and I sat on a small flower print sofa. He stood at parade rest at the door.

"We found this in a cave in the high mountains in California." I handed her the book and continued to tell the story.

Her attention was absolutely fixed on the book. "Boy, hand me that scanner over on that table." She pointed at the soldier who almost leaped across the room. He picked up a small silver box—she nodded—and he handed it to her. She held it over a dozen pages, then announced she was sending it to her linguistics program for ancient languages.

"I don't believe this is a contemporary tongue but rather an ancient one with variations. Languages are alive and change with usage over time. A group of native speakers, if they broke off from other groups, would alter the language significantly over the centuries. For a species to change, as you've inferred, would likely require centuries or even a millennium to pass in isolation."

I reached back into my pack. "Here are recordings of words as the young man spoke them so we get the right pronunciation, and a long list comparing modern day English words with his shared definitions."

We sat in silence for nearly an hour as she read and transferred what I'd given her into her language analysis program. She sat up suddenly, "Yes!" The soldier and I jumped.

"It's a form of Celtic, very old with touches of ancient Gaelic. Rather remarkable to find it in this book, in a cave, in the high mountains of the Sierra. It may have its origins in Ireland and Scotland from centuries ago."

"Can you...."

"Can I create a data base that will allow you to talk fluently with this mysterious young man? You don't want much, do you? Yes, I think so. I assume you want it in a form that you can upload into your brain and those of the Guardians?"

"Ah, yes, ma'am." I thought of something else. "It's likely the Guardians are gathering additional translations while I'm here, a kind of dictionary. Is there a way that new material can be added to what you're doing?"

"Again, you don't want much do you?"

I gave her a hopeful grin. Put my boyish innocence to some good use.

"I think I can make it work and add it into the programming. You'll need to put in a form that can be downloaded and is compatible. It'll will take me a few hours. Private, take this young man to a guest suite so he can rest. Would you like your clothes laundered while you sleep?" She wrinkled her nose. "Or perhaps new clothing?"

"I've been up and active for a long time. Do I, ah…"

"Smell? I'm glad my words were not too subtle. That's why I'm offering you answers. Now go with the young soldier. I will contact you when I'm ready."

• • •

Someone slapped my leg. I jumped up, tossing off the covers, in a fighting stance for what might be happening.

Captain Peters was in front of me dressed in all his immaculate military glory, including the smirk on his face.

I put my hands in front of my crotch and grabbed the sheet.

"Time to get up. Wylinda Topaz is ready for you." He held up a bag holding my clean clothes and tossed it on the bed. He also held up another bag. "Brought a late lunch so you can maintain your strength. Go ahead, shower, eat and brush your teeth if you want."

"Ahhhmmm…"

"Nice seeing you again, Darwin. I'll take you when you're ready."

"Thanks, Captain," I replied, running to the bathroom, one hand behind me to cover my butt.

• • •

"Sit, boy!"

Ms. Topaz, maintaining her same charm as before, pointed to

a chair in front of her desk, looking just like she had last night, same scarf over her head and the floor length robe. Captain Peters stood behind me.

"I trust you got some sleep and a shower."

"Yes, ma'am."

"That makes one of us. I've been working on this since our meeting. My first impressions last night were partially correct. It is mostly ancient Gaelic with a mix of other languages. Some Anglo-Saxon words that may go back to the early Middle Ages. I also find Germanic, Icelandic and, this really did surprise me, Old Castilian, and various African tribal languages, even some indigenous tongues from the Americas. What this tells me is that this young man you found is part of a tribe that has been on the move for centuries, perhaps millennia."

"Like the Jews, being forced to move because of prejudice?"

"Perhaps. But the Jews were mostly persecuted because of the Catholic view that they killed Jesus or just because they dared to be different. If you believe your religion is the only one, and they all believe that, you may not take kindly to different perspectives, taking it as an insult to your god. They mostly moved around the Old World. This language suggests they lived in the Old and New Worlds. Few people or tribes would adopt such a vagabond life unless they were forced. The physical characteristics you found would take hundreds if not thousands of years of evolution, changes forced because of intense ecological or survival pressures."

"Did the book make sense?"

"Yes. It's Medieval in age, except for some handwritten more recent upgrades, and deals with a mix of issues relating to health and travel. It's been passed around for centuries, thus the notations at the front from various owners."

"What you've developed, will it help us communicate with Haldir?"

"It should certainly make it easier. The programming should help. Plus, it can record new words and changes as you speak. A rather nice feature."

"Is it ready to upload into my head?"

"Are you willing?"

"Yes. I trust you because Katnu Hisman does. The young man's special and I want to be able to help him. But first we need to understand his world."

She opened a drawer, pulling out a half helmet like what Uncle His used on me months ago. "I assume you want to be fully functional when you return to your world. Follow me into a treatment room and we can begin."

We went through a door and there was a table with a pillow. "Lay on your back."

I stretched out, Captain Phillips watching closely. She fitted the green helmet over my head. I closed my eyes; it began to hum softly. Then darkness.

When I awoke, both were beside me. She removed the helmet. The first thing I noticed was that her hair was nicely curled, and she was dressed. I was obviously asleep for an hour or several.

The captain touched my shoulder. "How do you feel?"

"Sleepy."

"Follow me to the T-L," she instructed.

"What's a...."

"Honestly," she said with irritation. "Tongue Lab! Don't you study anything in school?"

"Actually, that may not come up for another five hundred' years."

The captain laughed. She didn't.

"It's an automated language practice booth. You will engage in conversation with a fully realized speaker in front of you looking something like the person you described yesterday. It will talk with increasing complexity; you will respond so you're used to how it works in a real-life situation. It will offer corrections, suggest how to use your new program, and help sharpen your speed and skills. After an hour or two, you may be ready to sit down with your new friend."

12.

Captain Phillips personally escorted me back to the transport booth while I did my best not to think of how embarrassed I was when I jumped out of bed naked. He'd laughed when I tried to apologize.

The two-part ride back to my Earth and century, as always, made my stomach churn and brain twirl. I opened my eyes; I was back on the hill overlooking what was left of San Francisco. Such a tragedy that did not have to have happened. Even worse, my world was going to let it happen again.

I stepped away from the curved stone booth and walked a short distance to the back door which looked impregnable, like it was made of iron.

"I am Darwin, Guardian in training with the permission of Guardian Katnu Hisman to use the Passageway. Open, please."

The door slowly swung inward. I ran inside, took the lift down three hundred feet, hurried through the mist and freezing cold of the doorway to my world. I hurried through the blue undulating flame to the elevator.

A quick trip to the bathroom, switching my clothes to something fresher from my stash at the cabin, grabbing a protein bar, a fast gargle since I was about to see Daruk, and I entered the chamber where *Canoe* was waiting and facing the right direction. All I had to do now was get it launched during daylight when people were about. I put my hand on the flat screen; it warmed and changed shape to match my palm and fingers. A light glowed and *Canoe* turned on.

"External view." There were several camera angles on the side of the park. A family walking on one side. A man with six dogs on leashes.

"Camouflage," I said, reading the instructions on the screen. A light breeze started according to the controls. Fog began to appear which was not uncommon being close to the ocean but commanding it to appear was very cool. An opening appeared before me, at the end of the tunnel. "Advance slowly," I commanded, feeling a bit giddy. *Canoe* lifted a few inches and we floated outside, passing through a redwood tree. Or at least a fake redwood tree that looked real. No wonder I could never figure out the opening. We drifted leisurely over Duboce Park, filled with a score of dogs off leash with their owners. No one looked up.

I put in the coordinates to return to the Russian Wilderness. At first I didn't think we were moving until I checked the dial and a camera view of the changing landscape. But not too fast, as Uncle His might say, well below the speed of sound to avoid any sonic booms. *Canoe* didn't have all the technical options of Mars. Within minutes I was over the site of our camp before I even had a chance to call my friends. We settled in next to the giant warbird like a leaf touching down in still air.

Daruk sprinted from the large tent, grabbing me by the waist as I exited, lifting me up and twirling me around. "I missed you beautiful Darwin," he said, kissing my cheek when he let my feet touch earth.

"Nice to be appreciated," I said and placed my lips on his.

"Radharc álainn," Haldir said, coming up behind us.

"Radharc an-álainn," I replied in agreement, *"agus blasta."*

Haldir laughed.

"What?" Daruk broke apart from my embrace. "Are you two talking?"

"Oh! Wow! It just happened, so natural. I had the program uploaded. I guess it's working."

"What did you both say?"

"He said 'a beautiful sight' when he saw us kissing. And I replied, 'a very beautiful sight and tasty.'"

"This's great!" Daruk said.

I looked at him in disbelief. "You used a contraction."

"Is that a question, beautiful Darwin? I promised you I would try if you joined me on this trip to the Russian Wilderness." He grinned. "Let us find Katnu and see if we can all learn how to communicate, full sentences or not."

The three of us ran, holding hands, toward the war bird. He needed reassurance and we wanted to connect.

...

"Silence would be appreciated," Uncle His said, his annoyance obvious from by his tone. No translation needed.

Haldir and I had been talking like two gossipy old friends meeting after a long absence. Haldir took my hand; being able to communicate made us closer.

Katnu was examining the helmet I brought back, uploading data into his own program, examining the contents on a screen. "The linguist is brilliant," Katnu said, turning to us. "I have downloaded our work over the last two days, so the database is up to date. Daruk, let us start with you. You can upgrade your language skills to a tongue that likely originated in pre-historic times through the present. It is a complex language but a relatively short program compared with the existing content in your brain. This means the transfer may be short. Ready?"

"If you don't need me for other work, of course."

Katnu nodded and Daruk went to the table, undoing his belt with its sword and sling. I came up next to him and kissed him softly on the lips. The helmet was placed around his head and the light buzz began. Within minutes, Daruk was asleep.

•••

"*An mbeidh orm dul i mbun a bhfuil á dhéanamh ag Daruk?*" Haldir asked as we sat outside the main tent, eating lunch and leaning against a rock. The female FBI agent, Amare Williams, and the anthropologist were squatting nearby, listening without comprehending. Agent Gorgeous was standing and eating. Would Haldir need to undergo the helmet? Katnu had told me privately that once we were all uploaded, he could use his own significant power of telepathy to transfer and engage with Haldir's brain. He'd been reluctant to use the device knowing so little about how the young man's brain was wired. I was pleased he was being cautious.

I looked at Haldir and considered my words in this strange language. "*Nílim cinnte. Ceapann Katnu go bhféadfaimis é a dhéanamh ag baint úsáide as do chumhacht telepathy.*"

He looked at me, nodding. "*Déanfaidh mé cibé rud is gá chun do theanga a thuiscint.*"

I set down my plate and took his hand, smiling. "*Ná tú féin.*"

"What the fuck!" Agent Sexy barked, spitting out bits of food. "How? You were gone less than two days and now you understand him and are fluent? How is this possible? I've never heard of such a thing."

"It's astonishing," the anthropologist added.

"You've seen many astonishing things since you arrived," I responded, unsure how to answer. "Technologies beyond anything you know. Daruk and Katnu have astonishing brain capacity and knowledge . They're working with me to increase mine. President O'Connor knows what we can do. Katnu Hisman's worked with her on several projects over the years and with some of her predecessors." I needed to be careful and probably had already said too much. Certainly I could not say Uncle His has been meeting with presidents for nearly two centuries. "Within a day or two, both Daruk and Katnu will be fluent in Haldir's language and will be working with him. Our hope is he can learn to speak English."

"This's insane!" Special Agent Gabriel Tomas protested.

I needed to start remember his name not just his physical description.

"You've seen enough to know why you were sworn to secrecy," I answered, trying to sound respectful.

"Please calm down, Gabriel," Agent Washington interjected. "I understand how you feel. I'm feeling a little dumb. We knew this was a highly unusual, maybe even unheard of, assignment. Agents over the years, we know they'vee been privy to remarkable things and maintained confidentiality. We don't know what other secrets are being kept. Remember *Men in Black*, that movie about a secret government agency that deals with aliens?"

He asked wryly, "Am I Tommy Lee Jones or Will Smith?"

She shook her head. "We've given our word and that's part of what makes us special. I'm not really sure how we proceed once we finish our work. That will up to the Director and the President. They made it clear that Mr. Hisman will give his own report to President O'Connor on what we did and how well we did it. This structure is certainly a first in my career." She shrugged. "But we work under the guidance of the president."

"Where do I fit in when you prepare your findings?" Wilkins Vardan asked. "As a forensic anthropologist, my specialty examines human remains, particularly bones, or more broadly, looking at the human species, searching for perceived links between the nature of a crime and the personality or physical appearance of an offender. None of that really applies in this case, the crime and perpetrators are obvious. What fascinates mc in my area of expertise, is understanding the world in which Haldir and the baby have lived. What are they compared to what we might think of as normal humans? The question for me is how their lives, their unique culture, their civilization, if you will, informs our work, gives us insights into the minds of the murderers. Answers could shake my professional world, and perhaps the broader American public."

"Well said, Wilkins. I agree," Agent Washington replied. "I

think we need to work with our hosts to find some answers, particularly cracking the language barrier with the young man. Hopefully in the next day or so because our hosts are so far beyond the normal. Meanwhile, Agent Tomas and I need to go through our photos and findings and begin a report to the president. You're welcome to join us, Mr. Vardan."

13.

aving spent the last two hours sitting on pine needles, my butt and back were numb. I'd been leaning against the only tree with a relatively smooth bark, a silver birch, nestled in a grove of what looked like Christmas trees, likely some kind of Spruce, all while reading Homer's *The Odyssey*. It was a summer reading assignment, the first of many, for my senior World Lit course and I needed to turn in an analysis in three weeks. No time off for summer for advanced placement, an honor I didn't seek. We had to use an actual paper book, turning a page instead of swiping it, which I kind of liked. Of necessity, I read and pondered issues for school when I could. Odysseus, the hero, a man of sometimes superhuman strength, dealt with gods, monsters, and magical creatures, also entering the underworld at one point, experiencing space/time travel, divine intervention, immortality. I kept getting sidetracked with what was happening in my life that had some elements in common with what was said to be one of the greatest epic poems ever written.

When the door on *Mars* opened, I stood and gratefully rubbed my behind, folding a page in the book to mark the spot, another new experience in this very long, complicated story.

As Daruk walked out of *Mars*, he was communicating with Haldir—telepathically. Their faces announced the connection in a big way—pinched eyebrows, smiles and giggles, their arms over each other's shoulders. I felt like a fourth grader dealing with grad students.

"Please," I asked gently, hoping I didn't sound desperate.

"I am sorry," Daruk said, sounding contrite. "Let us talk verbally while we wait for Katnu to finish his own download and joins us. *Lig dúinn labhairt ó bhéal.*"

Over the next three hours, sitting casually, sometimes with Daruk's arm over my shoulder or me leaning into his chest, we learned much about Haldir's world, only a few words in English, and we answered his questions about our own. He often shook his head in amazement. If his understanding of our life was limited, our understanding of his world was near zero. Slowly he helped build a picture of his radically different existence. He was straightforward, almost guileless, readily giving an intimate portrait of his reality. We had established that some would kill to control him and his people, and I worried he might reveal too much in communicating with anyone who might want to exploit him or the baby.

Some of the books in Haldir's room and elsewhere in the compound, we learned, dealt with the history of his people and their travels in the Old and New Worlds. His history, the story of his tribe, again reminded me of Odysseus, a traveler facing endless conflict. The more we learned about Haldir and his contemporaries, the more questions we had. I found his life incomprehensible when compared with my own. Who is to judge which life is richer? I found myself wanting to protect him from the evils of my own world. He surprised me when he said he had read the King James Bible and other versions, translated into his language. King James, who sponsored the creation of a new Christian bible, was known to have had male lovers, Haldir mentioned with a smile. He indicated that books on his own history likely contained many myths and contradictions, much like the Bible. This was not a revelation I was expecting.

...

Uncle His came down from the warbird and announced with a smile, "I feel comfortable in his dialect." He switched for Haldir. *"Mothaím compordach ina chanúint."* He gestured to the spot where Haldir sat cross-legged; Katnu dropped down in front of him, their knees touching. Clearly, the session would be telepathic. The two touched their foreheads together with Katnu's fingers touching the boy's temples. Haldir did the same to him.

Daruk and I watched, silent. "Are you listening?" I whispered in his ear.

"No. This is a private conversation."

Daruk offered his hand and we walked toward the big tent. Inside the agents and anthologist were squatting around the low-slung table, papers in neat piles, three computer screens scrolling photographs. Their voices were low but animated.

Agent Washington turned toward us. "Has Mr. Hisman emerged yet?"

"Yes," I answered. "He's working with Haldir to see if telepathically he can reach an understanding on English translation. Best we leave them to their efforts in private."

She looked at me, shook her head in disbelief and smiled. This was all way out of her reality and barely in mine.

Daruk and I walked together into the woods. My head was roiling with all we'd experienced in the last two days and all we've learned. We climbed a rock outcrop and perched atop it, having a view of mountain peaks and valleys going on until the earth curved and dropped them from our sight. There were low clouds on the horizon, the air clean and pure, the temperature cool, the sun glorious as it set, offering a splendid red sky. Red sky at night, sailor's delight, I thought, remembering an old seafaring proverb. It was impossible to imagine what delight might mean.

"I know you must be troubled by what our day long vacation has turned into," Daruk said, squeezing my hand. "This is an adventure I would never have anticipated. So, I think being a bit disoriented, a little confused, searching for sanity is what should be expected in the madness we have stumbled upon."

I put an arm around his waist and leaned my head into his shoulder. Just doing that, my lover as anchor, made me feel more stable in this wobbly world. With him, we would figure this out.

"May I use the satellite phone?"

Daruk nodded and took it out of his shoulder pouch. I texted my parents that we were still camping and would stay a few days more. I didn't want them to worry. Camping they could accept, all the rest of what was happening, not so much. I'd warned them before we left that regular cell service was nonexistent where we were going and I would use a special phone with a different number. I thought about my best friend, Miguel, back home with his new boyfriend. I texted him that we were having some new adventures here that I would tell him about when we returned in a few days. No emoji options on this phone. Too bad, I could think of a few nasty ones.

"Do you have a reaction to some of Haldir's revelations?" Daruk asked. "I am still struggling."

"Would it be acceptable with you," I responded, not ready to answer since it was almost too much to comprehend and we were just beginning to learn details, "if we just continued to gather data, let his words sink in and we go with it for the time being? I need to step back and think about what it all means." I lifted my head and kissed his cheek.

"Perhaps we can go to our tent and find something distracting to do while we wait for further developments."

•••

"Hell. O. Dar-Bin. Beaut-ful daey" Haldir said, a bit sheepishly, looking down and shrugging. He held the baby in the cloth sling he'd been using. He was perched on a cabinet at the back of *Mars*. He seemed to readily accept this new reality.

He was so innocent looking, a description I was more than

willing to abandon for myself and grant to our new friend. Just thinking that made me grin and I hugged him.

He giggled. *"Caan took?"*

I gave him a blank look.

"I think the transfer and upgrades have done much of what needed to be done," Uncle His said, leaning against the wall. "Now he needs practice. We need practice. Once we work out the kinks, and before we let the agents talk with him, we should decide if there are parts of his story best kept hidden from an official report, indeed from the public if this gets wider attention. He understands that the agents are part of a murder investigation. He understood it from the beginning, even when we had limited communication. It is still unclear how his people handled such things but there apparently was a process." He picked up a back-pack. "We have two bottles of baby milk in the blue container, all warm and ready to go."

Haldir listened closely, nodding. "Thank you," he said, taking a bottle from the warmer and moving the baby from his carrier to his crib by the main control panel. The child giggled as he was lifted and opened his mouth to accept the warm nipple of the bottle. A happy baby was always a delight.

"Daruk," Uncle His said, "let us take *Canoe* and scout for the professor's camp. It is likely well-hidden so it may take some effort to find. Based on my cursory exam of the clothing they wore, they may have tried to hide their presence from common heat reading monitors, much like criminals and terrorists. I suspect it is within a few miles so they could keep a close watch on Haldir and his family and remain hidden. We need to see what they have gathered and regain the medallions."

"Plus, any knives," I added.

Daruk kissed my cheek. Haldir whooped.

"Shall we talk here or go outside?" I asked Haldir as Uncle His and Daruk left us.

He watched me for a moment, trying to translate, then pointed outside. Taking the baby, the door sealing behind us, we returned to our blanket near a stand of trees on the edge of a ravine, a hundred yards from the ship. He adjusted the baby against his chest as the boy continued to feed.

Canoe slowly lifted and hovered. The craft slowly floated north. My lover and favorite non-uncle uncle were likely already scanning for life forms and any signs of an encampment which might include tents, metal, ammunition, a latrine, or anything not native to a forest.

The agents and anthropologist continued their work in the big tent. I could hear some high-octane debates but exact words were hard to decipher.

"What do you call your people?" I asked. "Your tribe?"

He watched me, considering my English words. He licked his lips, taking this very seriously, looking nervous, considering his own words, all foreign to him even a few hours ago. "Darwin... my people...called many names over thousands of your years."

We talked, haltingly, for an hour or more, the baby falling asleep in his lap. He never answered my question; maybe it wasn't easy. The number of lapses in our exchanges seemed to diminish. New words not in our dictionary seemed to pop up with frequency and we had to work on finding definitions. Gradually we seemed to be making it work.

The two agents eventually came out of the big tent and stretched. The woman headed to the nearest latrine and Agent Gabriel Tomas touched his toes, stretched high, squatted down, dipped his hands in a bucket of water and washed his face. He saw us and walked over, dropping down cross—legged beside us.

"How goes the instruction in English?" he asked with a wide, gorgeous grin, reaching out and offering to do a high five with Haldir.

Our new friend looked at the agent's hand, cocking his head to one side, trying to figure out what he wanted. I reached over and slapped Mr. Perfect's palm with mine and we shook. Haldir smiled then did the same. "How is the baby?"

Haldir smiled and gently turned the child toward him. The baby was asleep and both Haldir and the baby looked angelic.

Moments later, Agent Washington walked over with Hat,

our anthropologist. "May we join you?" she asked. I pointed to the now crowded blanket, putting a finger to my lips, then to the child. They nodded understanding.

This was a different dynamic. What could I talk about with our special guest that would not violate the warning Uncle His gave on not divulging certain aspects of his people's history?

"Have you finished your report?" I asked the agents, my voice quiet, stalling for time while I tried to figure out a safe set of exchanges with Haldir.

"Much of it," Agent Washington responded, wrapping her arms around her knees, the tips of her shoes almost touching mine. "We still need to understand what happened from Haldir's perspective. How do we explain four bodies, killed violently? Does it all remain a mystery, the bodies disposed of, the families never notified? Do we contact next of kin, provide the human remains for burial, but offer no explanation? An autopsy will show they died from arrows or blunt force trauma. How do we explain that if part of the story is kept secret?"

"National security is a possible reason for secrecy," I answered, having second thoughts about Uncle His' call to the president. This was getting complicated.

"We didn't have to look you up on the Internet," Agent Tomas admitted, a bit sheepishly, "to know you have quite a presence in news articles—kidnapped, declared a hero by President O'Connor, operating in secret because of our ongoing war on terror, declared a genius in your IQ test. You crack an obscure, perhaps even dead language in less than forty-eight hours. You're still in high school. You're more than handy with a bow and arrow. Your boyfriend and Mr. Hisman fly around in aircraft unlike anything on this planet—you're probably the source of all those UFO sightings in the San Francisco Bay Area. This young man Haldir might be the last adult member of a lost civilization. Wow. Did I miss anything?"

"Wow, indeed." Wilkins Vardan sat cross-legged next to Haldir. He took off his hat, setting it on the blanket, running his fingers through his hair. "There is such a richness of topics we could discuss."

Raising his arm, tilting his head Haldir pointed to the child to remind them of volume. "No understand all you said."

Gabriel laughed. "Sorry, Haldir. I'm just frustrated. Forget what I just said. We would love to talk with you."

"Gabriel, my apologies for all the mystery," I said, rubbing my palms over my eyes. "Only President O'Connor, Katnu, Daruk and myself knowall that's in play here. Even the Director of National Security is out of the loop on this one. For good reasons."

"So says the high school senior," Wilkins barked, irritated and ready for a fight. "What gives you the right to withhold secrets vital to solving this case?" The way he said my name was condescending, and he crossed his arms over his chest for emphasis.

"Mr. Vardan—keep your voice down," Agent Washinton snapped in a harsh whisper and shook her head. "Your tone and volume aren't helpful, nor your accusations. Sometimes certain facts are withheld from even members of an investigative team. Our work here is unique in my experience too but I follow the orders of my president. You should too."

"Apologies if I sounded stressed. I am," he replied with a dismissive growl. "We all should be. We've examined the bodies of a tribe unique in human history—or at least recorded history. I say that without exaggeration. The cave they lived in is more palace than cavern. What technologies built it? This is not a Native American tribe. It's not a group of mountain men. More like a hidden civilization, a secret society of quasi-humans. We need to provide thorough answers to President O'Connor. That means we need full comprehension of what happened here and the history of Haldir's people. I want answers!" His voice rose as he talked.

"Well stated," said a man emerging from the Christmas tree forest at the edge of the gully behind us, dressed like a horror film creature, covered completely in a forest green suit made up of thousands of tiny strips that moved easily in the breeze. His face, deep in a large hood, was difficult to see. What was real was the automatic rifle in a sling over his shoulder, the barrel pointed at us, his gloved finger on the trigger.

We all jumped to our feet.

"Who are you?" demanded Agent Washington, swiveling around, both surprised and pissed. "I am lead agent on an FBI team. You are not to interfere with our work. Why the hell are you dressed like?"

"Sit down, now!" barked another man dressed in the same Abominable Snowman attire, emerging on the other side. He swung an impressive looking weapon at us. "Sit down now or I'll shoot."

The baby started to cry. Haldir began singing quietly, patting the child's back, an angry stare on the intruders while somehow maintaining his serenity and focus on the child.

We slowly dropped down. I noticed the butt of a pistol partially exposed under Washington's jacket next to where she was sitting. Vardan and Tomas had no weapons I knew about. I had a knife strapped to the side by my calf. So did Haldir.

"Bí socair, Haldir," I said. Be calm. *"Tá na fir seo contúirteach."* These men are dangerous. *"Lig dom é seo a dhéanamh amach."* Let me figure this out.

"Leanaim do luaidhe, a chara." Haldir nodded and smiled, sitting serene and alert, cradling the child. "Thank you, my friend."

I had no idea what he was capable of or how he might respond. But he trusted me and would take his cues from me before acting.

"What did you just say?" the first gunman said, pulling back his hood. The man was white, maybe fifty, his pockmarked face with several day's growth of beard. "You can talk his language?"

"I urged him to remain calm. He agreed. Yes, I am learning to talk to him in his native tongue."

"Identify yourself!" Washington demanded. "There are consequences in interfering with an FBI investigation."

"I don't think you're in a position to demand anything. But I'll tell you who we are." He stepped closer, facing us head on. "I'm Dr. Dean Roshoff. A colleague of Professor Whitacre who's apparently been captured or murdered since I've not heard from him. My friend here is a former Navy Seal, Sergeant Daryl Seamus. He knows how to shoot so be warned against taking any action."

They were about three hundred feet from *Mars* and seemed not to notice its existence. They must have been in the camp Uncle His was searching for and missed what happened. I wondered if they were dressed in some kind of anti-thermal camoflage to mask their heat signatures. I'd read that there were some new developments in this field, great for terrorists, murderers, the military and anthropologists willing to kill to tell the story of a new type of humans.

"Cuff 'em," Roshoff said to his guard. "Roll onto your stomachs, hands behind your back."

"You first," the sergeant said, pointing his weapon at me. With his hood back, he appeared also to be white, maybe forty, several days of scruff, and handsome in a hungry vampire way. For some reason I thought of Arnold Schwarzenegger being pursued by that alien who read body heat signatures. He'd had to use mud but managed to slay the creature. Knowing that was probably not helpful, I began slowly moving as if to respond, not sure what to do. I could set fire to one or try to grab them, but the other man had an automatic weapon and there was a baby with us. For now, best to comply so no one was at further risk. I sat up on my knees and stretched forward, my arms behind my back.

"Good boy," Seamus said, pulling off his backpack. As he knelt to pull out cuffs, Agent Washington went for her pistol faster than I thought possible. She fired a shot, hitting the sergeant in the leg and swung to face Rossoff who fired at her, hitting her in the chest. She dropped to her side and curled up.

"Fuck!" Seamus shouted.

The baby started screaming.

Haldir started another song, cradling the child, but his expression was murderous. He looked at me, indicating he wanted me to take the child. So I sat up, and obeyed.

Tomas was bent over the agent, cradling her head. "Bastard!" he said. "Where're you hit?"

"Right side," she managed. "Chest."

He pulled a handkerchief from his back pocket and placed it over the wound and applied pressure.

Haldir looked icy calm as he moved to the agent. "Allow me help," he said haltingly. "Roll on back." The agent nodded to Tomas who backed up and helped her move.

"Tá mo scian ag teastáil uaim."

"He needs his knife," I translated carefully. "He will pull it out slowly from the sheath on his calf. He's going to help her. Please let him," I pleaded, hoping they would allow it, whatever special talents he had. The child was still crying, adding to the turmoil.

"Shit! This is your fault, lady. Go ahead, slowly!" Roshoff looked panicked. "How's your leg?" he shouted at Seamus.

The former Navy Seal had pulled a roll of gauze from his pack and was wrapping his thigh. "Just a nick," he said.

With care, Haldir lifted up his pant leg, and unbuckled his knife. As he pulled it from its sheath, the blade gleamed in the sunlight. He dropped to his knees and leaned over Agent Washington. He removed the bloody handkerchief and pressed the side of the blade directly over the wound and began to quietly chant. His eyes, dramatically larger than my own, were intense, and somehow the pupils were expanding, turning dark green, engulfing the whites even in the sunlight as he stared closely at the wound, almost as if he could see within it. We all watched, captivated by the scene. With yelling and gunfire over, the baby quieted.

Was it my imagination or was the agent covered in a barely visible green haze?

"What the fuck is happening?" Seamus said behind me. I turned to see him pull a bottle from his pack, take out a pill and wash it down. "This whole mission is creepy. That kid is creepy."

"That kid, both of them, are amazing," I answered, pissed. "What's happening? I wish I knew. Just let him do whatever it is he's doing."

Haldir never moved, frozen over the agent, chanting. The agent was silent, breathing quietly like she was asleep. Haldir straightened, held his forearm over the wound and pushed the knifetip into his own flesh. A trickle of blood flowed from his forearm and dripped into the bullet hole. He returned the blade to her chest and began a more animated chant.

Haldir finally stopped, sat straight up, lifting his arms to heaven, the knife in his right hand. "*Leighis!*" he shouted. "*Leighis!*"

Heal, he was saying. Would it work? Did something happen?

Haldir stood, ignoring the intruders, the knife still in his hand. "Must sleep to heal. Let us take her to tent."

Tomas stood, his arms raised. "I just want to help her. I am not armed."

"Seamus. Can you keep an eye on them while I follow those two?"

"Sure," the sergeant said, on his knees, his rifle up and ready, the gauze on his leg red with blood.

The two gently lifted the comatose agent and carried her into the big tent and placed her on top of her sleeping bag, a blanket over her, another folded and placed under her head. Haldir placed a palm over her forehead and spoke words I couldn't hear. Next he waved his knife blade over her. He then exited the tent with Tomas. The knifetip was facing down, his arm relaxed.

What was he doing? What didn't these men know and how could we turn this around? I could fight and had a talent for pyrokinesis. But that talent wouldn't work on two people far apart, at least I didn't think it would. Should I risk lives to find out? Tomas was skilled in fighting, I assumed. No idea about the anthropologist. Of course if we were handcuffed, that would be a moot point. Uncle His and Daruk could return any time or be gone for hours.

"You have shot an FBI agent in her line of duty," Tomas said, anger just barely below his words. "Turn over your weapons or…"

"Or what pretty boy?" Seamus challenged. "Drop the knife, freak."

Agent Tomas seethed in helpless fury.

Haldir looked at him then turned his gaze to his accomplice. "You done evil. Drop weapons. Leave. Stay and die."

"Don't you threaten me, you fucked up elf boy!" Seamus shouted, lifting his rifle.

Haldir looked unimpressed. He snapped the knife up, said something, and a flash of light hit Seamus in the chest, lifting him off the ground and smashing him into a nearby tree. He fell to the ground, dead or unconscious, hard to tell.

As our jaws dropped he turned to the professor. Haldir tilted his head at an angle, waiting for a response.

"Ah, let's talk about this, guys," he said. But he raised his rifle.

An even brighter flash sent him hard against a large redwood, sideways. There was a sickening sound of cracking bone. A last gasp from Roshoff and he rolled lifeless onto pine needles. No question about his condition.

"Dead," Haldir said slowly, pointing to Rossoff. Lifting his arm to the sergeant he said: "Head...bleeding...will...live." Turning and pointing back into the tent. "Female...recover. Awake next day."

What had we just witnessed? The anthropologist had his camera out, snapping photos as he stood with the rest of us. Tomas, standing by the front of the big tent, looked stunned, his mouth agape. Then he straightened, his expression grave, perhaps remembering he was now the agent in charge.

"Better cuff this guy," I suggested, "he may be even less friendly if he regains consciousness." It seemed to spark Agent Beauty to action. He ran back into the tent and came out with a backpack.

"Darwin," Haldir said in a soft voice. "Go home?" He bent down and put the knife back in its sheath and reattached it to his calf before placing the baby into the cloth sling. He held out his hand and I took it.

"To woods," he said, pulling me along. He knew the pathways well.

...

Keeping up with Haldir took serious work. He was taller with longer legs and an effortless, elegant stride. Rocks, logs, plants— the stuff of the forrest—was for him like walking on a carpet while I had to keep my eyes on the ground to prevent tripping. He still gripped my hand like he needed the connection. Maybe he did.

We had gone only a half mile when he stopped. "Contact Katnu now," he said, looking north, placing his fingertips to his temples and closing his eyes.

The sat-phone, I realized, was back on the blanket. Even if I had it, there was no point in calling Daruk. Katnu was getting what was likely a visual report on what happened. My boyfriend would be next to him and also getting the message. I really needed to up my game on telepathy. I also needed to learn how to take on multiple assailants with the skills I had—or, more likely, learn some new ones.

I sat with my legs straight out, my arms back on a rocky ledge admiring the tranquility of the forest while he did his mind-com. Not a bad name for it. I tried to make sense of what I'd just witnessed. This younger boy/man had killed one man and disabled another using a long knife and a few words. Didn't I have enough weird stuff in my life with the Passageway, three earths, pyrokinesis and an athletic, sexy, indigenous boyfriend who could move things with his brain?

I jumped when an arm circled my shoulders. Guess I was just too caught up in my mental adventures to notice Haldir had finished his mind-com.

"Katnu...Daruk evil camp found. Ten miles," he said pointing to the north. "Knives. Medallions." He lifted his own bronze pendant as he talked. With a smile he leaped to his feet, loaded the baby gently into the sling, offered his hand which I took, and began moving at a near run for his home on the other side of this ridge.

14.

We sat on the edge of his bed, the only sound our breathing and a snort from the infant sleeping beside us. Haldir leaned back, legs under him. I did the same, sat cross-legged facing him. He lifted his hands, palms toward me. I met them with my own and he squeezed them tight. It was clear that he was nervous about something important, working out the English words in his head.

"Dar-win."

I looked into his eyes, the irises wide and intense in the low light. "Yes. Please tell me."

"I...you...trust." He swallowed and looked down at my hands and back up to my eyes. "More...anyone." His dark forest green pupils were staring at me, alive, vibrant, almost mesmerizing in their remarkable size and mixed colors. "Please...no betray me or baby. Only him as family. We last. Please..." He stopped, the tip of his tongue peeking out, and swallowed. "Please make me your family?" The plaintive look in his face was mournful and yet full of hope, more question than request.

"Yes." My voice was a whisper, I was still processing the scope of his request, the depth of his need. "Yes," I said louder, feeling more comfortable. "Yes!" I shouted and wrapped my hands around his neck, laughing, tearing up, and pulling him tight to me, kissing each cheek. "Yes. I'll be part of your family and you part of mine. We'll be brothers. All of us." I reached over and touched the sleeping child.

He looked down, tears cascading. "I...alone. World gone." He was breathing deeply, working to regain control. "You and Daruk and Katnu are good men. You save baby. Kill terrible men. Thank you."

He slipped off the bed, standing as he glanced at the sleeping child, and held out his hand. We walked deeper into the cave into what I would guess might be his kitchen. He took two cups from a shelf, purple in color, likely some type of clay or ceramic, and filled them with water from a swirling pool in a recessed area of a wall, perhaps part of an underground stream captured and somehow pulled into their home. He handed me a cup and I drank. Icy and pure. Katnu would proclaim it delicious.

We sat in chairs covered with a soft, thick cloth, woven in the colors of a green meadow. I asked, "Do you want to stay here, just you and the baby? Go back to my world? What will happen about all the murders and the investigation, we should know soon. Katnu will talk with the leader of my world."

He held his cup, looking into it as if for answers. "No want alone. Too much death here." He leaned his head back and closed his eyes. "But history here," he sighed, pointing to a stack of brown leather covered books on a shelf. "Some come me if go."

I nodded. "Of course." How would it work, I wondered. He looked different from the norm although I thought he was beautiful. He was not exactly feminine but there was a softness, a vulnerability to him. Kids, even adults, might make fun of him, call him a freak. Tall for his age, he was lean yet muscular, with segmented ears that moved although you had to look closely to notice, bigger than normal eyes with a pupil that covered the whole eye in low light, a smooth chest with no nipples. Able to kill with a word. Bullies might try to hurt him. What would he do? Cruelty seemed ingrained in many humans; high school kids were no exception. His life experience was so different from my world. The downloads could help give him a sense of our history and customs. That his ability to speak modern English would improve and become nearly flawless I had no doubt.

Would it be a step backward for him in terms of his life development? Was my world more backward in every way than his? How did I know? I only knew him and a little about his family and friends. Not much about how they lived, nothing about their sense of family and joy. Did they share equally? Did they have money or jobs? Was there a hierarchy? Were there others like him elsewhere on the planet? Did they have sex like we did? How were children raised? How would we take care of the baby?

We only knew some of the broad strokes, not the day-to-day. I feared for his future here if it was only him and the infant. What if something happened? An accident or if other men, hungry for fame and to exploit him, came looking, came hunting, perhaps familiar with what the two professors were doing. He had no practical way to feed the child. How would my family react if he came home with me? With the baby? They'd need a believable explanation. How could I describe my world, the world they did not know, and not be considered a nut job? Uncle His was rich. Could I ask him to help my parents financially if Haldir came to live with us? Maybe Mom could quit her job at the corner store and help raise the baby. She might love the idea. Or feel we were stereotyping her and resist. Would he go to my school to learn more about our ways? Learning how to fit in might be more important than what he studied in the classroom. We had more than our share of bullies and thoughtless kids. How strong would he be emotionally, having lost his family, when he found modern kids were often just jerks? He couldn't just go see a therapist. After one session, the therapist would need a therapist. Keeping him isolated at the cabin, hiding him, would not be useful if he were ever to try and integrate into my world. Risks in any direction.

My phone buzzed. Daruk and Uncle His were near.

"Hello, Daruk."

His tone was dry. "Another body. A badly bruised, bloody and angry ex-Marine in handcuffs roped to a tree. An unconscious FBI agent with a bullet wound. A panicked male beauty. A snarky anthropologist demanding to leave. You left quite a scene here."

"Thank you, boyfriend. Thank you also for showing your ability to speak in incomplete sentences when you want to. Haldir needed to get away and talk. Everything seemed stable there despite what you found. We've been having some important exchanges in his home. Stuff he wanted to share. I'm glad he did. We have some big decisions ahead of us. I need to talk with you and Uncle His."

"May we come there?"

I put the phone aside. "Haldir...Katnu and Daruk would like to come here and talk. I know there's more to discuss between us."

"Yes," he said quietly, nodding with a tiny smile.

...

Katnu and Daruk walked directly to us in the kitchen area, directions, I assumed, given telepathically by Haldir. My new friend took two more cups from a shelf and filled them with the sparkling spring water.

"Delicious," Uncle His said with a smile. "Thank you. I am assuming you have reached a decision on the question we discussed."

The young man looked down at the table, his fingers around his cup. This was an important moment for him. He looked at each of us in turn. "Yes. I not wish stay here alone with infant. Ghosts. My people...close. Everyone raising children, gathering food, preparing. Everyone for each other looked out. Baby needs surrounded...loving community; I need as well. We look different. No provide milk child needs. You can. His survival crucial. Do anything him grow and become man."

"I admire your devotion to the baby. Also, don't sell yourself short," I said.

"I no understand."

"It means you have more skills, more talents, more capacity than you think you do."

"Thank you, Darwin. Wish part of your family. In world most humans evil, you three kind. Want to protect us. I grateful."

Katnu lifted the pack he had carried in over his shoulder. He pulled out three medallions on chains, like the one Haldir wore around his neck. Then three long knives in leather sheaths.

Haldir gasped, reaching out and touching one knife, larger than the others. He fought to control his breathing. "This... this...ohhh...belongs to leader. Seeing bring back memories of his life; his murder. You avenged him. Grateful. I loved him as all tribe. The power of blade inspiring."

I put my hand on his, still covering the knife and sheath. "These belong to you."

He pulled the knife back to his chest, unfastened it from a raised hook on the side that fit into a leather hoop on the sheath. Slowly he pulled it out. The handle was bone, just like his, and the blade alone must have been a foot long. The silver blade was covered by dozens of symbols, some etched on top of others, some black, some red, others silver. He turned it over. Same on the other side.

He brought it to his lips and kissed the side. "This...this weapon and tool. Amplify natural world, forces hidden, hidden to humans based on history and stories for generations told, forces protect us and shape world. I keep this and train you, others. Not know if work with you three. I can hope."

He selected a different knife and presented it to Uncle His who made no effort to hide his grin. "Thank you, Haldir. I am honored to accept it. We—I think I speak for all of us—look forward to learning about the knives, the markings, how they are used and about your culture and life. We have just met and already you are precious to us."

Haldir smiled, his cheeks a bit pink. He took another knife and handed it to Daruk. My lover smiled, kissing the blade. Our Fae friend then pulled up his pant leg and unstrapped his knife, setting it aside as he attached the large black one to his calf. He joined his hands together as if in prayer and lowered his head to Uncle His and Daruk. He then picked up his own knife. As he placed it in my hands, he said one word: "Brother."

We were quiet for a time, pondering what just happened, his generosity. Uncle His broke the silence: "As we seek to better understand each other, would you allow me to examine you with the machine I used on the child and your adult friends who were murdered? It will help me understand the physical differences between us. Perhaps it will suggest ways to make us closer."

Haldir looked at me as if wanting my approval. "Do it Haldir. It may serve us well to know more about each other."

"Yes. You examine me." He handed each of us a medallion. "May be useful or not. Not know. If medallions accept you, serve many ways." He rose and offered a hand to Uncle His.

The two walked out of the cave and up into *Mars* to conduct the tests. I wondered what they would find. I put a medallion around my neck. Surprisingly heavy, its craftsmanship was extraordinary, the sharper edges of its carving worn down by age. How old? I hoped they'd work for us, whatever that meant. What about him joining us back in our world? How were we different, how the same? Would he go to my school? Knowing the popularity of cruelty with many students, the hunger to be unique even as they dressed, groomed, and acted the same, I was worried how people would react. Could the President order a fake birth certificate and school records or some way to make him acceptable for school admission? I was confident telephathic downloads on American history, customs, and culture would be extensive, yet he was still an outsider who would have to learn to fit in. High school could be fun or treacherous, and sometimes just boring. Of course, the same could be said for society at large. Was I already so cynical? Haldir was an amazing guy. He was also now my friend and maybe soon a family member, like a brother. How would my bros react? Could Mom enjoy having a baby in the house or was she happy to have those days behind her?

15.

Uncle His knew I wanted to talk and took me outside for a walk. What we'd learned or thought we'd learned, what he'd said before, still circled in my head. I felt unsettled and wished Miguel were here to talk with me, someone with my own American lower middle class, regular kid roots. The issues before us seemed too fantastical. Of course, so were three earths.

We ventured out the opening in the cave wall and down the rocky path to an ancient tree laying on the ground, smooth and warm in the sun.

"Young warrior, what is troubling you?"

I looked at this special man in my life, smarter and wiser than anyone I knew. "Warrior? Right. I'm just trying to pull the pieces together and make sense of it. Haldir a future human, his tribe living in isolation in a cave that reminds me of photos of Egyptian tombs. How's this possible?" My questions just kept coming. "How did our species beat out the Neanderthals and where did Haldir's ancestors come from? Simple stuff." I laughed, but in frustration. "I'm supposed to be worried about school and an upcoming math test, not all this fantastical stuff."

"True if you were just anyone. But you are not. I can only speculate until we learn more and that may take time. What created this young man has roots in the ancient past. Just how ancient is the issue." He rubbed his hands over his face and took a deep breath. "How did homo sapiens come to rule the planet? Are Haldir and his people an offshoot of homo sapiens?"

"Not exactly simple."

"Indeed. Some anthropologists contend that Neanderthals were the dominant species of *hominin* from roughly 400,000 years ago to about 40,000. They did have large brains and great physical strength. There are numerous theories about how our species came to rule but one I think has merit argues that environmental instability and constant disruption in daily life were key. Our species was able to cope and turn it to our advantage. There is speculation that our complex brain itself is an organ of adaptability. It allows us to assess information about our world, our environment, our social alliances, and raise the probability of survival. We learned to carry food from one place to another, to make complex tools, make fire and dozens of other steps that increased our probability of survival. Eventually we learned to make crops and change our environment to grow them, to make shelter, altering our surroundings at a time of habitat instability."

"Hearing you talk makes me wonder if our species has lost the ability to survive and think beyond the current generation. I wonder if our ability to change our environment may be what might someday make earth uninhabitable for humans. But not roaches."

"Dark humor. I am not sure our ancient ancestors made decisions thinking about future impacts, only what was needed in the moment to survive. Humans today have the tools to look ahead but policies remain mostly short term. Look at E1 five centuries ahead of where we are now where only a small part of the planet is habitable and even that area is shrinking. That Earth endured wars of survival as millions, billions starved and moved from continent to continent, generated wars, and mass killings. Humans can be strategic but rarely if the reward is not immediate. We have the capacity and tools to understand how we can shape the future but concern for grandchildren often loses to politicians and activists seeking power. Charlatans often do well in politics, and people seem willing to accept lies as truths if delivered with a certain swagger. This age of hyper connectivity, endless numbers of channels, works against good sense, it seems to me. Mass media no longer really exists. Now you can find any channel you want that reaffirms your views even if they are irrational and work against your best interests. The age of Twitter, a much more accurate term than X, exemplifies the problem. Messages are short which demands simplicity and allows those skilled in deception to prevail. The courts in this country see money as a component of free speech, allowing the wealthy to drown the messages of less well off. Campaign donations are often little more than bribes. Integrity is seen as a loser's game. Any tradeoff of short-term rewards in favor of long-term benefits is unlikely and because of that, our long term future points toward extinction."

I shook my head. "You're a pessimist. How I wish you were wrong. Those several theories you mentioned on how our species became dominant..."

"There are several hypotheses with no definitive answer. Survival may have had something to do with climate. According to some anthropologists, when glaciers invaded Europe, Neanderthals moved south. They claim development of the needle for making clothes gave homo sapiens greater adaptability to live in the cold. Our species was also apparently able to maintain social networks over great distances. Neanderthals were perhaps more habitat specialists than we were. We developed the ability to live most anywhere and as climates changed, they had few options and died out."

"And what else? What other theories?"

"Some say Neanderthals simply intermarried with homo sapiens and are alive today in our genes. Still others suggest that homo sapiens were better fighters with deadlier weapons and simply eliminated Neanderthals or drove them away."

"I'll read up on this when we get home. But based on what

you say, Haldir's ancestors must stretch back to hundreds of thousands of years ago. Am I right?"

"I believe so."

"How could his people have evolved alongside us and be so different?"

"One theory I have been considering, and this is only speculation, Haldir's people, perhaps millennia ago, or even a million years back, were separate and began to develop differently, just like Neanderthals did. Perhaps they were excluded from working with homo sapiens or Neanderthals and kept their distance, perhaps advanced beyond them. Many histories tell of strange people, often the stuff of legends, that existed near but separate from us.

"Scientists have developed a Neanderthal genome," Uncle His continued, "based on DNA from the teeth of three individuals that suggests homo sapiens and the Neanderthals had a common ancestor who lived about 600,000 years ago. Could Haldir's ancestors date back that far or further? Given their burial practice, has that kept scientists from discovering any remains? Perhaps when we understand their history better, we can better understand how it all came to be."

"Even his magic? I saw what he did to those two men with a few words and a flick of his knife."

"I doubt it's magic. To a primitive tribe, our airplanes, rifles, and even a cigarette lighter, appear to be magic. It was Arthur C. Clark, the scientist and science fiction writer, who said: "Any sufficiently advanced technology is indistinguishable from magic."

"You're suggesting his ability might be part of his brain development?"

"It could be that. My scanning of his brain confirmed what I found earlier in the members of his community, an odd growth, perhaps the size of an apricot in the forward part of Haldir's brain. It is not found in our species. It is not in the baby so it may develop in puberty and grow further in adulthood. Given its placement, is this something that gave them a special advantage to survive? Until I can do more research, I do not have an answer.

But his magic may just be part of normal brain activity in an extraordinary species."

"So he's more advanced than we are?"

"I think he may be. He certainly has shed some redundant organs still common in us. That could be because his ancestors may predate the common ancestor of Neanderthal and homo sapiens which would make his origins six hundred thousand to a million years back. If so, perhaps they never inherited those useless organs like an appendix or nipples on a male. What is important now is protecting him, finding a way for him and the child to survive. That will not be easy."

I asked a question I'd been mulling over myself: "Do you think our species will survive?"

"Not if we make the wrong decisions, or make no decisions, the status quo being easiest even if it is deadly long term. Plus, as the earth changes, will we have time to evolve as a species? I have my doubts."

"Then if we don't survive, might any other human-like beings exist?"

"Perhaps Haldir's people if they are found elsewhere. Or, given the hundreds, perhaps thousands of years that it might take, perhaps a new species unknown to us today will step forward. And if they do, what will they think of the mess our species left behind, the plastics and pollution?"

I shook my head, sighed. "This conversation will keep me up nights."

• • •

"I like visit this place," Haldir said pointing at the map. "Important go before leave mountains."

"You three should go. Take *Canoe*. I will remain here," Uncle His said, "and work with the agents on their final report."

"Is Agent Washington strong enough for that?" I was worried. She was sitting up and talking but it was only a day since she was shot.

"Whatever Haldir did fast-tracked her healing, almost miraculous." Uncle His pursed his lips, hiding a smile as he watched our man from tomorrow. "Would you care to repeat what you told me earlier today?"

Daruk stopped his research, closed the screen on his computer and swung around in his chair. Haldir, Katnu and I were sitting at a table that once held the body of one of Haldir's tribal members. Now it had a basket with a baby. Haldir had woven the new carrier out of sticks he found in the woods. It was elaborate and given his speed in twisting, stripping, and twining, it was obvious he'd done this many times. Haldir held a bottle to the child's mouth.

"I trained as healer. Bullet through Agent's chest. I able to pull out bullet, seal wound to discourage infection, as you call it. All our children examined for potential skills. I having affinity for healing and instructed as boy. I not know how works, no detailed, but have treated many wounds, some more serious than hers."

"You three should go," Uncle His repeated. "Leave the baby with me. I will talk with President O'Connor and make my recommendations. Hopefully Haldir will find some closure at the site that seems to have such meaning for him."

•••

"*Tá sé,*" Haldir shouted, pointing through the clear wall of *Canoe* at a plateau a mile across, covered in a massive pile of rocks. It was backed up to an almost verticle cliff a thousand feet high.

"There it is, indeed," I affirmed. What horrible incident happened here that so upset our new friend? There were tree trunks sticking out from the rubble, ripped lose when the mountainside collapsed in the not too distant past.

"*Crith talún a bhí ann,*" he said.

"Yes, an earthquake makes sense," Daruk responded as we floated over the site, looking for a place to land.

"There," Haldir said, gesturing to an open spot a few hundred feet from the base of the hill and relatively free from rubble.

As we exited *Canoe* and gazed at the mountain, Haldir had to take several deep breaths to steady himself. I put my arm around him to help keep him from collapsing. "We're here with you. We're your family now." Given all that happened to his world, he was holding up well.

He led us to what looked like a solid slab of granite a hundred feet high and wide, and waving us to follow, he disappeared behind a hidden cleft in the stone. He said, *"Bíodh solas ann,"* and there was light. It was the soft kind that lit his home or at least the place we thought was his home.

The room was at least fifty feet high and running deep under the mountain. Part of the ceiling had collapsed but I could still see the giant stone figures, sentries around the edge of the room, statues painted so realistically that it was as if they were about to step forward. There were also major pillars, stalactites carved with various motifs and symbols. The air was stagnant with a faint smell of rot and decay. What horrors might we find?

His breathing became gasps and he began to tremble. We held him and moved him between us onto a stone bench, our arms over his shoulders. He must have lived here once. Where were the others? Certainly not just the six who inhabited the cave. I took a canteen from my belt and handed it to him. He swallowed some water and nodded his thanks. We both rubbed his back. He leaned his head onto mine. There was no rush to do anything more. We were here for him and would follow his timeline. I looked around at the dozens of chairs and tables knocked over. Pieces of clothing, broken dishes. Not far off was what looked like a wolf, crushed under part of the fallen ceiling. Was he a pet?

"This where born," he said, his voice rough. "Lived as boy, moving other site study healing. This," he said gesturing with an arm, "home for centuries. Numbers small, only hundred left. Birthrate decline for generations, I told. We holding spring festival every year. Earth screamed…opened, swallow everyone giant rift…covered in stone. Six of us returning when happened, carrying sacred elements for ceremony. All lost except us. Evil men found us. We cursed. What do to deserve destruction?"

When his breathing seemed to normalize, I attempted to engage him in conversation, thinking it might help. "A language expert told me a few days ago that there were elements of your language that indicated your people lived in many different places on this planet. Do you know much about your ancient history?"

"Know what elders taught...have read ancient books. Existed alongside people like you but attacked because different. Learned to live near but stay invisible. When come into contact, driven away. Could defeat most but were peaceful. Also, more you. More them. Paintings show my people in giant rafts with sails, moving over great waters. Few hundred years back, skirmish with tribe on coast, we move onto mountain and created new home. Now all gone."

He looked like he was shutting down again. "Haldir," I said, pointing to the decaying body of the crushed wolf.

He got up and walked over to it, touched the snout, running the back of his finger gently back and forth as if saying goodbye to a friend. "He was part of family. His name '*Caomhnóir*.' "

"Guardian. Nice. We love dogs." Although a wolf might be a stretch.

He began to walk through the rubble, stopping occasionally to pick up a piece of pottery or cloth, sometimes slipping something into his pouch, often just putting it back on the ground.. He held what looked like a leather ball and grinned, lifting it overhead, twirling it around on a fingertip and pushed into my stomach, like a handoff in a game.

I gripped it. It was heavy. "What is it?" I asked.

"Play game on flatland. Call *Thrump* for sound ball when goes into hole." He turned to us and took back the ball, spinning it. "Two teams, five each...you win getting ball into hole. Carry, toss, kick. If run, must leap, twist around in circle or lose ball. Must run fast. Most choose to kick. I played many against my age or older. I good." His eyes looked wet and he again seemed lost, haunted. I came up and hugged him. He leaned into it. "Thank you." He handed me the ball. "Keep."

"You mean you had to do a somersault high in the air?" I

could not imagine how one could do that in a tough and tumble game.

"Not sure, somersault? New word."

I tried to demonstrate. He laughed and I did too, thrilled to see this lift his spirit. "Yes, like that."

"What's this ball made of?" Daruk asked.

"Deer skin, from animal slain by puma and left. We no kill animals unless they attack. Inside moss, straw."

In the kitchen area the water was still running. There was no food sitting out. When they'd gone out to the spring festival, everything had been put away neatly.

We next visited a room with shelves and hundreds of leather-bound books. "I take as many as can that tell history so I learn, remember and child when older. Would be acceptable?"

"Of course," I replied. "We can always come back for more."

Haldir started pulling books, placing ones he wanted on a table. Soon there were dozens in stacks.

"I will bring *Canoe* up close to the entrance when we are ready. There is a lifting device. You should take as many books as you need." Daruk nodded and smiled at the young man; he grinned in response. When he found all that he wanted we continued our exploration.

We entered an area with shelves of finely woven baskets. One had spilled its contents revealing hundreds of pieces of what appeared to be jewelry. Daruk picked up an elaborate golden necklace, a thick chain with lions depicted on a curved band about ten inches long and two inches deep. Three dark red stones were embedded between the figures. "It heavy," he said, handing it to me.

Haldir picked up a handful of rings, arm bands and bracelets. Took one arm band and slipped it over my wrist and up to my bicep. It was covered in various symbols and a twisted vine. It looked ancient.

"This protect you if allow me active power." He smiled.

"Thank you. I like that idea. I need protection given all that's going on in my life."

Haldir picked up another and turned to Daruk who extended

his right arm. Haldir slipped on one with a snakeskin design and a red stone embedded next to a series of squiggles that looked like runes.

"Thank you, Haldir. I'm honored." More smiles.

This seemed to pick up his spirits. He was doing something for us, his new friends and family. A distraction from what had happened. I hoped it would last.

He pulled out another basket and set it on a table. Inside was a variety of exotic jewelry. Haldir picked up what appeared to be golden leaves forming a crown, like something Alexander the Great might have worn when he conquered the Persians. He placed it on my head and looked at me thoughtfully, like an artist might do with a painting. Daruk pointed at me and laughed.

"Don't be rude, Daruk. Where did this come from?" I asked.

"Members of tribe, skilled, made what needed. Most from travels across waters over centuries."

"Am I right in assuming this could be from ancient Greece or even Egypt?" I took off the laurel wreath and held it, admiring the craftsmanship.

"Yes. Not know story on each but books give background."

Daruk wandered down the aisle lifting different lids. He dipped his hand in one and lifted what appeared to be dark, cut jewels. "I assume these are real," he said, shaking his head in disbelief, "and they are worth a staggering amount of money on E2 or even E1."

"When we return to our world, one issue is finances." I wasn't sure how to explain it but this was potentially a breakthrough solution. "In your culture—if I understand it—everything was shared, you were like an extended family, looking out for each other, sharing resources. In my world, people are mostly on their own, family units work together to raise money to support themselves. I know one of the programs Uncle His said he activated for you deals with these kinds of issues. This jewelry, if you are agreeable, could be used to make you a very wealthy man in our society. With wealth comes the ability to do much of what you want. It will insulate you from the substantial problems of being poor."

"We take back to your world as you wish. I not know what means be wealthy. I follow your leadership."

Yet how do you show up with ancient Etruscan or King Tut era jewelry and not create a sensation and law enforcement issues? "I suspect Uncle His will have ideas on how we can make this happen." This would also solve the problem of Haldir living with my family. We would likely need to hide the source of his wealth and the extent. He didn't need to deal with the difficulty of being a rich naïve visitor to a strange and sometimes ruthless world.

We loaded nearly a hundred books and two heaping baskets of jewels and exotic stones into *Canoe*. I was interested in some ancient Roman and Greek breast plates, helmets, and swords. We carried in several of each. Haldir visited a room he said he'd lived in at one time. He gathered some clothes and two golden rings, one with the head of two lions facing each other; the other winding vine with a dark red stone in the middle. He kissed each as he meditated. He reached for my hand and slid the lion ring on my right second finger. He held my palm and admired the ring, grinning. He turned to Daruk and took his right hand, adding the golden vine to his finger. Still smiling, he reached into a small compartment above the bed and pulled a thick gold band with a circle of red and yellow stones. He slipped this one on his right-hand ring finger and laughed. "We brothers!" He raised his clenched fist with the ring extended and we did the same, touching them together. A kind of ritual.

"Brothers," we said in unison.

"It is possible others might find this place," Daruk said, "should your story go public. What if we make the entrance impossible to find or breach? We can use some 26th century magic to mask the open space inside. We can make it look like solid rock."

Haldir agreed and Daruk, after we were finished loading, used pincher beams to lift an enormous rock in front of the entry, then an electronic opaquer program to mask the interior of the mountain.

"In my opinion, we must not mention any of this to the agents or the anthropologist," I said. "It has nothing to do with the murder investigation. We should also not wear this jewelry in their presence. Another thought…we need to decide what we can tell them about your own background, Haldir. There's something about the anthropologist I don't trust."

16.

Back in the war bird, we hid what we brought back, removed our jewelry, and updated Uncle His on our findings.

"How," I asked, "did your discussion go with President O'Connor?"

"She was shocked. As shocked as might be possible for someone so smart and centered. I assume when she gets a call from me, she assumes the worst. She agreed with my viewpoint and wants the agents to find a way to handle the deaths and keep the secret while somehow respecting the needs of next of kin. She also does not want this discovery of an advanced race of humans to go public as yet."

"I assume there was yelling when you conveyed her message?" Daruk asked, grinning.

"Indeed. As Darwin might say, Beauty and Hat were close to fisticuffs. I am surprised we cannot hear it now." He gave me a smug look.

Shaking my head, "Isn't *Mars* soundproof?"

Uncle His just smiled. "Haldir, I have my own suspicions about what your people are called," he said, serving us a pre-made vegetarian lunch, just the four of us. "It is what your people were known as in legends through the centuries."

"As I understand," Haldir said, taking a bite of quiche, "we called Fae or faerie. Longer name denotes craft. Craft of enchantment. Some called us elves. We seen as beings from parallel plain…supernatural creatures. We not. We lived real world, this world. Abilities beyond humans created legends based on capacity to manipulate natural world. What people not understand they call magic, or evil. Some saw us Satanic monsters and sought to kill us. We kept moving, hiding. Stories about magic grew and of little people with wings."

"Like Tinkerbell?" I asked. I was impressed by how quickly his English was improving. His lessons with Uncle His were showing results.

Haldir looked at me quizzically. "I do not know that word."

"I'll show you when we get back to San Francisco. I wonder, were there ever any of your people, another offshoot perhaps, who were tiny and had wings?" I wanted to make sure I wasn't missing anything.

"No, Darwin. I told ability to direct parts of natural world confused some, may made imaginations wild. Our history told by elders suggests humans, your kind of humans, enjoyed exaggerations to enhance own reputations, to make people interested in them, to make feel important."

"Yes," I replied with a laugh. "Great story telling is an art. Sadly, dishonesty is common in my world. So be prepared." I looked at our new friend again. It was clear that with his ears and eyes he was unusual. He could fit the image, fit the legends. It would be best if it were never suggested. "Let's hope your secret stays safe with us. Please don't mention any of this to the agents or the anthropologist."

. . .

Agent Washington was lifted inside *Mars* and lay flat on a table. Haldir examined her wound again, brought out his knife, gave some chants, and said it was safe for her to walk if she was cautious. Uncle His used his all-purpose silver tube to examine the wound. Shaking his head, he announced, "Never has such a serious chest injury improved so quickly. I concur with my special friend; you can cautiously move about. Haldir, I would be pleased if you would give me some insights on how you did this."

Our new friend seemed pleased with the question. "Wound not finish healing. Is close. I no understand why works, how I use natural sources, focus them. It just does. I need to review books if can find answer."

Daruk was ready to move on. "May we now discuss the final report to the President?"

"Yes," Uncle His responded. "Let me invite in Agent Tomas and Mr. Vardan."

The two had been outside waiting to be called and seemed a bit miffed at being excluded. Agent Washington was now sitting at the table; the two sat on either side of her while Katnu leaned against a wall. Daruk and I hopped up to sit on a counter. Haldir sat in one of the pilot seats and swiveled around to face them.

"To open our discussion and for the benefit of my comrades, perhaps you can summarize the report," Uncle His stated, crossing his arms, his expression and voice no nonsense.

"I've been tasked with that and wrote the report after considerable discussion with Agent Williams and Mr. Vardan," Agent Tomas said, looking stressed but handsome. "The four bodies will be taken to our offices in Los Angeles for an official examination and certificate of death. The prisoner will be placed in a holding cell while we continue to interrogate him and determine what charges will be brought or if he will be taken to the site where terrorists are held. He claims no immediate family so there is no one to notify. The Director of Homeland Security and the head of the FBI will make the determination on his future."

"Does this mean the prisoner will not be able to talk to the media or anyone outside our circle?" I asked.

"Yes. That is likely, Darwin. We assume that few know where he went as a hired gun. People who employ such talent tend to be secretive, for good reason." He picked up the report and continued. "The bodies will be returned to their families. Causes of death will be accurate. Arrow wounds and blunt force trauma. The reason they were up in this wilderness area was unclear but we'll state that we believe it was their futile search for legends of a lost civilization and treasure. When the crew failed to find either, it's speculated that a fight broke out, perhaps over money owed the hired guns, and they killed each other or died in accidents as they fled. There'll be no one to counter the findings and if any of the research done by the anthropologists emerges in other sources, then it'll fit easily with our storyline."

Vardan growled. "So dishonest it is unworthy of the FBI and scholarship."

"Does that mean you will publicly disagree?" Katnu asked, the threat obvious in his tone.

"No. I've agreed to follow the decision of Agent Williams and President O'Connor, assuming she concurs with the final details. But I'm not happy with it. Truth should mean something."

"No mention of the three of us or our technology?" Katnu asked in the same cold voice.

"That is part of the agreement," Vardan said.

Williams and Tomas nodded.

"We will set you down in the same meadow where you were picked up. You may want to arrange ambulance service to transport the bodies and a van for you three and your equipment. You will be dropped off before anyone arrives at the site. *Canoe* will remain there, hidden, to make certain the transfer happens. Agreed?" Katnu asked.

"Very fair," Washington said, her voice quiet. "We're grateful for this extraordinary experience. Mr. Hisman, you're a remarkable and insightful leader, as are you, Daruk. Good luck to you, Haldir. And you Darwin, our high school warrior. May your life continue to be full of wonder." Her face stretched into a warm smile. "I shall never forget you. Any of you."

17.

Uncle His and Haldir had another long telepathy session to finish implanting the English language program in his brain. It was apparently less effective than the program they used on my brain but they'd no choice because Haldir's head was wired differently. It was still remarkable how well he was doing.

We tried to explain to him what he'd see as we returned, what a modern American city looked like: roads, bridges, buildings, homes, cars, trucks, taxis, self-driving cars, airplanes, subways, grocery stores, streetlights, crime, orchestras, marching bands, football, stadiums, space flight, homelessness, begging, street gangs, racism, bullying, elections, protests, taxes, rallies. The list was endless when you thought of all that made up our world. Humans from birth have a decade or more of shelter and protection to make sense of it, one thing at a time, before they're expected to function. He was dumped into the middle of the madness. I used our computer screens to show examples. He thought at first we were being funny, trying to make him laugh. He couldn't believe the numbers of people who lived in our world, hundreds of millions. His life was with a hundred, all existing in harmony and friendship, looking out for each other and sharing, no individual ownership of spaces or things. Eventually his face darkened as he came to realize we weren't joking, that this was our world, maybe his new world.

When we dropped down over Sacramento, his face was glued to the clear walls of the plane. We'd intentionally taken a high-altitude trajectory. He let out a kind of primal yell and tried to jump up but was stopped by the seat belt, something else that made no sense to him. He was in *Mars* with me, the baby and Uncle His. Daruk piloted *Canoe*.

"Haldir, it's okay." I held him tight from the next seat. "Our world is strange and crazy, even those of us who've lived here our whole lives sometimes have a hard time making sense of everything. We'll take it slow. You're very smart and we'll go step by step so you fully understand how it works and how you can succeed."

"Promise?"

"Yes. I'll be with you and work with you." I held his face to my chest as he breathed heavily, until my closeness brought him some measure of relief. He trusted me and I must make certain I earned it. Dropping below cloud level and seeing freeways with thousands of cars, thousands of houses, giant aircraft overhead, must have been beyond the possible. I pointed out San Francisco Bay, the Golden Gate and the Bay Bridges. Had never seen the ocean, only heard stories it existed, and now he was flying over a human-populated land with giant bodies of water. He withdrew from me, fear replaced with wonder.

Miguel was waiting for us inside what might be called the aircraft hangar, just a large space for *Canoe* and *Mars*, not far from the Passageway flame. He wore gray jeans and a purple and orange checked shirt that seemed to move even as he stood still. Next to him was his boyfriend Luther Isley, whose hair was just starting to grow out, dark fuzz, hard to say what color, no more shaved head now that he was out of the jungle and the paramilitary. He was dressed in jeans and a blue pullover sweater, a much better look than his jungle fatigues when we'd met him as captives back on E3 in that previous adventure when I'd discovered these parallel worlds. Only he and his commanding officer had come back from the battle with the Aztecs, the colonel likely executed by now back on his own future earth, the rest of his troops dead or enslaved. Luther we'd claimed as our own and brought him to my Earth after he and Miguel developed an intense interest in each other when we were prisoners. Without his help, we might not have survived, so we owed him. He seemed like a genuinely good man. Of course, as someone who knows what will happen for the next five hundred years, he has to be careful in his comments to strangers or be seen as nuts.

Miguel ran to me with such force he almost knocked me over if it weren't for Daruk holding me upright. "I missed you and want to know everything that happened! Your messages were scary and didn't make sense!"

"Sorry. We'll tell you inside when we've a chance to shower and change. I haven't had a real bath in days."

"Obviously. You could've warned me."

"Don't be rude. There's much to explain. Hey, Luther, nice seeing you again. I hope E2 is agreeable and Miguel doesn't wear you out." He turned red and looked down. I reached out and he embraced me along with his boyfriend who didn't let go.

"Gentlemen," Uncle His said in his authoritative voice. "I would like to introduce our new special friend, Haldir. He will be staying with us."

Miguel and Luther looked up, jaws open. They both extended a hand to shake. Haldir looked at them before taking one of their hands and examining it, letting go and looking confused.

"It's called shaking hands, something popular in our world as a means of greeting," I explained. "You clasp each other's open palms and squeeze lightly. Supposedly it originated long ago to show you had no weapon and were peaceful. I read about it in Homer's *Odyssey* from, like, the eighth century." I shrugged, unsure if he understood and worried I'd talked too much.

Haldir gave me a curious look. "Explain later." He reached out and gently took Miguel's hand, palm to palm. Miguel squeezed and Haldir squeezed back. Our friend let out a happy yelp. "I like!" When Miguel let go, Haldir turned to Luther and did the same. "This excellent custom for peace."

"Let us go up into the cabin," Daruk said to the bewildered Miguel and Luther, and headed to the elevator.

When the door slid open, everyone except Haldir got inside. He just stared. "Why get in tiny room?"

"Please come in, Haldir," I said, "we'll explain." Fortunately, the elevator rose quietly with no obvious movement until the door opened. He seemed stunned to find himself at a new location. I noticed his eyes were closed at first. Stepping out he shielded them and looked down.

"Light bad," he said.

"Let me look at them," Uncle His said. Haldir's eyes were watering. "You had no problem coming through the flame, correct?"

"No, Uncle His. Light good there."

Katnu grinned. "I like being your Uncle His. The light from the flame is closer to what was in your home in the Russian Wilderness." He stepped back. "Give me your hand and keep your eyes closed. We shall go into a room with good sunlight and keep the electric lights off."

Haldir was led to a room at the side of the cabin. "The light is off. Open your eyes and have a seat. I will call an old friend, an ophthalmologist. That is a medical doctor who specializes in eyes. He may have ideas and has been here before."

Miguel had brought sandwiches to the cabin and we ate them in the small room, sitting on the floor around our special guest.

"What is green plant?"

"That's called an avocado," Miguel said. "I like avocado, lettuce and tomato sandwiches on whole wheat."

"Good. Very good. Explain later about hole in wheat, please."

After we finished, Daruk and I took Haldir plus the baby to our bedroom for clean clothes and to take showers. He kept his eyes closed in the hallway and we put the lights real low in our room. He still didn't like it but said he could squint.

It had a large shower which often accommodated Daruk and

me. He seemed inquisitive about the toilet and sink. I explained and demonstrated. He ran hands over each. The toilet paper confused him at first and he giggled when I pretended to demonstrate.

"May use?" he asked and almost immediately pulled down his pants and sat on the toilet. I turned around and walked out the door.

"Of course you can use it, Haldir. In my world, what you are doing is done in private."

"Why?" he asked. "Everyone must do this. This efficient."

I didn't tell my boyfriend that I was curious about what Haldir might look like naked. I saw the bodies of his clan members so I kind of knew what to expect. We found some shorts and a long hoodie that should work on Haldir. We needed to go shopping without him until we figured out how to introduce him to our world. The eye doctor was on his way.

When we stripped, he watched us, curious about our own bodies, his expression inquisitive but also detached, like he was studying us and not at all shy. He undid the small rope holding back his hair and it flowed midway down his back and over his shoulders. He then stripped and prepared as I was, he was not what I expected. No nipples but a powerful looking chest and arms. Reasonably thick calves. Almost no body hair. Was that because he was younger than we thought or just the way his people developed over time? But what I tried not to stare at answered the age issue. Several inches taller than me, no question he was sexually mature. He had the largest penis I'd ever seen. Same with his low hanging nuts. He looked at ours, reached over and lifted mine, inspecting it, not at all uncomfortable or embarrassed, then back at his own and shrugged. I just stood there and let him do it, not sure if I should be uncomfortable or humiliated.

He loved the shower and hot water. He was used to bathing in cold lakes and streams. He said they could easily heat water for special purposes such as cooking, at least some could, using the power of concentration or with his knife. Shampoo had him shreiking in delight.

Introducing him to our world would be a challenge, a fun

one—or a disaster. We had to do it right.

Plumbing fascinated him. Electric appliances got him whooping and jumping up and down. But not electric lights. Fluorescents were the worst, which we had in part of the hallway, but incandescent was also bad, even the newer LED lights. He was able to produce light in his world and knew how to make it happen, not explain how it worked.

While we were showering and admiring Haldir's manhood, Uncle His called his attorney and printed out a non-disclosure form, having it ready when the ophthalmologist arrived.

Dr. Wolfdon, the eye doctor, was portly with a short gray beard, and friendly. He was surprised about the form but seemed to know Katnu well and agreed to sign. He let out a high-pitched whistle when he examined our friend.

"I've never seen eyes like his. The boy can literally see in the dark, like a mountain lion. But he has what's called photosensitivity or photophobia. Many people have the problem but not like he does. His eyes are a wonder. I suggest adding dimmer switches and getting lower lumen bulbs. LEDs are a problem but perhaps not warmer-toned ones. Try smart bulbs and experiment with different lighting intensities and colors to find the best variation. I also think dark glasses especially designed to filter out the problematic spectrums to help him see in bright artificial light. You said he may go to school. They are notorious for florescent lights. Let me take some measurements and I'll have a prototype made, maybe goggle like but with a designer flourish. If they work, we can manufacture more as backups, perhaps in different styles and colors."

Thank you," Katnu said. "I would also like a no-nonsense letter from you for use in the school that lays out what a serious issue this is and any denial of his use of these special glasses would be detrimental to his health making the school liable for any damage."

"A kind of scare the shit out of 'em letter."

"Exactly."

Afterward, I went out and bought clothes that would fit, jeans, sweaters and T-shirts, and multiple pairs of wrap-around dark glasses just to see what might work while we waited for the special lenses. I got some that were large, curved, dark but not mirrored, with arms as wide as the glass frames to hide any side views.

Katnu got the name of the school principal and the Superintendent of Schools and had his lawyer draft a letter to use when he was enrolled, suggesting possible legal action if anyone denied Haldir this reasonable accommodation. He liked one pair I got and we added an elastic band on the back to hold them tight. The light still bothered him but not as much. We figured once people got over the initial surprise at seeing a student wearing this kind of designer glasses, they'd ignore them. The idea of fashion made no sense to him. Utility was his benchmark. From his point of view dark glasses were sensible and pragmatic.

18.

went home to visit my parents for dinner, for conversation and roughhousing with my brothers. Mom wanted to know about the Russian Wilderness. She even had a map out that showed where it was and wanted me to point out where we visited. Describing the beauty and wildlife was easy. I said we did a lot of hiking. At some point I'd need to explain Haldir if we were going to bring him into our household. Spending the night was good politics. They wanted to share time with me and I liked it too.

The next morning, I asked to borrow the car, an old 2002 Volvo station wagon. We'd bought it used and it was roomy and dependable, one that didn't get a lot of usage other than trips to the grocery store or cinema. I explained, "Uncle His needs to pick up some household goods and electrical parts." We wanted to drive Haldir around the area, semi-hidden by a car that wouldn't draw attention, to give him a sense of the city and our crazy civilization. Dad was fine with it.

Haldir came outside the cabin for the first time and had to walk through the woods to a nearby street to get to the car. He was wearing his sunglasses. As soon as we left the tree line, a red TV news helicopter flashed low overhead. He held his ears just as a long, articulated bus came by, covered in the friendly faces of animals at the zoo and bending in the middle like a giant centipede as it turned and went up the road. A police car careened around the corner with its siren blaring.

He shrieked, his hands pressing against his mouth. *"Biast mòr!"* he shouted, pointing to all this craziness before he retreated into the woods, leaning with his back against a tree, breathing heavily. "Tell, please." He looked at us as we stood around him, touching his shoulders in comfort.

"No. There are no giant bugs flying overhead or going up the street. We are not under attack. Please trust me. It's just our weird and noisy world." I hoped my words reassured him. "Nothing to worry about. It will eventually make sense."

"Make no sense! Noise terrible."

His ears were hyper-sensitive. Daruk and Uncle His tried sending pictures of buses and helicopters telepathically. He looked from one to the other. "Too much."

We'd explained earlier what he would find outside the cabin, including some photos and video we found online. Why did everything happen all at once? A noisy twisting bus may not have been in the mix, nor a helicopter or a cop car chasing bad guys. But living our reality was different than being told about it. Uncle His was gentle as he pointed to the homes, the paved streets, cars, electrical poles, sidewalks, garages, and many other parts of life we accepted because they'd always been part of our own existance. Haldir had grown up in a forest with herds of silent deer, not honking automobiles.

"Let us walk around the neighborhood," Katnu suggested, holding out his hand. Haldir accepted it and slowly stepped forward. I gave him a blue and gold Golden State Warriors knit cap with a logo on the front. He put it on and as I adjusted it over his ears he winced and then seemed to accept it.

With Daruk and I beside him and Uncle His leading the way, we walked several blocks, taking turns to explain workmen trenching for a sewer repair, carpenters working on an apartment under construction, street venders, dogs on leashes, overhead electrical lines, street cars, skateboarders who were mostly rude as they whipped past, garage doors opening. It was endless novelty for Haldir, and the poor guy looked to be on sensory overload.

We reached Haight Street and stepped into the Fifties Rock Café and found an open table. A gum-smacking woman in a blue stripped uniform dropped off four menus and asked, "Coffee?"

"What coffee?" Haldir asked.

"That's cute, Steph Curry," she said and popped a bubble with her gum.

"Four orange juices, no coffee," I said quickly.

"She thinks I Steph Curry? What is that?"

"No, Haldir," I said, "she compared you to a famous basketball player. Remember we talked about basketball when asking about sports you played and were played in my world."

"Basketball? Her lips puffed out and broke…"

"No. It's something she was chewing, a weird habit some people like. It's called bubble gum. It exercises your jaw."

"Why? Strange." He picked up his paper napkin and placed it in his lap as we had done, looking at it with confusion.

I demonstrated the purpose. He shrugged, obviously considering it another odd and pointless human custom.

We ordered four vegetable omelets and wheat toast. He liked the idea of putting strawberry jam on his toast. He'd never had either and was now a big fan judging by the grin and the heaping amount of jam on each slice and it dripping down his chin.

The good news was that no one seemed to pay any attention to him. With all the weird people and things happening in a big American city, particularly this city, he fit in just fine. But I knew it would be different in a high school setting if we decided he should attend.

After breakfast, we got in my family car and I drove us around the city to give him a sense of it. He felt safer in the car in part because it was quieter, more forest than city for sound. At Fisherman's Wharf, we watched ferry boats dock, unload passengers and take on new ones. He wanted to do it so we did. He hooted as the boat pulled into the bay, leaning over the rail and watching the water. People looked at him and grinned seeing an excited, exuberant young man, not a freak. At least that was how I chose to interpret it.

●●●

When we were having lunch, Uncle His announced that the president was coming to San Francisco for a meeting of the G7. Group of Seven, a political forum consisting of Canada, France, Germany, Italy, Japan, and the United Kingdom with the European Union as a special participant. "She wants to meet you both and Haldir, also Miguel since he was part of the terrorist incident we made up in that public announcement. She also wants some private time with me. I think we should schedule a meeting with your parents, Darwin, and also Miguel's father so she can thank them for having such brave sons. Separately, and with just Darwin's mom and dad, to introduce Haldir and ask them to give him and the baby a home."

"Wow!" I responded with a cough. *Really?* "My parents will be thrilled. Would this be in private?"

"Probably so. A public setting would just complicate things. The world does not know about Haldir and we don't want a national press event to bring him out to the world. Perhaps at her hotel. We could get a suite and clear it with her security team."

"Should we talk about the issues we discussed before?" I wanted to make sure my mom wanted to do this. She should not be pressured. My sense was she would be responsive but it had to be her decision.

"I have looked at the astonishing array of jewelry and precious stones you brought back. It is, in my opinion, worth hundreds of millions of dollars. Given that much of it is from antiquity, there is no easy way to sell it in the open market without documentation of how it was obtained. My financial resources are extensive as we once discussed and I could set up a trust fund for Haldir that will have a substantial amount of money, maybe ten million or so, which should be more than enough for his immediate needs. Since he has no experience with such matters, I could sign off on it, perhaps as his guardian, or your mother or father could. I am open to either."

"I know you're a brilliant investor." I gave him a big grin.

"Yes. Do not make fun of me, young man. Knowing the future makes it easy to have a hundred percent success rate in investing. It is always useful to have money." He punched me softly in the shoulder. He was a playful man with a deep love of Daruk and me. At least I liked to think so.

"You should know that I own several pieces of real estate. Three houses and two condos in San Francisco. One free-standing home, just outside the park on Buena Vista Terrace close to your apartment and near Miguel's, was upgraded a few years back. It is quite large, and the tenants left recently and it is empty. I am having some minor repairs and painting done now. It is part of my investment portfolio. Five bedrooms on three levels, a family room, den, and office, four baths, magnificent views of the bay. It is relatively private and security is easy or as easy as it can be in a big city. I would be open to letting your family live there if that would enhance the possibility of Haldir staying with you. I would be pleased to forego any rent. I do not need the money. You and your two brothers could have your own rooms. So could Haldir and the baby depending on how you organized the space. Do you have any reaction?"

I just looked at the man. He could do anything. I leaned in, wrapping my arms around him. "Thank you, Uncle His!"

The house would be fantastic, but if not handled right it could look like Mom was being offered a bribe. She had to want to do it and then be offered a new place to live. Also, Dad was proud of what we had, what he'd worked for, and we couldn't do anything to diminish that. Maybe if President O'Connor put it to them as a personal favor, or helping with an important national security issue or something. How much could we tell them?

...

The new eyeglasses were a hit. They fit perfectly over Haldir's nose, around his eyes like designer goggles and back to his ears. Like a glove fits a hand, these fit his face. They were a bit boxy and surreal but I could see some celebrity like Elton John wearing them. The prescription worked well and even florescent light was no problem. Katnu ordered five more pairs in different colors so he would also have spares for special occasions. For the cabin Uncle His ordered a case of smart light bulbs and dimmers so we could experiment with colors and light intensity. It would be good if he could go without his glasses when he was here. I assumed we'd do the same thing at my home if he lived there or in Uncle His's rental home.

19.

What do you wear to meet the President?

My parents were in a panic, at least my mother was. Dad announced, after spending thirty seconds looking at his wardrobe, that he would wear his only slightly frayed gray suit with his one white dress shirt and his only tie, a blue/red/white stripe, appropriately patriotic.

"Mom, nice job getting rid of the gravy stain," I commented about the tie.

"It was a challenge," she replied.

Given that President O'Connor liked to wear slacks, Mom decided that was good for her too. She pulled out various options as we watched and she described the colors: Azure blue slacks, a Tiffany blue and turquoise scarf, tasteful French Blue three-inch heels, and navy-blue blazer. I'd never really thought about all the different colors of blue until Mom had on most of them. She looked great.

I settled on my regular and only dress up outfit: black jeans, green button-down shirt and my always fashionable midnight-blue blazer that still kinda fit if I didn't stretch out my arms. My brothers were split. Reggie, at eight, had heard of the president and opted for a T-shirt with the five colorful *StoryBots*—Bing, Boop, Beep, Bang and Bo. When Mom objected, he insisted it was educational. She finally relented and I teased that he had a future in politics. Markus was twelve, more boy than many on the cusp of puberty, and knew the president's name. After a long and sometimes loud conversation with Mom he opted for a black vest over a green Spongebob T-shirt. He claimed this would make him look *authentic*. Not sure what he meant but she bought it or didn't want to argue anymore.

Uncle His had booked a large suite at the Fairmont Hotel on Nob Hill; three bedrooms, a kitchen and living room. President O'Connor's entourage was in a massive set of rooms in the penthouse. We were four floors down. Not the kind of hotel room I'd ever been in. Fancy and expensive was the vibe, a bit too decorated for my taste.

We had special placards around our necks to get past a dozen security types and upstairs to the suite of rooms. An African American man, tall and in a form fitting black suit, met us at the door, eyeing us like he could read our brains. He checked our ID's, talked into his wrist, waited, listening to the device in his ear, and said we should step inside and go to the room on the left. I knew that Uncle His, Daruk, Haldir and the baby were on the other side of the suite in a separate room. There were three agents posted in front of that door. That likely meant the president was inside with them. That had been the plan. Two other guards were in the living room, looking at computer screens, glancing at us as we came in with the same x-ray-vision stare.

Not five minutes after my family settled down, the door opened and Miguel and his father stepped inside. Miguel wore a faded black sports coat, white shirt and red bowtie, a startling look for him. His dad, a horror comic artist, had on a black jacket with lightning bolts across the front and around the back over a T-shirt emblazoned with one of his canine superheroes, yellow, green and brown. It was quite a statement and altogether quite a contrast. Maybe that was the point. They were both perfect.

Miguel and I hugged and giggled at what was about to happen.

The head of Homeland Security entered moments later. I'd met Ciara McCloud at the press conference back when we'd returned from dramatic events on E3. A former Marine general, she looked strong, someone who didn't tolerate fools. Her thick hair was severely short with a carved part, like a marine in basic training; maybe age fifty, her face lined from years in the sun.

I jumped up and extended my hand. "General, wonderful to see you again."

"You too, Darwin. I briefly met your family at the media circus. Miguel, nice to see you too under more pleasant circumstances."

I did the re-introduction to my siblings. Reggie asked about her hair and she bent over and let him feel it. He announced he wanted a haircut just like it. My dad just nodded. He was the barber for us kids. Reggie wanted a selfie with her and got one.

She stood, pressing a finger to the white plug in her ear. "The President will be here in three minutes. A photographer will take photos for your personal use, then exit."

The Secret Service guard opened the door and President Barbara O'Connor stepped into the doorway, lights from the living room giving her a bit of an ethereal glow, kind of like a new character from the Avengers, Super Grandma, except she held the nuclear launch codes and carried a small purse over one arm, much like the late Queen Elizabeth II. I closed my eyes and then looked again. It really was her, not on television but in person, maybe five foot seven, short white hair, in her early seventies. She was a former university professor, slender, in a midnight-blue pants suit with a red scarf. Her chin up, supremely confident, she carried a black cane with a silver lion handle, probably useful in fights with errant members of Congress. Her eyes were sparkling blue-green with "don't mess with me" eyebrows. She exuded both warmth and power.

"Darwin, Miguel, we finally are face to face. I've been looking forward to this. Also to meeting your parents. How proud they must be to have such remarkable boys." She stepped inside followed by another guard, this one female, and a photographer, a young man.

I was grinning and immobilized, not sure what to do. She answered that question, coming up to me and giving me a hug. *The President of the United States just hugged me!* "Thank you, ma'am." She then walked down the line and shook everyone's hand, stopping to give Miguel a hug. He squeaked in excitement. I could use this against him for years.

She was patient in the taking of the photos. The photographer grouped us in different ways. My parents with the three of us kids. Miguel and his dad. Miguel and I with her. Her with my brothers. Then all of us together. I noticed General McCloud exit the room quietly, apparently listening to a message in her earpiece.

My mom asked if she could reveal any more information about what happened when Miguel and I were kidnapped. The president said she could not because of the ongoing fight against the terrorists. We talked about our lives for nearly a half hour, then a guard pointed at Miguel and he stood with his dad as had been planned. She rose and thanked them again with handshakes, and they exited. A guard came over to my brothers and asked if they'd like to see some of the special Secret Service equipment. They squealed and left. Now just Mom, Dad and me. I knew what this was about and hoped we could handle it right.

President O'Connor sat and looked at me, then at each of my parents. "We cleared the room," she said, "so we could have a private conversation. At my insistence I'm about to reveal some of what happened in the Russian Wilderness that you don't know about, and I'm going to ask your help."

My parents looked at each other, and then at me. I just nodded. I knew my parents would hear only a tightly edited version.

"As you know, Darwin and Daruk went up there to camp and see the wildlife. What you don't know is that they came across a horrific scene. Eight people had been killed. The FBI just gave me its report. Daruk contacted his adopted father, Katnu Hisman, a man you know well as Uncle His. What you may not know is that Mr. Hisman and I have known each other for several years. Katnu called me because of what he found, both the dead and the living: two people, one barely in his teens, the other an infant, just a few weeks old. The child's mother was one of those murdered. They were all slaughtered, we believe, because greedy men were looking for a legendary lost treasure and a secretive tribe living in the wilderness. They found four members of the tribe, including the mother of the infant, and shot them, apparently in anger when they found no treasure. Then they apparently killed each other in frustration.

"Darwin, Daruk and Mr. Hisman rescued the two survivors. The boy, maybe fourteen years old, has lost everything. His family's dead. He's taken the child as his own. The boy's name is Haldir. He and Darwin have become close, like brothers. As the boy struggles to make sense of his new life, Darwin has become his anchor. Knowing a little about your son, I can understand that. He's a special young man."

I was sitting on a sofa between my parents; Dad punched my shoulder and Mom squeezed my knee and kissed my cheek.

"Here's the shocking part. I ask your discretion in not revealing this to anyone outside this room. One reason Katnu called me was to bring in the FBI. Beyond that, the larger reason was because he believes the young man and child are from a subspecies of humans different from us in some ways but similar in most. In terms of anthropology, if he's right, this is an eight-point earthquake upending scientific belief. We have no definitive answers yet...and I'm jumping ahead of any final expert analysis, but this is the early guessing: Haldir could be part of a group of early humans that broke off from the *hominin* or human family tree maybe a million years ago. They developed independently of other homo sapiens groups. I'm told they may represent an advanced form of humans, what the rest of us may look like far in the future. Haldir's eyes and ears, like other members of his tribe, are a little different and helped them survive, living near but often hidden from other humans who feared and hated them because they were different. Perhaps not unlike racial differences in much of our history or the ugly politics of today which seems to forget our basic founding principles of equality. Finding difference a threat seems a sad but common human trait. He's tall for his age, seems mature and very smart. But his world, living in hiding in the mountains, is radically different from ours. Imagine growing up in an isolated village with no contact with the outside world. Most of our world and way of life are a mystery to him. He desperately needs to be surrounded by a loving family. The baby also needs a family to love and to love him. They have no one. Except Darwin."

Mom let out a cry and covered her mouth. "The poor child! Are you asking us to help, to take them in?"

"Yes, I am." She reached over and touched my mother's hand. "If you're willing to take on this awesome responsibility, Mr. His-man has offered to let you occupy a large house he owns in the neighborhood, free of charge."

Mom gaped at her. "Uncle His owns a house other than that cabin in the park?"

"Yes," she replied. "He's a savvy investor, a wealthy man who's chosen simplicity and humility in an age of arrogance and ostentation. I admire him for that and many other reasons. He's happy to make the offer to lift some of the load off whoever takes the children in. He cares for them, feels a responsibility, knows he can't provide what they need and wants them to have as good a life as possible given their circumstances."

My parents looked at each other. "Can we meet Haldir and the baby?" Dad asked.

"Yes, but here's more detail to put this in perspective." The president nodded to an aide, the door opened and Uncle His entered. Mom gave him a hug and Dad reached over and shook his hand.

He sat down next to the president across from us. "As you make your decision," Uncle His began, "you should know that anatomically Haldir and the child, indeed his people, are not exactly like us." He related in careful detail all the anatomical differences we'd discovered, then the stark cultural differences in Haldir's world. "He is learning English," Uncle His concluded, "which is still a bit rough at times, but soon will be near perfection. I hope all this information is useful as you make your decision. This is a big ask. He needs to learn our world which he finds crazy and a bit frightening. We have discussed enrolling him in school with Darwin so he can learn the social skills he will need to succeed in our world. We know school will be challenging, not for the curriculum, but the social interaction. Being different can make you a target with teenagers."

President O'Connor: "Your first sight of them may surprise you. May shock you. But I hope you'll look deeper than appearance and know their good hearts and need for love." She lifted a hand. The door opened and Haldir walked into the room with the baby in a sling across his chest. His eyes and ears on full display. He wore gray jogging pants, tennis shoes and a blue sweatshirt, not unlike many teenagers.

Mom got up and walked over to Haldir and wrapped her arms around him. "You poor child." He towered over her, looking surprised. Dad rose and did the same. He lifted a cloth from the baby's face. Gazing at him she reached in and ran the back of her fingers over the child's face. Then wiped tears slipping down her cheeks. Haldir offered the infant to her. She held him, kissing his forehead. Dad came up next to her.

"Your offer of a house, Uncle His," my dad said. "We don't take charity."

"It is hardly charity," Katnu responded. "You would be taking on a serious responsibility to help raise two unique beings. I feel responsible for them and I cannot provide the kind of family environment they need, nor can the state. There will be challenges, some perhaps extreme. I have a house that I think would be perfect. I feel obligated to help these two beings. Haldir is close to your son and depends on his judgment. Some items Haldir brought back from his world are likely worth a great deal of money. I will use them to raise funds in his behalf. A trust fund will be set up to defray any expenses you may face even if one or both of you choose to step away from your current jobs to take on this opportunity. I use the word 'opportunity' on purpose. You would have a chance to raise a unique pair of humans, unlike any on the planet. With the help of President O'Connor, we will have paperwork prepared that indicates he has been home schooled, thus no school records. You could be named his guardians, or I could, legally, with the help of the talented people who work for Barbara."

President O'Connor stood and then we all did. "Everything Katnu said is true. I back this proposal with all my heart. This is not without its challenges, given the physical appearance and learning curve here." She indicated Haldir and said quietly, "Our world makes no sense to him. People will probably be cruel to them, both high school students and adults. But if the public understands what he represents, a future human alive today, the publicity would be intense, savage without letup. We must do our best to keep it out of the media. Please give it serious thought and I will leave a number to reach me with your decision."

Mom looked at my father, communicating silently. I knew the look. "I think my husband and I are of the same mind. We would be delighted to take Haldir and the baby into our family, to become his new family with Darwin as his brother. I suspect my other two sons will be thrilled. The option of a larger home would make it easier. Thank you, Uncle His."

Haldir's voice cracked with his words: "Thank you."

President O'Connor raised an arm and snapped her fingers. Two aides immediately entered the room. "Sarah and John will work closely with you as planners and liaisons to me and my office. Thank you very much for your openness and generosity. There'll be challenges but also an immense sense of satisfaction for helping two children in need."

She opened the purse hanging over her forearm, and pulled out two small pouches. Now I was really paying attention. What was inside? "Please give this one to Miguel, something for him and his father." She handed it to me and opened the other larger bag. Several beaded bracelets fell into her palm. They dangled a miniature White House and a unique tiny angel wing, some black, others silver or white. "In my spare time, particularly on some conference calls or endless staff meetings going over what we've already gone over, I like to make jewelry, colorful beads and accessories. It's better than knitting. What makes these special to me is they were blessed by the Dalai Lama." She handed one to everyone, each bracelet different. We all looked as startled as I was. "And this one is for Daruk," she said, slipping it onto my palm. Being blessed by the Dalai Lama was cool, a major religious figure who urged peace rather than war and opposed the subjugation of women. Cool.

"Even me?" Haldir asked.

"Especially for you," the President said, stretching up to kiss his cheek as he bent down to her. She slipped the black onyx beaded bracelet with a white angel wing onto his wrist. "Now, I must attend a G-7 Conference." With that she hugged me, both parents, Uncle His and Haldir, rubbed a finger on the baby's cheek and stepped smartly from the room followed by her detail. No wonder she'd carried forty-two states.

...

We sat for an hour with the president's aides, reviewing options. The head of Homeland Security, Ciara McCloud, joined us.

In a written agreement with the court, Uncle His will now be the legal guardian for both Haldir and the child. My parents, Harold and Eva McQuaid, will be the godparents with legal authority to raise the children. There was also be an option to adopt. General McCloud guaranteed that her staff would make it happen with no fingerprints on how it got legalized. The story would be that Haldir was home schooled and privacy issues were keeping his background secret. He'd need to pass some tests to get into my school and establish his grade level which Uncle His said should be no problem. His age would be set at fourteen, an eighth grader, just a guess since his people used a different calendar. Having seen him in the shower, I would have guessed older. He would certainly stand out in gym class and get lots of attention for his height. I looked it up. The average height of a boy that age is five feet six inches. He was six foot-three.

Dad was holding the baby. He looked a little apprehensive as he rubbed the boy's cheek. The child giggled, and coughed, his spit catching my dad's forehead. He grinned and laughed, wiping his face. Yes, we had a baby in the family, again.

"Do you want to see your new home? Uncle His asked us.

My parents smiled, a little embarrassed if I was reading them right. My brothers were brought in. They stopped dead and stared at Haldir, looking up, up at him in wonder. He smiled at them. He was now wearing his special dark glasses and the Warriors knit cap down over his ears. Mom explained that Haldir and the baby would soon be living with them in a new home. Haldir squatted down and invited the boys to come to him. Reggie ran over, never shy, and jumped onto his lap, arms around his neck. Haldir effortlessly picked him up and stood, spinning him around in a circle. My little brother screamed in delight as he was lifted overhead. My mother looked shocked, but not my brothers.

"My turn!" Markus insisted.

"More!" Reggie demanded.

Yeah, no problem with Haldir being part of the family.

Daruk joined us to see our new home. It was only a couple of blocks from the cabin. What I could see looked Victorian, with the typical peaked roofs, lots of gingerbread, and a yellow and blue paint job. A painted concrete block fence maybe eight feet tall held a tall pair of metal gates which opened as we turned into the short driveway. I thought that's where we'd park but a wall of the house opened to reveal a garage. Uncle His pulled the van inside and the wall slid back. I'd never seen anything like it.

With my brothers wrapped around Haldir, we got out of the van and were led toward two doorways. "You can take the elevator or stairs," Uncle His explained. "Some of the house is below us, down a steep hillside on three additional levels all with a full or partial view of the bay. The garage has a Victorian façade and essentially a one-bedroom apartment above that can be used as an office or security. I bought it many years ago and re-modeled it for a wealthy bio-med CEO, obsessed with security, who has since moved to Europe."

"*El-E-va-tor,*" Haldir said, sounding out the syllables, as he stepped inside. He was now an expert since riding one at the cabin. He held Reggie in one arm and held Marcus's hand. Mom now had the baby, who seemed content in her arms.

The elevator opened into a large living room with a view of the Bay Bridge and beyond. We all stopped and admired the upgrade from our current two-bedroom apartment with its view of an old wooden fence. Examining the open kitchen floor plan with the same view, a built-in barbecue, range, oven, dishwasher, granite counters and a dining room, Mom seemed overwhelmed. "Wow," she said, her grin even wider. An office space or perhaps den was next to the living room, it even had a large fireplace along with a large bathroom. On the two lower levels were the bedrooms. The master suite got some appreciative sighs. It was large, with great view, an antique four poster bed, a highboy with lots of storage, a walk-in closet and large private bath. "I purchased some of the furniture from the previous tenants. If you don't like it, it can be put in storage," Uncle His explained.

"I think it's beautiful," my mother said.

The boys laid claim to two small bedrooms, also with views, and a shared bath. Two more bedrooms and a bath were at the bottom level. I pulled Haldir to follow me down the stairs. Daruk right behind us, to two rooms, a bath in between, with lots of space and good views. I suggested that Haldir take the larger room so we could put in a crib. I pulled up a picture of one on my phone, explaining how it worked. He was excited, grinning ridiculously when he saw the queen-sized extra-long bed in his room, leaping onto it and rolling on his back, laughing. Yeah, fourteen was about right, not a sophisticated seventeen. I suspected Uncle His had something to do with the bed.

Daruk pulled me back into my room and closed the door, using the opportunity to pinch my butt, in approval, I guess, of my ass and the room, both good. He then tried to get frisky just as there was a knock on the door.

"What do you want, Haldir?" I asked, opening the door. "Oh, hi, Mom."

She too was exploring. There was a small office or den by the elevator with a sofa, chairs, a fireplace and a kind of mini kitchen. We all watched a freighter, stacked high with multi-colored containers, pass under the Bay Bridge.

Outside our window there was a small, landscaped garden featuring, at this level, the amazing cinnamon-red bark of two modest redwood trees, green ferns, a large clump of bluish hydrangeas, yellow and pink impatiens and red hibiscus.

Yeah. We could make this work.

20.

nclle His paid movers to help pack up our old apartment and get us situated into our new home. Our busybody neighbor was videotaping it all, hiding behind her drapes with just the camera lens and part of her head exposed. I'd miss her silliness and waved, I knew this was important to her.

Daruk helped me unpack in my room, constantly pushing the door closed. I liked it but also didn't want Mom to come walking in again and catching us. "Later," I kept telling him and realized how magical it was to be able to say that, having something and someone to share my future with and certain body parts.

"Why are you smiling?" he asked.

"You know," was all I said and needed to say.

• • •

Haldir's recall from listening and watching was impressive, perhaps from his curiosity about his new life, his training as a boy or maybe because of the way his brain was wired. It had to be extraordinary if he was to have any chance of fitting into our world.

138

We obtained audio and video programs explaining math, history, politics, law, fashion, customs, money, and anything a high school student should know. Paying money for food or other services made no sense to him but he was intrigued and asked questions. He seemed surprised when I told him not to touch anyone else's body or stare, like he did when lifting my dick in the shower. Everything was open and trustful in his world, not sexual, his people were just curious and much more open than in our more puritanical society. We watched movies and television series which helped give him a sense of life but cautioned that much of what he saw with teenagers was exaggerated. They provided lessons on how not to act. We also listened to music by singers popular with teens.

Unclle His hired a retired teacher to coach our new family member on how to take a test and read questions critically. Haldir was already an avid reader of ancient texts and his telepathy time with Uncle His helped him adapt to English. My dad visited the school to register him and paid his tuition from Katnu's trust fund. An academic test was scheduled.

After several intense weeks of cramming, he took the test and apparently did well enough to meet the school's standards although full tuition and a large donation from Uncle His before the exam may have offset any deficiencies.

Principal Darling's office called to set up a meeting with my parents and Haldir. I added myself. We came separately. When Haldir and I arrived, I stopped us before we entered the building. "Are you still carrying your knife?"

"Yes."

"See those metal pipes on each side of the doorway?"

"Yes."

"They're part of what is called a metal detector. It's designed to make sure that no one brings in any weapons, like guns and knives. It will set off an alarm when you go through it and security will run up to stop you. We do this because sometimes, rarely, there is violence in schools and this helps protect students."

He walked up to the door, squatted down and inspected it. "Go through so I can see how it works. Please."

I went past the machine and there was a beep. He listened, watched and nodded before pulling up his pant leg, touching the knife and whispering something. He then released the knife, pulled down the pant leg, and walked through the door. There was a beep, just like it did for me. No alarm.

"How'd you do that?"

"Make knife and sheath invisible to this machine and any like it. Electricity easy to manipulate."

I was still shaking my head as we entered the outer room of my principal. Inside were my two favorite FBI agents sitting in Darling's office behind the glass window, Agent Washington and Agent Heartthrob Tomas. They both stood and offered their hands.

"Good to see you again Darwin," she said in her take charge agent voice. She wrapped her arms around Haldir. "Wonderful to see you again." He seemed surprised but hugged back, as was his way. She turned to Darling: "This young man saved my life after I was shot by one of the men who murdered his family." She stood on tiptoe and kissed his cheek. Not exactly how I pictured most FBI encounters.

Darling looked stunned. "Wha...What'd he do?"

She shook her head and slid an arm around Haldir's waist. "Case privilege." She returned to her seat, her message delivered that her commitment and the FBI's to Haldir ran deep and personal. A *don't mess with him or else!* kind of warning. Cool.

Darling stood when my parents entered. "Glad to see you, Mr. and Mrs. McQuaid, Darwin. Hello Haldir." He stepped over and shook his hand, now one of our new friend's favorite activities.

"No weapon!" Haldir proclaimed proudly as he opened his palms as proof. Darling just stared open-mouthed, again. A good look. Yet I also knew this would lead to endless inquiries from my mother.

Agent Beauty finished for his partner: "We've been briefing Principal Darling on our agency's interest in Haldir. The teachers are here this week for orientation before school starts. We'll be meeting with them later this afternoon to make sure there're no problems. He can wear his special prescription glasses any-where, anytime. Someone with a complaint must contact us, not him, ever. Because of his differences, he'll be a target for bullying. Teachers have to be on alert and intervene. Principal Darling is fully behind this approach."

"But you're not going to tell me what happened?" Darling asked.

"We cannot," Washington stated flatly, her tone of finality making it clear it was beyond Darling's pay grade.

He nodded acceptance. "Darwin, my secretary has the sylla-bus and books he'll need for fall semester so he can have time to study. Also his locker number and combination. You may want to take him on a tour. Here's a list of his classes and room numbers."

"Thank you, sir," I replied. "I'm so glad we had this chance to talk."

With that we left the room. Finding his classrooms was good so he knew where they were. The lock combination on his locker seemed ridiculous to him. He just shook his head, put his hand over the lock and whispered something and it snapped open.

"What purpose of lock?"

"It's a device used to protect your personal items and keep other people from stealing them."

"Stealing? Mean what?"

"It means to take someone's property without permission."

"You not share?"

"Some things are shared, but in this world, people own cer-tain items and lock them away to use later. It keeps them safe."

"In Fae world, everything shared. You said 'own'. That is a new word."

"Wow. I didn't realize how different our societies are. Here individuals have exclusive control over many things. They own them, like clothes and furniture. For some people, the more they own the happier they become. Other items, like streets and public spaces, are shared, owned by everyone."

"Must think about this. Your ways strange."

A few students were wandering the hallways, likely seventh or eighth graders, and they stared at him. He looked back.

"This what I be in school with?" he asked quietly. "They tiny."

We visited the gym. He asked about the high ceiling, the bleachers, basketball nets, weights and other features. He listened intently as I did my best to explain.

Entering a classroom, he looked doubtfully at the combination chair and desks. I explained and demonstrated how to sit in one. He tried and it didn't go well. Eighth grade desks and Haldir did not easily fit.

We went back to Darling's office and reported the problem and the need for accommodation. He considered it and nodded. "I'll have maintenance find individual adult tables with separate chairs for each of his classrooms. In fact, I'll put a few in all classrooms since he's not the only tall student or student who'll need a little more room. That should eliminate any complaints about special treatment."

"Thank you, sir." A good decision, I thought. Darling doing the right thing for all students who may not fit the standard size.

On our way home, we stopped by a sporting goods store and bought a basketball hoop and ball as well as a football to familiarize him. He might have to deal with both. I called Miguel to come over and help us practice. His skills in sports matched my own.

• • •

Haldir better understood the concept of a grocery store because it echoed his own experience at gathering food in their greenhouse. Until I pulled a grocery store cart from the rack.

"What this?" Haldir asked, running his hands over the metal bars, stooping down, examining the wheels as people stared. He used woven baskets in his village. I did my best to explain. He shrugged as we walked into the store. I pushed at first and then he wanted to do it.

We headed to the vegetable counter of the chain grocery store. He grinned as he saw a hundred different offerings. "So many," he said in awe, pulling his hands to his mouth. He ran to the nearest bins. *"Cairéid,"* he said holding up a bunch of carrots. *"Pónairí glasa,"* he shouted with glee, picking up and feeling a handful of green beans.

"Practice your English," I advised.

"We grew many these. Wonderful many here." He continued walking up the isle as I selected different items and put them in the basket.

He picked up an eggplant, feeling it, sniffing it. "What?"

I explained and put three in the cart. "Mom makes a great eggplant parmigiana." He started to ask and I cut him off with, "Trust me, you'll love it."

We came around the corner to the milk aisle. Holding up a gallon of two percent, I said "Cow's milk."

"What is cow? For milk? We goats."

On the cereal aisle, he just shrugged so I picked several different kinds. He was in for a treat. At the sight of the meat counter he froze, staring at the various kinds of packaged animal flesh. His face contorted. He picked up a cellophane wrapped container of ground beef, felt it, sniffed it and then threw it down, twisted around and ran from the store hand to his mouth as if he was about to hurl. No meat on this trip. What if they served hamburgers or hot dogs at school? Maybe we'd brown bag it and try and organize a vegetarian table.

•••

We attached the basketball hoop and net against a wall inside the garage. There was no garage door that looked like a garage door, so no place to bolt it in. The inside worked. It was a large space with only one vehicle, so plenty of room for a half-court game.

Before we practiced, he needed to learn the game. We studied an instruction video before watching professional basketball games, generally the Golden State Warriors. He had endless questions: "Why three-point highest value? So close to hoop."

On that I had no answer. "That's just the rule." I looked up one stat on the Internet. "The Guinness World Record for furthest throw made by someone on the court was 64 feet, 3 inches in 2022. It was by a coach in Louisiana."

"What Guinness? What Louisiana?"

He needed more work on his verbs. Every answer led to more questions. But that was how he learned.

"This is a game similar to *Thrump* only you must bounce ball up and down and throw into metal hole on a wall instead of ground hole."

"Basically, yeah," Miguel added, and we went into the garage so he could demonstrate dribbling or trying to and driving in for a layup. "Darwin, let's show him how two can play."

We tried to block each other from getting to the net, only tripping once.

"Ball light," Haldir said, twisting it around in his hands. He tossed it toward the net and it dropped in. "Dribble no sense."

We played for a half hour, both of us trying to block him but he was faster, taller, and the first time he vaulted over our heads in a tight roll, we fell down gasping. Did he just do that?

"Must leap in *Thrump;* better than dribble."

Football tossing did not go well. I really didn't know how to throw the ball in a spiral. Miguel either. My dad and brothers came out and did it perfect, all three of them. Gloating was not a good look.

21.

"**K**atnu, I must learn how to dance as a high school student."

"I assume you are not asking me how to do it. I really do not like modern E2 music. Give me the soft chants of our world."

"Agreed. It is too loud, often with lots of screeching. Yet I must learn because Darwin expects me to be his dance partner at the senior prom with a smile on my face. I have looked up the term and watched videos of teenagers dancing, either jumping up and down or squeezing tight together and rocking slowly back and forth like they are trying to procreate. Very odd behavior. It will be a challenge. I do not want to embarrass him."

"There are dancing schools you could attend. It would be just you and a teacher. I'll check Yelp for reviews."

"What is Yelp?"

Katnu looked at him like he was joking.

"I will also need a type of clothing called a *tuxedo*. I looked it up online. They are ridiculous to look at and likely uncomfortable, maybe even painful particularly around the neck. He will need one too. Shiny lapels. Who needs lapels?"

"No worry. Your two-hundred-year-old plus adopted father will help you be a success at this high school extravaganza."

"I like him best naked."

"Really not an option for a school dance."

•••

"Miguel, what's wrong?" We were hanging out like the old days at our favorite hamburger stand on Valencia. If I wanted to eat meat, it'd have to be when I was out of the house and not with Haldir. Mom had made the decision that we were going vegetarian. My brothers were not happy.

"Luther is bored with me." My best friend looked desperate. "I think he's adorable and smart even if he hasn't had much education. I guess when you're poor in the twenty-sixth century, you're only good for cannon fodder and manual labor."

"Did he say he was bored?"

"Not in so many words."

"Does he initiate sex?"

"Only two or three times a day. Down from twice that. That proves it."

"You have sex three times a day? Sometimes six times? How are you walking?"

"Hey! No making assumptions!"

"Is he going to enroll in school with us?"

"He's intrigued but embarrassed. He's nineteen and would be older than any other student. We'd need to make up fake background records and a phony birth certificate so he could be younger on paper. He doesn't want to look dumb. He doesn't know anything about twenty-first century life, or history, or math or movies or music. He'd be lost in the daily chatter of kids at school. He has a good handle on what happened in his century. Not too useful back in these times."

"No one would guess nineteen. He's cute, he could pass for fifteen or sixteen."

"All true. You forgot stamina in bed."

"I wouldn't know and take your word. Maybe you're lucky he's cutting back."

"I worry he feels trapped. He's dependent on Uncle His's generosity for a place to live and food. He came back through time as a guy I had sex with. He may feel he can't move on if he gets bored with me."

"My family is now dependent on Uncle His' generosity," I told him. "We live in one of his properties. But this is important so listen close—no one could get bored with a hottie like you."

"True. I'm irresistible. But he's sampled this fine product many times. He can't go back to his own time because he'd be seen as a traitor. He'd still be dirt poor just like he was when he joined the militia. He'd be a pariah. The twenty-sixth century is not a nice place to live."

"Yet that's the future of our planet and the human race."

"I don't want a boyfriend who feels forced. That's not a loving relationship or a healthy one."

"Let me think about this. He needs to feel good about his situation, feel a bit independent. Hmmmm. A crazy idea just popped into my head. I need to explore it with Uncle His."

"*Wait!* Are you planning on discussing my sex life with him?"

"Only the good parts."

•••

Mom was going to make macaroni and cheese, a favorite. She'd put a large pot under the faucet to fill it with water when she got a call on her cell. She left the kitchen.

"What your mother doing?" Haldir asked me.

"Boiling water to cook."

"Seem odd. How hot you want?"

"Boiling." I took the pot from the sink and put it on the stove.

He lifted his pant leg and took out his knife. Waved it over the pot and said something under his breath. The water started to boil vigorously. "Much easier." He slipped the knife back into its sheath.

This was not something my parents could know about. "Please don't say how you did it, or do it again." He was supposed to be just a big kid for his age with a tragic story and from a rural background, not a magical creature. But the more I learned and watched, the more it seemed like he was. A legendary Fae. My life already held endless adventure and complications. Plus I had a hot boyfriend. Life was good.

"That was fast," Mom said coming back.

"Ahhh. We'll slice the cheese and prep the greens for a salad." I turned around to avoid eye contact. "Help me, Haldir."

My brothers came running into the kitchen shouting, *"Cheese!"* They had a sense. Haldir gave them each a piece.

"Play with us!" They each grabbed one of his arms and pulled him into the living room. He laughed and lifted them up and held them against his hips and twirled around, faster and faster. The boys screamed.

22.

aldir was able to fold his ears back close to his head and hold them there without having to constantly think about it, as if he could click them in place. Handy. We pulled his long thick hair over them and wrapped it in a carved bone barrette at the base of his neck. That held them tight and camouflaged the pointed tips. His hair hung to his waist and those special shades, a modified rounded goggle with designer styling and an elastic strap behind his head to hold them in place, were also useful for the same reason.

He wore typical teenage clothes now, strategically ripped jeans, high-top tennis shoes, size fourteen—and what they say about big feet was obviously true—and several old sweatshirts with various versions of the school's name and logo. The face of the howling coyote seemed appropriate. He liked it. Nothing bright or flashy so he could fit in easier. Just his height and dark designer shades made him stand out. We considered trying to modify his walk—more of an elegant male model's glide—but decided we had enough issues to worry about.

Uncle His continued to work with him on his English and was making remarkable progress.

At my suggestion, Haldir started listening to radio stations, mostly those popular with teenagers. Pop. Rock. Punk. Rap. Hip-hop. They were far out of his experience but he listened to become familiar. I tried to explain them to the extent music needs interpretation. He liked to sing, he informed me, something he did within his elfin community. His voice was surprisingly good with considerable range and power. Some songs were ethereal, others more melodious, ballads about life in his world in his native tongue. When I found a classical music station he touched my hand.

"Wait, please."

We listened for several minutes as he leaned toward the radio. The longer he listened, the bigger his grin. *"Bach."*

I looked at him and shrugged in confusion. He repeated the name.

"You mean Bach as in Johann Sebastian Bach*?"*

"Yes, yes."

"You know about classical music?"

"Know *him.* I read many of our *Fae* history books. Long ago, my people lived in Holy Roman Empire, now you mostly call Germany as well France and other countries and kingdoms after fall of Rome and through beginning of Renaissance. Their music and instruments popular with my people. Music handed down, generation to generation. I like play lute. Enjoy his music."

"A lute? Like that pear-shaped guitar-thingey you see in historical movies about knights in armor and damsels?"

He just looked at me. So I opened my cell phone and did a search for lute. One came up.

"Yes. Yes. I play."

"Mom! Dad!" I said leaping up and heading to the living room. I showed the photo to my parents. "He can play the lute and knows Bach!" I felt proud for some reason.

"Oh, honey," my mother said. "Wonderful! We have to get one for him."

Three calls later and with some of Uncle His's trust fund money, we headed to a music store and got a lute. Very 1960s, very dusty, used in a long ago musical, then stored forgotten in a back room. Haldir was thrilled. He blew off the dust, adjusted the strings, replaced several, and strummed. The store gave us a stack of sheet music, not that he would understand it. At least not anytime soon.

In the car he started strumming a tune that sounded Christmasy. "Dad, he's playing 'Greensleeves.'"

"Wow. I think you're right."

This lute had sixteen strings and he was clearly a master even though I had no way to compare. He played all kinds of medieval-sounding tunes as we drove, riffing a piece from one song then jumping to another, often dropping in some words in his native tongue. I just grinned. My adopted brother had serious musical chops. Not that kids at school would care much about a lute or Bach.

Mom was instantly a fan when he played for her. She decided we should use more of the trust fund to locate and hire a music teacher. I was worried our new brother was already overwhelmed, but this was Mom. Finding someone who specialized in medieval as well as contemporary music was a challenge but once she set her mind on something, she succeeded. Or she made my dad succeed. The teacher ended up being a plump, middle-aged woman with wiry red hair named Mrs. Knox. She signed a non-disclosure form and started working with him.

After an afternoon of practice with him, she pronounced him talented, almost a virtuoso, suggesting he study a range of music including more modern pieces. She thought he might enjoy an acoustic guitar which was related to the lute and might work better with more contemporary music. What seemed most important to me was that playing and singing made him happy, helping him forget, at least for a while, the horror of what had happened in the Russian Wilderness.

I, unfortunately, had no talent when it came to instruments. But I could applaud with vigor.

•••

Uncle His worked with me on telepathy skills, the point being to be able to communicate with Haldir in case there was a problem when school started. Every evening for weeks Haldir and I would sit in his room or mine and practice giving instructions to do something and seeing if we each got it right. I was not as skilled as he was or the others, but I was vastly improved. It would be a lifeline if there were problems. Given all he had to learn and the unpredictable way teenagers could act, it seemed like a good plan.

He and I also discussed what he would do with the foot long knife he carried strapped to his left calf. He said it was part of him, something that all his people carried. Some Fae trick made it invisible to metal detectors and to everyone except us. "I just pretend to be slow in removing shoes. It fit in locker. Should not be problem."

•••

Luther and Miguel joined Daruk and me for dinner one night when my parents were at movie with my brothers and Haldir. They'd picked *Black Panther*, a story about a hidden kingdom and people of extraordinary power. Kind of like Haldir's story. Mom had made vegetarian spaghetti—a little odd but with enough cheese it was good—and we had plenty for the four of us.

Was Luther losing interest in Miguel? It didn't seem like it the way he sat with his arm around him, keeping him tight on the sofa, kissing his ear…wait…biting an earlobe. His workouts were building on an already strong body, bulging nicely in a tight blue T-shirt. His hair was getting longer, now over an inch, curly and medium brown in sunlight, clear light brown skin, hazel eyes. His jaw gave him a masculine look. Miguel leaned his head into Luther's shoulder, getting a kiss on his forehead in return. When we stood, Luther rubbed Miguel's butt, always a good sign. My sense was the guy was into my best friend. Still, there was some validity to worries that Luther was trapped in this century, in a small cabin in the park, with no prospects to work and be independent should he want that, because he didn't exist on paper. I watched them together, young love. Three times a day was amazing. Six times a bit excessive. Daruk and I rarely hit that mark, rarely being different from never.

"It's strange being at the before end of my future, knowing how it ends, if that makes sense." Luther spoke as we finished dinner, sipping wine, enjoying some carrot cake my mom made. Dad was fine with me having wine when my mother wasn't around and we limited it to two glasses. "My world is five hundred years ahead of us. Some really terrible things are going to happen to Earth, to humanity and life in general, in coming decades. From what I understand, it's obvious politicians refused to do anything that would inconvenience anyone even if it meant leaving a miserable world for their grandkids. Media was so splintered, facts so easily exploitable, that there were no longer any commonly held beliefs. Truth as a standalone ideal no longer existed. You made up your own."

"Yes," I said, elbows on the table, Daruk's hand rubbing my thigh, making it difficult to concentrate at times. But I wanted to use this time with Miguel's boyfriend to understand him better and also what was going to happen. Like Uncle His's investments, knowing the future makes the stock market a sure thing. "That's certainly already obvious today much less in decades to come. I'm almost afraid to ask…what's the worst thing that comes to mind during the rest of this century?"

His lips tightened, eyebrows pulling into a frown. His revelations would not be positive. We already knew about his world— our world in half a millennium—massive die offs of all life, including humans. A dead ocean, humanity holding out mostly in the last big city on the planet, in northern Canada. "I live in a difficult reality. First, you know I am not well educated. My family was poor and there were few opportunities for meaningful work or school. I liked to read, thanks to my mother, and studied books when I could. But that does not earn a living. That's why I joined the militia."

"You've told me some things," Miguel said to him, his arm over Luther's shoulder, "that would be helpful in understanding how it came to this."

"I'm not good on exact dates or names. I do have a general sense of what happened."

"Please share," I asked.

"Late this century, you—we—are in the twenty-first, dominos started falling and ever more terrible things happened, a combination of events with denial of pending environmental disaster holding people back from acting. When the worst did happen, then they shrugged and said it was too late to do anything. Weather patterns became so extreme that parts of the world were no longer habitable. In this country, the southwest, states like Arizona, were so hot and dry, few could survive. Islands disappeared in the rising ocean. North Africa became a graveyard, the land parched. Millions were on the march. Desperation in Central America and parts of Mexico led to mass migration north, in the millions."

Luther took a drink of wine, looking up like he was struggling to express what he may have intentionally tried to forget. "It was a defeatist time. People turned away from science and hope to pessimism and thinking small. Politicians invented scapegoats, distracted the public from truth. People were afraid of those massive numbers on the move, desperate to survive, threatening what Americans had. Anti-immigrant hatred, bad in the early part of the century, became a blowtorch of hate then a flame thrower. Wars were waged on all the continents. Politicians who were more interested in theater than solving problems made it all a dare game.

'Deploy the Army and shoot anyone who tries to cross the border!', he yelled in mimicry. *'Nuke 'em!'* The person who said that won the presidency and dropped a nuclear bomb on Central America. His base cheered. Christian ministers praised the murder of innocents so that their parishioners might not abandon their church. Millions died in the blast and the radiation that moved north and killed Americans. Eventually, civil war broke out between dozens of factions. Marshall law was declared, the President anointed

himself Supreme Leader, a handpicked Supreme Court declared America a Christian Anglo Saxon nation and white nationalism flourished under force of law."

Luther continued relentlessly despite our stricken, incredulous faces. "All other faiths were banned. If you weren't seen as a follower of Jesus, no one would hire you and gangs might kill you. Uber-Christian believers started getting tattoos of the cross on their arms to demonstrate piety. Forehead tattoos of the cross in multiple colors became common. Non-believers, even atheists, did the same to survive. Needless to say, anyone nonwhite faced great difficulties."

"How awful!" Miguel said. "Faced with that kind of choice, what would any of us do?"

Luther shook his head. "Narrow minded judges, really not much different from narrow-minded clerics, twisted history to please their congregations. The general public, not so much." He held out his glass for a refill. I could use one myself.

"Wow. Horrible. History repeats itself," I said. "In world religious history last semester one book we read was about medieval Spain, from maybe 900 to 1400 A.D. It was called *"Ornament of the World."* Muslims, Christians and Jews created this remarkable civilization in what they called Al-Andulus in what's now Spain. Muslims ran the country but tolerated Christians and even recruited Jews for their skills."

"In terms of science, medicine and tolerance," Daruk added with a grin, "it was perhaps the most advanced civilization in the world. Christians to the north, all devout Catholics, were in the full grip of Dark Age un-enlightenment, and their religious fervor kept them attacking to the south."

I gave him a look.

"What? I like to read how backward your world often was."

"Thank you, Sweet Lips. Spoiler alert. King Ferdinand and Queen Isabella won, kicked out the Muslims, and extended the Dark Ages for a thousand years, holding back the Renaissance and scientific advancement. They sent Columbus on his way but started the Inquisition that made non-Christians to hide themselves from the risk of death by public execution. Jews even ate pork in public to hide who they were."

"So Christian. Whatever happened to the Prince of Peace?" Miguel sneered. "History can be so instructive on how we never learn from it."

"Thank you for that," Luther said with irony. "Burning a cross onto your forehead can't save you from environmental disaster, dead crops, mass starvation, wars of survival, disease. The theocracy was eventually overthrown in what became known as the *Great Fumigation*, but it was too late, the world was beyond saving. Moving north made no difference. Massive rainstorms, toxic air, tornados, floods, heat waves, dead animals, dead land, billions dead. Leaders were reduced to trying to survive themselves. I wish I could give more specifics but I can't. Maybe that helps me maintain my sanity."

"It also explains the terrifying world that exists in the twenty-sixth century," Miguel added.

"What's scary is the sources of this catastrophe are in place today. Damn," I said. "Can we have more wine?"

23.

The first day of school.

Beckman High, a private school for rich kids in two fabulous old Victorian mansions in the Haight, was advertised as elite, mostly guys but more females this year. I had a scholarship as did a score of students, all smart and designed to help lift the academic ranking because wealthy and smart were not necessarily related. I was a senior, said to be a genius from my IQ tests and had been declared a national hero by the President of the United States. I was also more confident, not the bully bait I was before my life changed when I was pulled into the sci-fi world of Uncle His and Daruk. I knew how to fight, my muscles were a lot bigger and I had a new confidence. Losing my virginity and lots of sex were also a confidence builder and helpful in relieving stress.

Luther did not attend. By the time he indicated interest, it was nearly time for school to start. He claimed disappointment but I suspected he planned it. Maybe private tutoring. Uncle His said he'd be glad to sponsor him.

Haldir walked proudly through the front door of the school with me on one side and Miguel on the other. He stood tall, his full height. No point in trying to slump and minimize it. Big was good and might deter bullies from taking him on. People stared but there were other tall kids. But, just not in the eighth grade. His shades were what got attention. Several girls said "Cool glasses" as we passed.

We walked him to his first class. I could hear him telepathically groan as he looked at all the kids at least a head shorter. The teacher stood at the doorway, maybe prepped by the principal. "Welcome, Haldir," the slender young woman said, "I'm Ms. Mink, I set up a seat for you at the back at the freestanding table." She gestured and he walked over to his seat, thanking her. He was always so polite. The FBI visit with the teachers last summer had paid off.

Miguel and I ran to our class, World Literature, confident our friend's first day was off to a good start.

We met Haldir at the entrance of the cafeteria as planned for lunch. He had a brown bag as did Miguel and me. Several eighth-grade girls called to him, inviting him to sit with them but he smiled, thanked them politely and said he needed to sit with his family.

"The girls like you," Miguel said as we sat. "That might be fun."

"Darwin says rules different here than in my world. Cannot look too much or touch. Sex is special. Confusing."

"Yeah," I said. "You have to be cautious. You need to learn more about our society before you try dating someone."

"I don't even know," Miguel asked. "Do you like boys or girls?"

Haldir looked at him and tilted his head in confusion.

"I like everyone."

"I meant for sex."

"I just answer."

"You mean you like both males and females for sex?"

"Yes."

"Have you had sex before? With both?"

"Yes. You not?"

Wow, I thought. At fourteen.

"Actually, no." Miguel answered, suddenly looking a bit sheepish. "I'm only attracted to guys and I've only had sex with one. That's Luther."

"Sad," Haldir said, his voice deep and sincere.

"*Ahhh,* let's change the topic, all right, guys?" I took a bite of my peanut butter and grape-jelly sandwich. "How were your classes?" I looked at Haldir.

"They interesting. I understood most of what teachers said. I follow your suggestion and not raise hand to volunteer. Let others do that. Good advice. I learned a lot."

"How was P.E.?" Miguel asked.

"We played basketball after coach divided in teams. Coach seemed excited to meet me. Asked if I play. I tell him about playing at our house. After watching us, mostly just running back and forth, felt odd, everyone so little, he gave me ball and asked to shoot. He got agitated. Most strange."

"What happened?" Miguel opened his milk carton.

"He asked me to shoot at basket. So I did. He ask again and again."

"How many times did you shoot?

"Twenty."

"How many baskets?"

"Twenty."

"*Really?* Where were you standing?" I asked.

"In middle of court. Coach start to cry. Students laugh and applaud. Most fun."

•••

My parents got a call that night. The basketball coach asked if Haldir could be on the team.

"You mean try out for the team?" my dad asked, putting the phone on speaker. "He can hear you now."

"No, Mr. McQuaid, I saw what he could do in gym class. He's an easy fit for the team," Coach Quimby said as we all listened.

My dad looked uncertain, glancing from me to Haldir and back.

"This is Varsity, not J.V.," Quimby added, perhaps spooked by the silence and anxious to close the sale.

My dad said, "He'd be playing with mostly juniors and seniors, wouldn't he? He's fourteen and they'd be sixteen and seventeen."

"Yes. But he's a natural. When you shoot a hundred percent, that makes you special. We're a small school."

Dad was quiet for a moment. "You don't know if it was a fluke."

"Coach," my mother said, "this is Mrs. McQuaid. He is so young and hasn't played the game much. Surely there's a lot more to it than shooting baskets."

"That's very funny Mrs. McQuaid. Tell that to Stephen Curry. *Please say yes!* I haven't had a winning team my whole career and I'm getting ready to retire."

•••

It was agreed that Haldir would start practicing after school twice a week with some of last year's returning varsity players and there would be no announcement that he was pre-selected which would show preferential treatment. Coach Quimby started teaching him the basics of the game: dribbling, passing, blocking, layups, fouls and everything he didn't know, which was most everything. He pulled Haldir aside in his regular gym class and handed off the regular class to an assistant, and the rest of the students mostly did laps. They were not happy.

We watched professional basketball on television and some college games. Haldir pronounced it interesting but he preferred to play the lute. I decided not to mention this to Coach Quimby. We talked about what might happen if he got bullied by members of other teams, perhaps to rattle him, mock him because of his age or glasses, long hair or any reason. We developed a code I could send him telepathically when I was in the audience—*Code One!* If I used it, he was to avoid any confrontation and use all his skills—speed, dexterity, reach—to crush the other team in the final score. We also developed a few other codes for different actions.

Tryouts were held for the varsity team. Miguel and I attended the session open to everyone after school. It was obvious Haldir was still a bit rough on dribbling but his layups and three-pointers were awesome. He could sink a basket from anywhere on the court, time after time. Everyone watching had to know he was going to make the team. No one seemed to care about his special glasses, accepting that he had an unusual eye sensitivity and needed them. When the team was announced, Haldir no longer needed us to keep him company at lunch. He sat with team members and groupies. I loved seeing him make friends.

Expectations for the team were low as the game calendar was announced. Our football team won only once, when there was a forfeiture last term, giving them their best result in years. The first game of the basketball season, a home game, was against a private school in East Bay, the Pleasanton Titans. I thought Haldir would be nervous but he didn't see it as all that important. He wanted to do well for his teammates and especially my brothers who were super excited, but it was less interesting to him personally than his music.

At the start of the game, after the teams were introduced to loud cheers, our guys did the traditional coyote howl. Haldir's voice was so loud and soulful that people stopped and watched him, disbelieving such a howl could come from a human throat. He got a rousing cheer from both sides and more than a few laughs. He just grinned and shrugged.

He scored sixty points in a 110-60 rout. He showed he was also good at passing the ball so others could score. That made him popular with the team, assuring they'd have his back. Coach Quimby looked like he was having an orgasm when the final score was announced. The next day the local paper, which had only sent a high school journalism student to cover the game, wrote about the team. They then assigned a regular beat reporter who did a quarter page story the following day that included a photo of Haldir doing an impossible across the court three-pointer, one of four. Having the school actually win a game was news in itself. The story also included a brief explanation of his glasses. The student reporter was thrilled that his photo got used. The paper announced they would cover the next game with regular sports writers.

Next week's opponent was a much bigger private school in Sacramento, Capitol Prep, filled with kids of lobbyists, high-ranking government and corporate executives plus assorted wealthy families. Our league was not statewide, just private schools in Northern California. This team called themselves the Capitol Players. Defending division champs for the fifth year in a row, they were often arrogant, putting us down verbally as well as always running up the score. They would have seen the news story about our big win and Haldir as lead scorer. The coach warned the team that things could get ugly at this out-of-town game, so be prepared and don't react to provocations. He didn't trust the referees, either.

Excited school alumni rented three buses to take as many students and parents as possible to the game. Uncle His hired a limo service to bring my dad, Daruk, Luther, my brothers and himself. Mom stayed home with the baby, pleased for quiet time. Miguel was with me in one of the buses. We wanted the full screaming student experience.

Both teams ran from the locker rooms into the gymnasium with students from both sides shouting cheerleader chants. Haldir teleped me—that was our new shorthand for telepathically communicating—that their star player, senior Reardon Baum, had already called him a freak and jabbed him in the kidney when they raced past each other. "He's hoping to provoke you," I teleped back, "so stay calm and smile. Actually, make this a *Code 1*."

At the jump ball, Haldir and Baum, close to the same height, were paired off. Haldir easily outjumped him and slapped the ball to a teammate who handed it to another player and then back to Haldir, who threw in a three pointer from mid court. Fifteen seconds into the game and the score was 3-0. Baum's face was already red, his fists clenched by his sides. Every time Baum got the ball, Haldir would glide up next to him and take it away, sometimes passing it on or just as often taking the shot and scoring. Our side of the bleachers was screaming itself hoarse. On the other sideline, the Capitol Players looked on open mouthed and in shock when the half time bell rang and the score was 56-32. Never had that team been so humiliated.

"Prepare for some dirty play," Coach Quimby warned in the locker room and Haldir teleped it on to me. "I love you guys!" coach gushed.

As play resumed, the Players got physical, shoving, tripping, punching and the referees ignored it. This so pissed off and energized our team that they played hard and kept the Players from scoring more than a dozen points. Haldir was everywhere. In one crush of players, Baum grabbed Haldir's glasses and tried to pull them off. My friend readjusted his shades, waiting a moment for his eyesight to return to normal under the florescent lights. The referees ruled it a delay of game foul by Haldir which was met with open derision by our side of the auditorium and shock by the coach. In a political town maybe a referee needed to be political, not neutral, if they lived here.

As Baum moved up to take his first of two free throws, he wore a self-satisfied grin despite the lopsided score. Haldir teleped: *"Fun now."*

As the student prepared to throw, he somehow tripped over his own shoelaces and fell flat on his face onto the court, drawing blood to his nose as the ball rolled away. Ducking his head in embarrassment, he stood, wiped the blood on his jersey, ignoring catcalls, and prepared for his second shot. This time, as he pulled his hands back and started to launch the ball, he slipped and stumbled backward, perhaps from the blood on the floor, his legs high as the ball flew to the backboard and bounced. The game having resumed, Haldir took the inbound pass, dribbled a few steps and launched another three pointer.

Three players ran at Haldir, teeth visibly clenched. Haldir sprinted straight at them and leaped high over them, going into one of his aerial forward rolls. As his head came around he threw the ball at the basket from half a court away, then tucked his head and continued the roll, landing on his feet and running ahead as the ball swished through the basket. Total silence in the gymnasium, everyone froze, including the players. No one had ever seen such a shot. Coach Quimby was open-mouthed. I grabbed Miguel and we jumped up and screamed, as did my brothers, Dad, Luther and Uncle His, shouting Haldir's name. Our whole section erupted and the cheerleaders led us in a loud and sustained chant: *"Haldir! Haldir! Haldir!"* He waved and bowed, ever humble and gracious, then turned and blew a kiss at the thoroughly dejected Baum. Sweet revenge.

Play resumed and the now spiritless Players offered little resistance. Baum benched himself and sat with arms crossed, refusing to go out onto the court and play. The final bell gave the Coyotes a sweet 172-52 win. We ran onto the floor and mobbed our team, hugging Haldir and all the players.

Numerous students and one reporter captured "The Jump" on video. It went viral and made newscasts around the state as sports reporters marveled. Journalists wanted to interview Haldir but, at his insistence, all calls were referred to a delighted Coach Quimby.

When we got back home, Haldir thanked us and went to his room and strummed his lute, doing what was more important to him, singing songs of his home world, remembering friends lost.

24.

Dancing with my mother was a new experience. I never realized she was *Dancing with the Stars* talented. Actually more talented. She didn't favor the broom handle up your butt style
popular in the show. She was more like Ginger Rogers although
I was certainly no Fred Astaire. This pairing of me with her was
an intervention by my parents to improve my dance game. I
could wiggle and jump with the best of them, sometimes in time
with the music, but actually moving as a couple to slower music
was painful to experience and worse to watch. She was good; so
was my dad. I watched them swirl, dip and laugh. Haldir watched
too, studying the moves and music, but did not want to actually
try it. Mom made it easy for me to lead. What would happen
when I was with Daruk? He generally topped. Did that mean
he'd lead? Maybe we should avoid slow dances.

Uncle His asked us all to be at his house on a certain date
and time. Luther, Miguel, Haldir, Daruk and me. An older man,
trim, little hair on his head but no comb over, with a tape measure
draped around his neck, was waiting in the front room. There
were dozens of fabric swatches on the coffee table and pages

from men's fashion magazines. Uncle His was buying and this man was taking our measurements for custom tuxes. We didn't want to all be the same so he suggested styles we might like. I knew Mom wanted me to wear a traditional black tux so it would be useful for years to come but we could pick something lively for the cummerbund. I wasn't familiar with the term. Just a sash worn around the waist, the tailor explained and showed samples. We opted for a traditional black tux, single button with a reflective, metallic silver sash. Miguel and Luther chose dark blue, double-breasted. They decided to wear the same cummerbund. Haldir thought the clothing style lacked any valid purpose but was convinced to get one if it could be made to have meaning to him. He chose snow white, like his mountain home, single button, and was able to get the image of a redwood tree sewn into the fabric up his right side, the trunk around his leg and onto the jacket, with a branch and leaves over his shoulder and down his right arm. He chose a forest green cummerbund and bowtie. We would make a statement.

On the big night, Mom had us gather for photos. Miguel's dad joined us. My favorite photo was my brothers each hanging on Haldir's biceps as he flexed in a Mr. America pose.

Uncle His rented a ridiculous stretch limo for us to ride to the Fairmont Hotel. We'd booked dinner in one of the fancy restaurants. It turned out lots of other students had the same idea so we spent a lot of time on our feet talking with friends until the manager, on loudspeaker no less, asked us to take our seats and order.

We entered the prom hall five abreast, arms interlinked and grinning. It was a *Frozen* themed décor, of course it was, which sort of worked. It seemed like everyone wanted their photo with Haldir, hero of the basketball division championship, our first. Coach had declared he could now retire with pride.

Daruk asked me to dance, standing and holding out his hand, all formal. I didn't know what to expect. But he waltzed me around the room, holding me tight, then apart, twirling me, dipping me, kissing me. Clearly he was leading. People were watching. He double-stepped us up to the group of students, thugs, who'd chased me in Buena Vista Park that day nearly a year ago.

"Hoodlums! Who wants to dance with me?"

The five of them looked at each other and ran out of the room.

As we walked to the refreshment bar, Daruk cocked his head, listening. "There are people arguing outside about Haldir. We should investigate." He turned and fast walked us to the hallway. Three members of the basketball team, all in tuxes, were surrounding and yelling at a woman in her thirties, dressed in jeans and a green jacket.

"Why are you asking personal questions about Haldir?" Mike Johnson demanded, looking pissed off.

"You offered a girl a hundred dollars if she could get a copy of his transcript. That's wrong!" Johan Marks yelled. "Are you trying to hurt him? What gives you the right?"

"He's our friend and a great guy," added Sam Smithers. "What's wrong with you?"

"I'm Veronica Stong, a reporter for the San Francisco *Mirror*. He's a major news story and we want to know more about him."

Daruk moved up next to her, crowding her space. "So you are offering bribes if a student will break the law for you? That is disgusting. You have no right to try and embarrass or injure him emotionally, making him relive tragedy. That is not what journalism is about, at least ethical journalism."

"He's not returning my calls. You seem to know his background. Why can't the public? They have a right to know." Her voice was self-righteous. "Is it true FBI agents briefed the faculty about him?"

I moved up next to Daruk. "Maybe he likes and deserves his privacy."

"You're part of the story, Darwin McQuaid. You're the guy who came back from some mysterious kidnapping and the President called you a hero. It's your family Haldir lives with. What's the story?"

"It's none of your business."

"I've heard stories that his family was murdered and you

found him on some mountain and brought him to live with your parents."

"What's happening here?" Principal Darling had come out of the ballroom.

Again she identified herself.

"A high school prom is about students having a good time. Haldir is a popular student and a nice young man. If I overheard right, you offered a student a bribe to get a legally protected document. That's illegal."

She tightened her lips. "Refusing to let a reporter do her job is a violation of press freedom. I'll get my story another time and place. But I'll get it," she huffed, and stalked off.

Inside, two of Haldir's teammates were talking to him and he looked stressed. He didn't need this kind of pressure. We went up to him and he put his arms around me. He was trembling. We needed to figure this out. He was now a public figure.

Several girls and a couple of guys tried to entice Haldir to rooms they rented in the hotel. We teleped about it and I gave him some pointers how to graciously turn them down. In fact, we all went to our respective homes. Keep the parents happy. Besides, we needed to talk.

· · ·

I briefed my parents about the reporter when we got home and Haldir had gone to his room.

"That's disturbing," my dad said.

"His teammates really went after her. I know I shouldn't be pleased by that but I am. Haldir's popular and students want to protect him."

"Good for them," my mother added. "What can we do?"

"The reporter said she tried to contact him and he never responded. So she called here, right?"

"Yes, there were messages and I ignored them."

"She looks the type to do anything it takes to get what she thinks is a big story. We need to be careful about anybody pretending to be a utility worker or someone monitoring us from a distance with a telephoto lens. Who knows? You heard what he went through from President O'Connor and Uncle His. Haldir's world was stolen from him by violent, crazy people. He's trying to fit in a new world. Now this."

Mom crossed her arms. "I consider myself his mom now. This woman should be careful coming between Mama Bear and her two new cubs."

"Thanks Mom!" I gave her a hug and went downstairs to see Haldir.

He was sitting in his desk chair, in his underwear, looking at photos we took inside his mountain home. I saw he was sketching faces of those who died. The baby was asleep in his crib.

I put my arm around him; he leaned his head against me. "We love you," I told him. "My parents see you and the baby as sons. You're my brother. So is he."

He looked at me and smiled. "They are good people. I am lucky you and Daruk found me. Allowing me be part of your family is honor."

"The reporter you heard about at the dance is going to try and figure out your history. But we'll do our best to limit what she can find out. You heard about Principal Darling kicking her out of the dance."

"He has been good to me."

"You doing three of those amazing leap and tumble basket stunts at the district championships got national attention," I told him. "People were amazed."

"Basketball so much easier than *Thrump* game in my world. "

• • •

"You outdid yourself, Mom. That was delicious." I spoke for all of us who were crowded around the family table. Daruk, Uncle His, Miguel, Luther, my parents and brothers. Our dinner was really good for being vegetarian, mushroom risotto with truffle oil. Even my brothers cleaned their plates without being hounded.. She was experimenting with new dishes to make Haldir feel comfortable.

"Yes. Most delicious and different for me. Thank you." Haldir was smiling, holding the baby in his arms, feeding the boy with the special milk formula Uncle His developed when we were still in the Russian Wilderness.

"The spicy mango ginger soup was amazing," Luther said. "I've never tasted anything like it. Thank you for inviting me."

"Okay." I said, "the purpose of the dinner with all of you here is for a big announcement from Haldir. He's has been considering names for our baby and himself. I say "our" baby because the little guy is part of my family now, just like Haldir."

Haldir nodded. "I have been considering names. American ones. Many different languages, forgotten and current. My name is a shortened version of very long Elfin name. Miguel told me that my shortened name is in *Lord of the Rings*. Having watched first movie, I am honored to be linked to it. I think I would like to select an ancient Gaelic name for my baby boy. He is not mine by my union with a female but mine by being the last of my people. I have chosen *Diarmuid*. It means 'without enemy.' Surely one so innocent and beautiful as he has only friends."

"How did you pronounce it again? I want to get it right." I smiled at him and he nodded.He spelled it. "It is pronounced *DEER-mid*. It was name borne by ancient kings, heroes and saints in your world."

"Lovely," my dad commented. "Do you want to have a middle name and do you want to use our last name or another when we formally file the adoption papers?"

"I want the name McQuaid if you allow for both of us. I want to be part of this family and would be honored to have your name. I would also like us to have middle names. I wish to select *'Darwin'* for me if that is acceptable, and *'Daruk'* for Diarmuid. You are like brothers."

I coughed, covering my mouth with a napkin. My eyes began to water. "You...you want to have my name?"

"If you will allow."

"I'm...I'm honored. Of course you can use it."

"And Daruk?"

It was one of the few times I ever saw his eyes watering.

"An honor."

Suddenly everyone was applauding.

"*Diarmuid Daruk McQuaid* and *Haldir Darwin McQuaid* it is," Mom announced.

25.

aruk and Uncle His spent the next week back in E3, dealing with some poaching issues by a tribe in what we would call in this world Monterey on the central California coast. I wanted to go too but had school. In checking my phone this morning, there was a text from Daruk that they'd got in late and both were fine, the situation resolved.

Miguel had volunteered to help with a special program in the gym for eighth through tenth grade students—so he could get out of class—about improper touching and other sexual harassment issues. It could be a traumatic topic for kids any age if not handled well. Haldir might appreciate more data on sexual norms.

Nearly two hundred students, sitting on the floor because the bleachers had been pushed back to be repaired, would hear from the most straitlaced, uber-Victorian teacher at the school or any school, Ms. Orwella Brightmeyer. She typically wore high-collared shapeless blouses and pencil skirts that came to just above her ankles, with a color range from gray to black. She thought kissing was gross even in marriage and should be avoided. The only purpose of marriage was to have babies and once you had them, abstinence only. She never discussed LGBTQ issues because there were a fair number of us in school and it was known that Principal Darling supported us. I suspected he'd picked her for this just to make students think how bad it could be if she set the rules and how reasonable the actual school standards were. Clever, that. Her face became pinched if you ever asked her about homo stuff. Or trans issues. Some students did it just for the show. Miguel would hate her lecture but it was better than attending Modern Political Theory, a course I sometimes liked but he loathed.

Halfway through my class I teleped Haldir to see how the sex lecture was going.

"If woman correct, how does your society reproduce? Her ideas on how girl impregnated nonsense."

"How's Miguel doing?"

"He giggled when teacher said slow dancing can lead to pregnancy. She demanded to know what was funny. He said, 'I know from my own experience, dancing slow and sexy with another guy does not make one pregnant.' Everyone laughed except her."

"Thank goodness he's a volunteer not doing this for credit."

"Would you like to watch and hear?"

"I can't get down there. I'm in class."

"I can make happen."

"Is this some new Fae comm option?"

"Close your eyes for half minute then open."

I did. When I opened them, I was viewing the auditorium and hearing her lecture through Haldir's eyes and ears. *"Wow. This is amazing. You...you're a dragon."*

"No make sense. I Fae."

I immersed myself in the good show until my teacher started to hand out something. *"I need to go. Take notes."*

It was a surprise quiz. The teacher, who liked to be called Mr. G, had a last name of Liddy, was a maybe MAGA acolyte and fan of Richard Nixon, although only someone familiar with Nixon and Watergate would catch the meaning of his "G" initial. Despite this, he was eager to argue with students, all of whom disagreed with his views. He was decent about it and never downgraded you for arguing. He actually liked and encouraged it. I just didn't really want to hear such stuff. He sometimes wore a red baseball cap with gold letters spelling out *Make America Think Again.* I sometimes wondered if maybe he didn't believe what he was saying and did it just to provoke discussion. If so, then painful but amusing. We did have some spirited disagreements that made us take a deeper look at certain issues, not necessarily accepting his views but giving insight into our own.

As I was looking over the quiz, a loud crash came from the front of the school. The windows in our room shook, one slammed down. Felt markers popped off the white board trays just as dozens of books launched off shelves. It felt like the entrance had been ripped apart. Everyone jumped up, shouting, speculating and then shushing so we could listen. Automatic gunfire. Two or three different weapons, some at the same time.

A siren blared in the hallways. A woman's stressed voice shouting on the loudspeaker. *"THIS IS NOT A DRILL! ACTIVE SHOOTER ALERT!* Lock all doors and practice the emergency protocol. Repeat. *This is not a drill! Lock your doors NOW!"*

Everyone froze. Then everyone was leaping around, shouting. "LISTEN TO ME!" Liddy yelled and waved his arms. "SILENCE!"

It worked. Who knew this quiet and irritating man could scream. Everyone stood still to hear him. Two students were wheezing. We'd practiced the protocols once a month since forever. The school boasted that it was one of the safest in San Francisco. Steel reinforced doors. Bullet resistant windows. Four highly trained security guards armed with semi-automatic rifles and wearing bullet proof vests. I hated reading that on the school website but that was our reality. So many people with grudges on every topic imaginable, and able to buy AR15s and large clips. Some cynical politicians even encouraged it, to bring them votes from fringe groups. We heard it so much we stopped paying attention.

In this class, I was the *"Close the drapes!"* guy and ran to the windows. Someone else turned off the lights even though it was still bright inside because the drapes were not blackout. Another student locked the door. Four others moved chairs toward the single door as a further precaution. Everyone was agitated and scared but were holding it together. No one spoke. Complete silence. Except for gunfire off in the distance.

"Who's in here?" a male voice bellowed from outside our door as he pounded on it. The knob turned. The lock held. A girl gasped. We waited and backed away from the door. Would the shooter go elsewhere?

Automatic gunfire shredded the lock and the door around it. A boot kicked open the door and pushed the chairs back. A figure dressed in black with a Smurf ski mask stepped inside, holding an AR15 or some kind of automatic weapon with a strap over his shoulder. He turned on the lights.

"Hello, you spoiled rich brats." A male voice. He walked in and everyone moved back against the wall. A couple of students burst into tears.

Mr. Liddy moved toward him, holding up his arms. "Please. These are innocent children. There are lots of problems in the world. These kids didn't create them. Please, I beg you, leave them alone."

He fired into the ceiling. Shredded soundboard and lots of insulation floated down. Everyone screamed and dropped to the floor. He laughed. Only Mr. Liddy was still standing. I was against the far wall, near my duty station. *What should I do?* What I had to do, regardless of exposure, regardless of consequences.

"Please. They have done you no harm." Liddy stared pleadingly at him.

I was awakening my pyrokinetic powers. Would they be enough? Could I act fast enough to stop him?

"Such a safe school," the gunman sneered. "That's why it's our target. No place is safe even if it has NRA approval. Move back, teacher, or I'll shoot."

Liddy complied. Bravo to him for sticking up for us.

The gunman slipped a backpack off his shoulder. "Hey Black girl in the red blouse. Catch." He tossed the pack at her. She and others scooted aside.

"Two security guards are dead. I guess the other two didn't get paid enough to stay. Maybe rethink minimum wage." He giggled—literally giggled—at what he thought was funny.

I could feel the heat rising, the intensity of what was gathering in my head, ready to strike. I could conceivably kill him with heat but better to catch his clothes on fire, distract him and then use that special talent Daruk taught me to run my fingers across his temple and pulse a power they planted in my brain to knock him out. I had to be ready before I took him on or he'd kill me and more would die because of me.

He walked over to our teacher, laughing to himself, drunk on his power. "You're the apologist for rich people who ruin society. Maybe they'll pay more attention when their babies die." He sniggered. The guy was nuts. "We, the *True Patriot Alliance*, have a manifesto you get to learn about today. Girl in the red, open my backpack. Take out the papers. Give everyone a copy."

The young African American woman, Pace Ruley, was a senior . I wondered if her race was why he'd chosen her. Squatting on the floor like most of us, she reached over and unzipped it, then took out a stack of papers. She looked at the first one and then handed out several to each student near her so they could pass them around.

"This is our roadmap to returning real freedom to America. Each of you, read one of the bullet points." No one did anything. "Dammit! Red blouse, read the first one now or I shoot your teacher." He turned to Mr. Liddy. "Unless of course you don't like him and want me to shoot him." He chuckled, clearly taken with his own wit.

Pace, in a defiant pissed off voice, which was cool, said, "Men and western culture are under siege."

"Next!"

Tom Franks, a white guy: "Immigrants are flowing into America to replace white people."

Then others continued without being pointed to.

"We oppose Jews, Muslims, Black Lives Matter and transexuals."

"The federal government is part of a covert conspiracy intent on stripping Americans of their natural rights."

"We are ready to carry out armed resistance to keep our freedoms."

I was the next one to read. It was about them being the local line of defense. The man was looking more deranged the longer this went on. He pushed the barrel of the weapon into Mr. Liddy's gut.

"Read, boy!"

My powers were up to full potency. I stood, my eyes glaring at him, my voice loud and defiant. *It is up to people of good will to stand up against radical insurrectionists like you who want to commit treason and destroy our country. I am part of that line of defense.*

"What? That's not what it says you stupid kid!"

My teacher stared at me. Classmates were on their cell phones, whispering.

I started to project serious heat towards the creep. He jerked when it hit him. This was stronger than I'd ever felt it maybe because I was so angry.

I started to walk towards him.

The gunman staggered as he turned back to me, his barrel headed in my direction.

"Move away!" I commanded students as I pushed through. They scooted aside, opening space between the two of us. I could feel the heat surging out of my brain, down my arm, into my hand.

"Do you feel it? Are you getting warmer?" I continued to push. "Did you ever wonder what it would be like to be torched?"

He looked down at himself. *"What? What's happening?"*

His shirt exploded in flames and scorched his face. He grabbed his gut, dropping his rifle. Students screamed and pushed even tighter against the far wall.

I walked up to him, staring into his eyes. Fire and heat were overwhelming him. I yanked off his knit hood, swiped my fingers down the side of his head and he collapsed to the floor. I picked up his weapon and handed it to my open-mouthed teacher.

There were sirens in the distance. Lots of 'em.

Haldir teleped me. *"Two gunmen in auditorium. Darling shot. Students screaming."*

"On my way. Got one of 'em."

I ran to the open door and turned to my classmates. "Close the door and barricade it. Stay here. We're on lockdown." Everyone was staring at me, jaws agape. I dashed into the hallway, surprised I was able to walk or talk given what just happened.

Half a dozen classrooms were between me and the auditorium. Through a window I saw cop cars in front of the school, lights flashing. An officer on a bullhorn was demanding surrender. At least a dozen police cars, an ambulance, a phalanx of men in blue. A burst of gunfire came from the school. So police weren't inside yet. How many gunmen were there?

A figure in military fatigues stepped around the corner of the hallway ahead of me. I pushed into the women's bathroom just as he fired. There would be no time for pyrotechnics. There was a counter with sinks to my left, the stalls across from me. I leaped on the counter, put one foot on the hand dryer and put the edge of the other on the molding around the door frame, holding myself up by pushing against the ceiling.

The door opened. I saw the barrel first then the man.

"Give up you punk rich kid."

He stepped inside. Pushing away from the ceiling I dropped down by. My feet smashed into each shoulder, launching his body, his head smashing against the corner of a short wall between the sink and the toilets. I rode him all the way to the floor and pulled off his knit cap. He looked to be still a teenager. Still alive but with a serious head wound. He'd be unconscious for a long time.

And for the rest of his life would be in prison all because he was pissed off with society and didn't have a clue he was being conned. Should I take his gun? Nope. Police would think I was one of 'em. I picked it up, put the barrel into a toilet and closed the stall door. So many thoughts rushed my head, I had to stop, take a deep breath and exhale.

Mary had a little lamb...there, my head was clear. This always worked.

I listened at the doorway. The police bullhorn and constant sirens outside, but quiet in here. I ducked my head out the doorway. I could see a terrorist in the distance to the side of an exterior doorway. Waiting for police, gun at the ready. I raced in the opposite direction, to the auditorium. Through the open door I could see Principal Darling on the floor, propped up against the closed bleachers, eyes closed. A gunman walked in front of the students who were pushed back against the opposite wall. I could hear wailing.

"Stay calm, please stay calm. Help is on the way." It was Haldir's voice, his tone calm but loud enough to carry .

"I'm here. Where's the other gunman?"

"Against wall on my left as I face you, hidden by the closed bleachers, guarding the only other door."

"Are you safe? And Miguel?"

"We are good. Just mouthed your name and tilted head to the main door. Miguel understands, he nodded."

"Forget what that tall guy just told you." The gunman was preening in front of the students. "Cops are outside and too chicken to come in. Are you spoiled children scared? Anyone peeing their pants hold up your hand. What? Afraid I'll kill you? I've got lots of bullets. A hundred in this clip and three more clips. Fast loading. I love the gun lobby. How many rich kids are here? How many will die?"

There were some shrieks but I thought the students were doing okay, considering. Some were were on their cell phones.

"I'll burn the talker. Give me a minute till he ignites. You take on the other guy."

"Got it. No problem. I am withdrawing knife."

The gunman was still ranting. "This is going to start a revolution. The time is now. Knock out the government. Bullies shoved me into walls. Tripped me. Pushed my head in the toilet. Rich kids, just like you. *Payback time.*"

I concentrated on building the heat in his body and clothes. I looked at Mr. Darling. He was lying in a pool of blood. He gazed at me in the doorway and offered a weak smile. I needed to go to him.

The gunman staggered. *"What the hell?"*

I ran into the room and knelt by Darling. Quickly stuffed the handkerchief I carried in my pocket over the wound in his gut, lowering him flat on the floor. I moved his hand over the wound. "Press down." All I could do, I was no healer. Haldir would do that.

"Thank you," he whispered.

The gunman turned as I stood. My arm up, palm at a right angle. I moved towards him.

"So you're taking it out against helpless kids you're never met. And shot a school principal who enforces no bullying." I moved closer. *"So brave,* using an AR15 against unarmed kids. I promise you'll never be bullied again. You're gonna *burn."*

He dropped to one knee screaming as his clothes exploded in fire. I ripped off his hood and ran my hand across his temple. He collapsed. I slid his rifle away, across the floor.

I saw Haldir holding the knife, the runes flashing. He was chanting, gliding from the students toward the other gunman who was floating, rising higher and higher. Then he flipped over, head down, and was twisting around faster and faster. His rifle dropped to the floor. My Fae friend walked to him and swiped the knife over him. Slowly the unconscious body descended to the floor.

The students looked stunned, a few looked like they were about to run.

"Don't leave! Stay here!" I warned them. "Two more are out there. Police are here. Haldir can protect you."

Haldir glided to the principal like I imagined a ballet dancer might do. He ripped open the Mr. Darling's shirt, tossed my handkerchief, placed his blade over the wound and began to chant. Students stared, many with phones out looking to record a Facebook post. Of course they were.

"You two," I demanded, pointing at the ridiculously handsome football quarterback and one of his players. *"Get over here and guard this guy! NOW!"* They ran to the unconscious terrorist.

Miguel bolted to me. We launched ourselves out the doorway.

• • •

A large SUV with a mangled hood and broken windshield had crashed through the doors of the main entryway. Someone we couldn't see was shouting.

'I'm telling you, stay away…we have a bomb in the truck big enough to blow up this school and all of you if you try and get inside!"

We worked our way around the truck and debris from the front entrance. I saw a man's leg under the wreckage. Sneaking past it, we saw the terrorist, crouching behind the rear tire, dressed in black, his back to us on a cell phone.

I held up my hand, one finger, two fingers, three. We charged just as he turned. His rifle fired; a series of bullets ripped my left side.

We knocked him to the floor. Cops certainly could see us through the smashed front doorway as we slugged him in the face. I kneed him in the balls. Miguel got the man's neck in the crook of his arm.

I grabbed the guy's hair and pounded his face while Miguel tightened his grip around the man's throat. He flailed, hitting me and my side flared in pain but I couldn't worry about it. I pulled back and slugged his gut as hard as I could. When he stopped thrashing his head, trying to bite Miguel, I ran a hand over his temple. The gunman now unconscious, police ran inside, their guns pointed at us. At first I thought they considered us part of the attack."You boys are amazing," A police officer shouted, grinning. Cops surrounded the SUV.

"Bomb secured!" someone yelled.

I collapsed onto the floor.

"Darwin! Darwin! My God! Look at all the blood! Medics! Here! Here!!"

I heard pounding feet. Then two medics were checking me over, running hands over my back, talking excitedly to themselves. No idea what they were saying. They lifted me onto a gurney, rolling me onto my back. There was a scream. Was that me?

They ripped open my shirt.

I could hear gunfire.

A needle slipped into a vein, a medic held a bottle over my

head. "The bullets pierced his lower intestines. Maybe other organs," a female voice said.

"Will he be okay?" Miguel squawked in panic. *"Please save him!"*

"Our principal," I think I mumbled. "Shot. Auditorium." The pain was intense. Another scream. I had to tell them. "Haldir helping. Don't hurt him." I wasn't sure they heard me. I wasn't sure what I said made sense.

Miguel put a palm on the side of my face and cried even as the medics did their thing, one of them saying, "Injecting 10 cc's."

I felt the gurney rise and get pushed out the door. So many lights and people.

Then nothing.

26.

Everything was dark. My eyes wouldn't open. I couldn't move my body. My muscles didn't work. Voices. My mother talking. "Turn that up, please." My father's voice.

A woman's electronic voice: *"Eighty to ninety percent of all the school shootings in the world happen in the U.S...."*

"Switch to a news channel, please." My dad again.

"Our lead story. Two security guards were killed, one student and the school principal seriously wounded this morning when domestic terrorists calling for a revolution invaded Beckman High School in the Haight-Ashbury neighborhood of San Francisco. The private school had just finished upgrading its security system when an SUV plowed through the front entrance. Principal Jerome Darling confronted two gunmen who ran into the auditorium where an assembly was underway. He was shot and remains in serious condition at St. Michaels Hospital.

"A student, seventeen-year-old Darwin McQuaid, personally eliminated three terrorists and joined with a friend to take out a fourth by the school entrance, enabling police to enter and defuse a bomb. Young McQuaid was shot multiple times but continued to fight the intruder

until police entered the building. He is unconscious, his condition life threatening, according to a hospital spokesman.

"Scores of videos taken by students inside the school, show remarkable scenes of the teenager challenging two of the armed terrorists, somehow setting them on fire before he rendered them unconscious."

Something cold pressed against my chest. Moving around. Creepy. Please let it be a stethoscope. More noise, maybe a bottle. I felt sleepy just as my mother's voice asked a question. "Nurse…" The voice faded to nothing. I sensed myself floating. Was this a dream? Was this death?

• • •

I'm awake again, at least I think I am. Or maybe more dreams. How much time has passed? I can't move any part of my body.

"Why isn't he showing any progress, doctor?" my father asked.

"We are doing all we can, sir. The three bullets that ripped his intestines were covered in some kind of unusual poison and released major toxins into his system. He's also lost a massive amount of blood…"

"Hey," I thought, wishing they could hear me. "I'm alive."

• • •

Another newscast grabbed my attention.

"Students from Beckman High School have started a vigil outside St. Michael's Hospital, waiting for news on a fellow student, Darwin McQuaid. A dozen showed up hours after the shooting yesterday. Today there are nearly a hundred.

"On this second day since the domestic terrorist attack on the school a hospital spokesman said the boy's condition remains life threatening. Staff asking not to be identified said McQuaid is not responding to treatment and his condition is deteriorating.

"The hospital put out a call for Darwin's rare blood type, A-negative, and over four hundred people showed up at blood banks around the Bay Area."

· · ·

I could sense Daruk, Uncle His and Haldir at different times, holding my hands, kissing my forehead. *"We are here for you"* Haldir said. *"Please telep me if you can. So far I have heard nothing from you."*

"I can hear you."

All three whooped and laughed.

"What is it?" my parents asked at once.

"His brain is active and can communicate," Uncle His explained. "Your son has remarkable telepathic abilities, as do the three of us."

"What?" my dad asked, sounding incredulous. *"He's never said anything about this."*

"What are you people saying?" An indignant male voice. "He's unconscious. Don't play games getting their hopes up. I may have to bar you from Intensive Care. I want to honor his parents' wish of allowing you in, given his deteriorating condition, but not if it makes him worse or disturbs other patients."

"It is no game, doctor. He is able to communicate telepathically." It was Uncle His in a no-nonsense yet quiet voice. "His mind is active."

"That statement is fantasy."

"The fact that you do not understand a phenomenon does not mean it does not exist," Daruk responded.

"He can hear you if you want to talk to him. I can interpret any response. All three of us can." It was Haldir.

Someone picked up my hand. "Darwin, can you hear me?" It was my mother.

"Yes, mother, I can hear you."

"He said yes," Haldir stated.

"What's the name of your favorite sixth grade teacher?"

"Mrs. Helen Blaufus."

"He said Mrs. Helen Blaufus." It was Uncle His.

"Oh My God!" my parents shrieked together.

"That's right," my father said, sounding stunned and breath-less. "No one else would know that. You can hear us, son. How do you feel? I mean, what do you sense?"

"Stop this nonsense!" the male doctor barked. "I'm calling security. You're interfering with his medical care and the operations of this department."

"We will leave for now. It is obvious you lack the knowledge or skills to save him," Uncle His said in a quiet, steady voice. "You see his death as unavoidable given his injuries and accept that outcome, confident other doctors with the same limited skills will agree. We do not."

"Get out!" the doctor growled.

•••

I could feel them doing things to me from time to time. Such as putting what might have been a bed pan under my butt or maybe something even more disgusting. Something was being done with my dick. Not the good kind.

I could hear another newscast. No idea how much time went by.

"An update on the mass shooting at Hartman High School. It has now been a full three days since domestic terrorists attacked the private school, killing two security guards and wounding one student and the school principal.

"Principal Jerome Darling is listed in stable condition. He credits the quick action of one fourteen-year-old student in saving his life. That same student later took down one of the armed gunmen in the school auditorium. We are not releasing his name because of his age. Videos of his action have gone viral.

"Disturbing news on the student hero who took down four terrorists. Doctors report they have done all they can for seventeen-year-old Darwin McQuaid and are recommending he be taken off life support. His parents have refused."

• • •

"I am here," Haldir said to me. *"Your parents have taken you off life support so that they can give me permission to do what I can to heal you. You are out of Intensive Care and in a private room. One nurse is helping obscure what I am doing from any doctor who might stick his head inside to see if you are still alive. Your parents asked her for help."*

"They have become friends," Uncle His explained.

"Your parents are helping block the view from the hallway." Daruk squeezed my hand as he talked.

Haldir: *"I have made it so anyone inspecting you from the hospital will not easily detect what I have done. A special doctor called an intern is also helping me despite the regular doctor ordering all medical care to stop. Prepare yourself, this will be cold."*

"Lie completely still, Darwin." Uncle His.

I could feel the pull of the bandage against the wound. Then a metal blade against my hot skin, still burning with fever. The chants were rhythmic noises, hums, foreign words.

• • •

At some point the newscast was turned up.

"The vigil outside St. Stevens Hospital has grown to nearly two hundred students, parents and teenagers from other schools after word got out that the hero of the invasion of Hartman High School was taken off life support.

"Police have declined comment on videos circulating on the Internet that show seventeen-year-old Darwin McQuaid setting fire to two terrorists before rendering them unconscious, and a 14-year-old student

somehow lifting up a terrorist without seeming to touch him. Police advise that the attack is still under investigation.

"Meanwhile, Beckman High School Principal Jerome Darling, who was also shot and is in stable condition, released a statement from his hospital room:

'Darwin McQuaid saved my life and the lives of all our students. He is one courageous young man. So are his two friends, Miguel Medina and Haldir McQuaid, a younger teen being adopted by Darwin's parents. A remarkable trio. I don't know how they did what they did and I don't care. They acted and saved lives, including my own. The teachers, school staff, parents, and students are grateful.'

"You may remember, young McQuaid was kidnapped by domestic terrorists earlier this year and declared a hero by President Barbara O'Connor. Another student, said to be his best friend, Miguel Medina, also charged the terrorist at the front entrance to the school.

"Reports from students and teachers confirm that the gunmen, at least two of them, have claimed they were once bullied, and the two in custody have reportedly repeated the claim. This matches invasions in other schools, angry men coming back for vengeance, even if they never attended the schools."

My mother was talking to me. "Can you hear me, Darwin? It has been five days since the attack and the nurse says you have made an unbelievable turnaround."

• • •

"You had no right to remove his bandages and let some high school kid treat him with chants." A male voice, one from before, obviously angry. *"And some indigenous witch doctor!"*

"Please lower your voice! This is a hospital after all, doctor. I have every right. First, I'm his mother and he's a minor."

She crossed her arms and glared at him, a scene I could witness courtesy of Haldir. It was weird seeing my body lying in a bed and I was viewing it from across the room. "Second, you *gave up* on him after three days. You said there was nothing more you could do. You recommended hospice care, you recommended I take him off life support. I took your word at that. *I, however, wasn't ready to abandon hope.* So I brought in two men I know he believes in. This high school kid, as you gallingly called him, is a skilled alternative medicine healer, a shaman. He saved the principal's life in his school--look at the report from the EMTs. Katnu Hisman is also a legendary healer among his people. Two days after you gave up, Darwin's wound is nearly healed. His vital signs are normal, his temperature is down to near normal. The color is back. The poison is gone from his system. He'll will wake up soon. You're just pissed off because Haldir and Katnu did what you couldn't. You should be celebrating that my son is out of danger. Male egos can be ridiculous."

My mother was on a tear. Don't cross Mama Bear.

"Mother..."

My first spoken word. She ran to me.

· · ·

I used my clicker to turn up the volume on the television in my room. It was kind of surreal listening to newscasters talking about me. I could also go to the bathroom with some help. No more catheter!

"A major update on the condition of teenager Darwin McQuaid, hero of the terrorist shooting at Beckman High School five days ago.

Because his condition was deteriorating so quickly, doctors had recommended he be taken off life support after three days. Sources say his parents then allowed an alternative medicine healer to treat him. His parents have now issued a statement saying their son is awake and talking.

"Nearly three hundred teenagers and parents, mostly from his school, have set up a vigil outside the hospital waiting for every update and cheering good news."

I skipped to a different news channel with a panel discussion on violence. Three suits: two men and one woman.

Male #1, distinguished looking, early seventies, gray hair:

"…fantasies of adolescent shooters take root in a desperate attempt to gain recognition. Often they're inspired by previous shooters and in a show of force, demonstrate they won't be bullied again."

Female, maybe thirty with bright purple glasses:

"There've been nearly ninety school shootings this year and most could have been avoided with more armed guards and armed teachers."

Male #2, maybe forty-five, black wavy hair, short beard:

"But there were four ex-military guards with semi-automatic rifles at Hartman and that didn't stop it from happening…"

Female: interrupting,

"But no teachers had firearms. That was what was missing!"

Male #1:

"Good point. Only a good guy with a gun can stop a bad buy with a gun."

Male #2:

"Isn't that what police are for?"

Female:

"In this country, you can't trust government. Cops want to take away our guns. We are citizens of Internet America now, we find our truths there. As I said in my new book, we are new frontiersmen

who know something vital has been stolen. It's an audacious scheme to disenfranchise and disrespect us hard-working citizens. Maybe we also need to arm students."

Male #2:

"Four hundred armed students, sixty armed teachers, maybe even the janitors plus four armed ex-vet security guards! That would be insanity. The guns are the problem!

Male #1:

"No! Guns are never the problem, they're the solution!"

"These people are insane!" I shouted and switched channels. Maybe CNN.

Host:

"Guns are now the leading cause of death among children and adolescents in the U.S. That figure comes from the Centers for Disease Control and Prevention."

MD #1:

"We often want to rationalize this type of behavior as the acts of mentally ill people. This creates an easy political myth, making it useful for politicians who've done nothing to limit the sale of arms, particularly high-capacity semi-automatic weapons designed for military use, to say such laws are not needed and there was nothing they could have done. Thus the popular statement of 'thoughts and prayers' in place of anything meaningful..."

I turned off the TV. I really didn't want to hear a circular firing squad debate on gun violence. The fringe was now mainstream. My gut was proof, was still healing from three bullets that made it quite clear what caused my near death. If not for Haldir, I would have died.

•••

Daruk accompanied Darwin's father downstairs to the small conference room where Mrs. McQuaid was meeting with hospital officials. The session included Darwin's parents, Dr. Harold De-cateur, the doctor treating Darwin and the guy who screamed at us, and Dr. Chatting Bruno, the hospital director, and Nurse Sally O'Brien.

"Who is this boy?"

"Daruk is Darwin's boyfriend. He belongs here. There will be no disagreement. *Clear?"* Mrs. McQuaid stated, raising an eyebrow, daring him to disagree.

"No problem. Welcome," Dr. Bruno said, waving them to seats at the table.

Daruk was surprised at the intensity of the conversation. Also amused.

"You can join me and my husband in making a combined statement to the press or we will give our own." Mrs. McQuaid was taking no prisoners in this standoff.

"You cannot expect us to say we gave up and some high school shaman cured him." Dr. Bruno was struggling to sound reasonable. He added, "I don't believe in miracles."

"This was not a miracle, doctor!" Mrs. McQuaid shot back. "This was a type of healing you simply do not understand. I'm prepared to say that and show his medical chart for when you gave up and for what it shows now." She pulled a clipboard from her purse and set it on the table.

The two doctors looked at each other and nodded.

"You will give Haldir credit," Darwin's father said, "or we will say you gave up and abandoned our son and we had to go behind your backs to bring in alternatives. And you fought us doing it. Trust us, you will sound like doctors afraid to admit failure, the life and death of your patient secondary to your egos. The licensing board might find this an interesting case. Before anything like that happens, it's not unreasonable to state that there are things you don't know. Honesty does have a place here."

"All right," Dr. Decateur said, deflating. "We'll give them credit for taking over where normal medicine had reached its end. They did things that are not well understood but obviously worked. Also worked for Principal Darling."

His mother added one change. "Katnu Hisman does not want to be mentioned. He wants all credit to go to Haldir. Clear?"

"Very."

"I want a public celebration among friends and well-wishers for my son's recovery. It should be billed that way with reporters invited. I want Principal Darling there. I've talked to him and he's anxious to take part. I want my son there in a wheelchair or stretcher. He wants this. So do we. So do students from the school. It will help give them closure from this horror." She reached over and took her husband's hand. "Let's give the media a specific time and location for tomorrow morning, say ten am. I'll let the student reps know so they can send out word. I suggest your largest auditorium."

She walked up to Daruk afterward. "I hope I wasn't too subtle."

He laughed and they hugged. She was a warrior too. Like mother, like son.

• • •

Principal Darling wheeled himself to the front of the stage in the hospital auditorium amid foot stomping and shouts of *"Darling! Darling!"* from the standing room only crowd after he was introduced.

"Please take a minute and understand how evil was overcome just seven days ago by three courageous young men. Few will ever face what most of you did that day. Most recoil when confronted with violence and threats. That's normal. Yet some in such a situation are compelled to act."

"You did!" a blond boy shouted from the audience.

"Yeah! Mr. Darling stood up for us in the auditorium!" The Asian girl's voice was strong, emotional. "He put himself in front of the gunman and got shot to protect us!"

"Darling! Darling! Darling!" the chants began. Students were cheering. The feeling was electric. Then someone shifted. *"Glad! Glad! Glad!"* before there was widespread laughter.

He was blushing and smiling as he continued: "I appreciate your enthusiasm. But I was a victim, not a savior. Others were remarkable and effective and we're here to celebrate *them*. Political science teacher Gordon Liddy confronted the gunman in his class"—there were scattered whistles and applause—"and tried to reason with him. When his life was threatened, it was a student who intervened, taking out the gunman then running down the hallway and taking out a second gunman. Then into the auditorium where he found me, then confronted another gunman at the same time as an eighth-grade student charged and subdued yet another gunman in the auditorium. As if this weren't enough, the first student charged the gunman at the front of the school and was shot with life threatening injuries yet held on till that man was unable to fight. *Now that in my book is true heroism!"* He pumped his arm in the air. *"Yes! Yes! Yes!"*

The auditorium erupted, pounding feet, applauding, laughing. The room could legally hold three hundred people seated. But there were no seats today and no one complained that the attendance was likely double that, with a large number of reporters and TV camera crews. Again he called for quiet and the room went silent. "Three young men, one only fourteen years old, two of them seventeen. They can't even vote yet, they're not old enough to even be classified as adults but they sure saved lives." He held up a hand to stop another round of cheering. "Save the enthusiasm for someone I will now introduce who will speak for *this magnificent trio."* Whistles from the audience. Darling grinned as he continued. "Someone given up for dead, so grievous were his injuries. I don't know how they did what they did for him to recover. Frankly, I don't care. That's not important. What' crucial to remember—*he acted, they acted and defeated evil.* Such courage deserves celebration." More whistles and applause. "May I present you a young man I deeply admire…senior *Darwin McQuaid!"*

As Darling rolled his wheelchair to the side of the stage, students were stamping their feet, whistling and calling out the names of the three students, almost like it was planned in advance. I sat in a wheelchair behind a drape.

"Darwin! Darwin! Haldir! Haldir! Miguel! Miguel! Darling! Darling! Heroes! Heroes all!" It was led by three football cheerleaders.

My mother moved my wheelchair to the front of the stage, patted my shoulder and handed me the mic. Eventually the room quieted.

"I'm a bit overwhelmed at the moment." People laughed. "The three of us just did what we could. The terrorists killed two fine security guards trying to protect us. Let us remember that, and honor them with a moment of silence. Thank you, officers Vojtěch Vlček and Sarah Washington. You died for our sake. We honor your sacrifice."

There were whistles and approving shouts, then everyone was quiet, heads bowed.

"A-men," I said after some moments of silence. "I appreciate the honesty of the two doctors who spoke earlier. They did all they could, all they knew, helped stabilize me, and were willing to step back when they could do no more and let Haldir perform his powerful non-traditional healing methods." I turned my wheelchair and gestured to the back of the stage. My Fae friend stepped into the light, came forward and took my hand.

Someone started chanting, *"Haldir! Haldir! Haldir! District champs! District champs!"* He grinned and blushed as it went on and on. I held up an arm. The room went quiet.

"May I also recognize and thank my best friend since we were toddlers. He charged the gunman at the front door of the school. I couldn't have done it without him. A quiet guy, a brave guy: *Miguel Medina!*"

He stepped from the wings, stopped and smiled to acknowledge the applause, and then walked to me, placing a hand on my shoulder. He blushed too, as people cheered, which was perfect. The three of us were still as a sea of phones and cameras were pointed at us. "The magnificent trio," Darling had called us. Hopefully that dreadful moniker wouldn't stick.

This had been set up as a celebration, showing us off, but not as a press conference. I didn't have the strength to answer questions nor did I have answers that would work in explaining—setting gunmen on fire, knocking them unconscious with a touch, lifting a terrorist off the ground without physical contact, healing with what seemed more magic than medicine. If only they knew.

Videos of the invasion from student cameras were already circulating. Answers would have to be given at some point. Some kernels of truth, maybe, but certainly not the whole story. My parents had questions too. My little brothers, thankfully, thought it was cool.

27.

was released to return home that afternoon.

A young doctor examined me, Dr. Adam Pincher, an intern who'd been a frequent attendant in the hospital, pronounced me nearly fully recovered and that I could be released. My original doctor apparently didn't want to deal with me. Miguel and eleven nurses walked with me to the front door of St. Michael's Hospital including Dr. Pincher, all of them having watched over me on different shifts, doing what they could even when I was comatose, thrilled when I started to heal. One called me a champion, another said I was a lionheart, a third one, a paladin, a kind of medieval knight if I remembered my history. I suspected they were also hoping to learn more about my miraculous improvement but were too polite and professional to press. They were my heroes and heroines. I heard a few whispered comments about a certain doctor, and muffled laughs. Even Pincher smiled. Interns probably needed to watch what they said about established doctors.

Haldir and Daruk were waiting for me as I was wheeled from the front door of St. Michael's Hospital.

As I was loaded into a blue SUV with a wheelchair lift, a television news crew rushed towards us shouting questions. I waved and shrugged as the door of the SUV slid closed and locked. Two hospital security guards held them back as we drove away. There were too many unanswered questions on what had happened at the school. Police could only say the terrorist attack was being investigated for so long. Gunmen bursting into flames were the most popular videos on You Tube and endless FB posts. There were also videos of Haldir saving Principal Darling with a green haze covering them both.

When we pulled in front of our new house, there were a half dozen television cameras and reporters waiting in front of the driveway. Three security guards from a private company hired by Uncle His came out and held them away from us as the gate opened and we drove inside the garage. Miguel wheeled me into the elevator. When we exited into the main living room, I heard voices that sounded familiar but that I couldn't immediately place. My parents stared, as did Uncle His, and there he was, Gabriel Tomas, the square-jawed, All-American quarterback sexy FBI agent with a dimple in his chin. Beside him was Senior Agent Amare Williams, still the wiry, tough-looking, no nonsense African American professional, looking fully recovered from being shot when we were in the Russian Wilderness.

It was wonderful to see them both and I'm sure my big grin made it obvious. My dad was holding the baby in his arms, Diarmuid Daruk McQuaid. I loved the child's name. For a newborn, he was surprisingly quiet and calm, his big eyes always watching, his ears turning to any sound, listening. Maybe these were Fae characteristics even in babies that helped them survive. If you are trying to hide, a wailing baby could be a problem.

"Wow! My two favorite FBI agents. Don't take this the wrong way…but why are you here? Just to say hello?" As I rolled toward them, they stepped forward, hands extended. They each took one of mine and leaned in to kiss my cheek. Not exactly FBI protocol but fun and welcome.

"You look remarkable," Agent Washington said, stepping

back. "Considering what you went through, it's a miracle you're here after doctors gave up on you."

"Ditto," said Gorgeous. "Given what we already know, what we're pledged to never reveal, I hope we learn what really went on."

Miguel pushed his fingers into my back, a gentle nudge to remind me he was here and wanted to meet the very special agent. I said, "Let me introduce you to my closest friend since boyhood, Miguel. Special Agent Tomas and Senior Agent Williams." They shook hands. He seemed to hold onto Beauty's hand a bit too long.

"I think you can be read in on most details," Uncle His stated.

I was wheeled near the sofa and we all sat, my mother bringing me a protein shake.

"Thanks, Mom." I asked the agents, "So why are you here?"

The agents looked at each other before Washington answered. "After Katnu talked with President O'Connor yesterday, the decision came down that the FBI would take the lead in this case because the terrorists, arguably, were part of a larger group scattered in various states. The FBI director notified local police this morning. All calls for information they receive will be forwarded to us."

"Any relationship between what happened in the Russian Wilderness with this attack at my high school?"

"Not that we know of, and no comparison will be made. My director wants to put a lid on any wild speculation. We'll gather what the police have and try to figure out how to explain it all in a way that's at least partially true."

"I suspect that 'all the truth we think you can handle' isn't part of the FBI motto.."

"What truth can't we handle?" my father asked.

"Before we get into that, where are my brothers?"

"Over at Aunt Ruthie's," Mom said. "They've been with her since you were taken to the hospital. She's happy to keep them as long as we need. We kept them out of school this week. She kept them entertained as only she can."

My next question could not be stated aloud. I asked, making

sure I teleped to all three *"Uncle His, can we tell them everything?"*

"At some point they would need to know unless you want to remain deceitful. This seems like an appropriate time."

Folding my hands in front of my chin, I considered where to start. "I think a demonstration might be a good place to start. Then we'll explain how your son got to be an enhanced version of what you think you know about him."

My father chuckled uncertainly. Mom turned her head slightly and squinted at me.

"No, really." I pointed to the wood in the fireplace. Haldir, if you could remove the screen." My parents gaped at him as he pointed to the fireplace screen and it slowly lifted up and away from the opening, settling down to the side.

"What the fuck?" my dad yelled.

I pointed to the wood and ramped up my special talent. "Wait for me, Dad." In less than a minute, the wood burst into flames. "Please return the screen." Haldir levitated it nicely and set it in place. My parents, open-mouthed and wide-eyed, leaned forward in their seats.

For the next hour I explained as much as I could. Uncle His added in details as appropriate. Haldir talked about his people, breaking down in tears twice but finding the strength to continue. Daruk and I enhanced the storytelling several times. The agents talked about their findings at the Russian Wilderness. Miguel spoke about his adventures in E3. Then the trip into the future and E1.

One more piece of evidence would dramatically make this real. I asked Daruk to bring up a still-drying painting from my closet downstairs.

He handed it to me, two feet square, covered with a piece of cheese cloth. "One thing we didn't mention after our adventure in Daruk's world, E3. He wanted to take me on a special vacation. You thought we were going camping. Until now, there was so much you didn't know, couldn't know, I had no idea how to explain my reality. From E3, we flew to Italy, to seventeenth century Rome. Daruk had developed a relationship with a painter famous in our time, Caravaggio. Daruk brought him twenty-sixth century medicine for the lead paint that was poisoning his system through cuts in his fingers caused by mixing paint with a knife. He liked me and did this painting." I lifted the cloth. "Here's a twenty-first century teenager painted by an artist dead five hundred years and famous for his baroque style, emotional intensity through the dramatic use of light and shadow to define three dimensional objects." I looked straight ahead in the art, into Caravaggio's face. Beside me, partially hidden by a hood, his eyes glistening, my own personal Guardian, Daruk.

My parents and the two agents looked at it with an intensity that made me nervous. All four of them came closer, my mother just a few inches from it.

"Is that his signature?" Beauty asked.

"Yes," Daruk replied. "It's only the second painting he ever signed at that point in his career. As you can tell by the perfection and glow of Darwin's face, the man had a crush on him. It was beautiful and amusing to watch."

"It's too exquisite to leave in your closet," my mother said. "May we hang it somewhere where we can see this? It's magical."

"Of course, Mom. At some point we'll need to figure out how we explain it. The Caravaggio angle may not work with people outside this group."

My mother turned to Haldir. "Are you human?" She was ready to move on, her voice quiet and respectful. "Is Fae human?"

"Yes," Haldir responded, looking surprised "We are part of the human family but isolated for centuries, perhaps even thousands of years, from other *Homo sapiens*, so we advanced differently, gradually changing in minor ways, our genes mutating to enhance our survival, generation after generation. As Charles Darwin found with other isolated species on the Galapagos Islands after which he developed his theory of natural selection. We are a people of legend, often persecuted by those who feared us for our differences and we learned to live near humans but mostly out of sight. There are many stories about us, good and bad, throughout history, often exaggerated. To survive we evolved, developing certain capabilities others homo sapiens don't share and didn't need for their survival. Healing is what I was trained to do, it is my vocation."

He opened the leather strap at the base of his neck that held his thick hair tight, shook his head, and extended his distinctive ears. Next he removed his special goggles. His voice started to break. "This is who I am and the child as well. Does this mean you do not want us here?"

"Oh no, darling!" my mother exclaimed, bouncing out of her chair and over to him. He stood, looking unsettled, until they hugged. She kissed his cheek. "You are part of this family as long as you want to be. There is no need to hide who you are here. Soon you will legally have our last name and officially be part of this family. Darwin and the boys are your brothers now. We love you and the baby. This is new and surprising information, almost unbelievable. Actually, it *is* unbelievable but I respect all of you and accept it. Mostly."

"Uncle His, you're two hundred years old?" Dad asked, looking a bit shaken.

"Give or take a decade or three."

"Any other questions?" I asked.

Everyone laughed.

• • •

My parents again were speechless as they stood on the peak of what we called Buena Vista, looking toward East Bay in the 26th century. There was no Oakland or San Francisco, just the wreckage of a once thriving civilization. Both my parents were teary eyed. "Does this mean our future is set and nothing we do changes it?" My father asked the question holding my mother in his arms as they stared at the world of any future grandkids.

"I think the destruction—or perhaps a better term is degradation of earth—is set and well underway," Uncle His said. "At both a political as well as individual level. At some point denial in place of action makes this future inevitable. Cynicism is a dangerous human characteristic. Some businesses, politicians and individuals have benefited in their lives at a cost of dooming humanity in the long run. Each generation keeps making excuses, cynics all, as the planet faces bedlam. Our segmented media channels help redefine truth to make us feel smart and superior when in fact we are often fools. The question is how bad will it get? Some incremental changes in our environmental efforts can make a difference at the margins. The real danger is believing our future is hopeless, so why bother doing anything." He rubbed his chin, as if considering whether to say his next statement.

"Please say more, Uncle His. This is useful," I said, always amazed at the man, wanting to hear more of his perspective that spanned centuries.

He smiled at me. "History overall is not a long epitaph of our actions, good and bad, ending in the annihilation of our species. We can control our destiny. What is a tragedy is that the West has given up on progress. You need optimism, like that which existed in the Industrial Revolution, to tackle today's challenges. A more recent example might be in the nineteen sixties when President Kennedy announced the plan to put a man on the Moon. He believed it could be done. The nation believed it and united behind him. He was a charming man, by the way, and we had many remarkable conversations. Another example further back: the creation of the smallpox vaccine in the early nineteen hundreds had the world coming together to eliminate a scourge. A recent example: the creation and distribution of the Coronavirus vaccine. Most vaccines take five to ten years to develop and manufacture. The remarkable mRNA shots appeared in less than a year thanks to the work of thousands, teams who believed it could be done and did it. Those vaccines saved nearly twenty million lives in the first year. Then politics intervened and the effort became less effective and many needlessly died. Those anti-science, anti-vaccine activists died in greater numbers than the nation as a whole. So sad and unnecessary. Now the cynics rule. Caution, turning away from science, risk aversion, a sense of grievance for what you don't have rather than what's possible. If you believe you cannot do something, you are probably right. I hope the day returns when we can believe in ourselves. Now, I think we should visit the past."

Twenty minutes later we were at the same location, five hundred years earlier. Lush savannahs, thick sweet air. My parents were mostly struck dumb. The FBI agents just stared, asking a few questions but mostly overwhelmed. "My world," Daruk said with pride.

We returned to our century.

"How about a plane ride?" Uncle His offered his most bemused smile. At this point I think he could have suggested jumping off a cliff and they would do it given what they had just experienced. Their brains were on overload, just like mine was the first time.

He piloted *Mars* with Daruk next to him. My parents sat behind him, with Miguel and me. The agents had seen the craft before and bowed out of this trip. With six of us aboard, and once we left the fog bank until we were high above the Pacific Ocean, the aircraft didn't slow. He flew over North America, a slower ride over some major cities and national parks. Again my parents were mostly silent. Occasional questions on geography but otherwise they just observed. He crossed over the North Pole and back through Canada, slowing and lowering altitude to observe herds of elk, wolf packs and a remarkable Inuit village. "The people you see," Uncle His explained, "are descendants of the Thule people who emerged from the Bering Strait and western Alaska around one thousand B.C."

Back in the cabin, he served tea with almond biscotti dipped in dark chocolate that we got at a local bakery. I had milk, never having developed a taste for tea, and it was perfect for dunking.

"You and Daruk are boyfriends," my mother said, not a question and unexpected by me. She knew the answer so why ask it?

"Yes," I responded. "I love him. We share three worlds and have deep affection."

"Amazing adventures, too," Daruk added. "On my Earth, we seek to preserve the richness of the environment and life. Europeans are kept out of what your world calls North and South America and can continue to fight wars and destroy their own lands unless it creates problems for us, then we intervene."

We were quiet for several minutes. There was so much to consider. The way Mom stared at me I know a zinger was coming.

"I have a question. You've presented evidence of whole new worlds we didn't know existed. But I'm still old fashioned and, frankly, family focused. I'm still your mother. Are you sexually intimate?"

"MOM!"

"I take that as affirmative." She just looked at us, her face moving from me to Daruk and back. Did she approve?

"I think you make a wonderful couple and I wish you both every happiness," my father said, and walked over to hug me, then my boyfriend. My mother said nothing more but stepped over, took my hand, then Daruk's and placed them together. She nodded, her eyes wet.

As Mom and Dad left the cabin to head home, we stopped in the area out front. "The boys will be home soon," my father said, putting a hand on my shoulder and squeezing. "I have no idea if they can ever be told any of this. But we have to figure out how to explain what happened at school since other kids will know about it when they return to class. Thank you for sharing these worlds with us. We need time to process."

My mother kissed me on the cheek and gave me a bear hug. She did the same for Uncle His, Miguel and Daruk. Then they left the park, holding hands.

Uncle His texted the security team at our house to be on the lookout.

• • •

My one effort to leave the house and meet friends at Spike's Coffee ended with our car being tailed by half a dozen reporters. So we just returned home. To visit Uncle His for the tour with my parents had required using a decoy car to draw off the reporters while we left in a laundry van for the short ride to the park.

School had been cancelled indefinitely for the FBI team to continue processing evidence and evaluating the scene and to give people time to absorb the tragedy and decompress.

Now, to figure out how we explain everything. Today three of us were sitting with the agents in the common area just outside my bedroom on the lower level of our home. I hoped they had suggestions.

"We're considering various explanations," Agent Williams said. "So far none would pass close scrutiny. The issue is how to explain it and sound convincing, without saying anything."

Darwin: "Maybe we need to hire a politician."

Daruk: "Or think like one. While I am not native to this country or world, I have observed how politicians here change the subject, distract from the question or make up something that is not easily disproven or replicated. I also recognize that some politicians want to solve problems for their constituents and others are simply congenital liars. There is nothing to be learned from this other than that many enhance problems rather than solve them."

Agent Tomas: "So the green glow seen over Haldir when he was healing Darling was perhaps an unusual reflection of light from a faulty overhead fixture."

Darwin: "Can you find such a light that theoretically could do that and plausibly say it was in the ceiling of the auditorium? If we find one that could do that, do we put it in place? I suppose telling the truth is out of the question. I have pyro-kinesis abilities that somehow manifested in me; Haldir has what we might call, let me make up a word, how about curative-kinesis."

Tomas: "Interesting idea. Maybe analeptic-kinesis. It might sound more scientific. A dictionary definition of analeptic often refers to a drug that stimulates the central nervous system but can also used more generally like restoring a person's health or strength."

Miguel: "I've never heard of the word. It might force people to open their dictionaries or at least their dictionary app. Maybe they'd just accept it as real because that's easiest."

Agent Washington stood and walked in front of us, hands behind her back. "How would it be possible that both powers— one unproven and one unheard of—came to be practiced at this school on this day?" She moved to the window and then did an impressive military about face, one forearm up as if lecturing students in a class. "The FBI *will not plant evidence* to prove something that did not happen."

Daruk nodded, perhaps in agreement or not. "Another question that will likely come up…how did we meet Haldir and the child? I assume we don't want to explain what happened in the Russian Wilderness. If we did, it would need to match the stories told to the families of the dead scientists and guards."

"What if we do? At least partially." I felt inspired. "This special mental power drew me to want to visit up north. His mind and mine connected. Then the murder of his family, the FBI coming in to investigate. And Haldir comes here." As I talked, my enthusiasm slipped. Too many impossible coincidences. A mental connection over hundreds of miles? "Naw."

My lover looked at me, likely reading my mind which was not always a good thing. "I wanted to go to the Russian Wilderness because of the wildlife and the lack of humans. It was to relax with the man I love. No connection with Haldir or his people."

"How about Haldir's medallion giving off a green glow or the overhead light reflecting on it giving off the glow?" I raised my eyebrows to the group.

We agreed on lunch.

28.

Miguel remained worried his boyfriend was bored and felt useless in our world. He also feared Luther had no choice in dating him. He could hardly drop Miguel even if he wanted to because his life revolved around the cabin, Uncle His, Daruk, Haldir and me. He wasn't a legal resident of this Earth although that could be managed. He lacked self-confidence, worried about his poor education and too nervous to attend school.

Even with all that, Luther seemed enamored of my friend. Miguel was over-thinking this.

"You said you had an idea, my brilliant best friend. Care to share?"

"I've been talking to Uncle His about how much detail on our future history is readily available from the twenty-sixth century and its accuracy. How can we access it with confidence?"

"Who cares?"

"I think many will care and perhaps pay money for accurate predictions. Katnu said there is a detailed record of news stories, books and other sources. We need access and analyze it for useful content."

"Can you cut to the idea?"

It was just the two of us at the cabin as we discussed this. "People who can predict the immediate future, or pretend to, are often highly paid. We would need to get him a track record of faultless predictions without him seeming like a fortune teller or other type of huckster. If Luther were to do it, with near one hundred percent accuracy, he would be sought after. People would pay handsomely for his time. This has worked rather well for Uncle His and his investments."

"Uncle His has access to the stock market."

"I'm guessing we'd need to go into the future and download databases and bring them back here to sort through and organize. Topics might include politics, weather, war and a host of more complicated issues we could track."

"If he did this on some major issues, could that alter history?"

"Good point. We might need to figure out which questions, if answered in a way that altered a major decision could impact events and change the immediate future. That complicates this but I still think it's a solution to his issue of feeling valued and having a way to make a living in this strange century."

"If you could figure out all this, would he be yet another superman in our little group? Couldn't that cause added problems?"

"Perhaps. But I was thinking of it being low key. Word of mouth, not a public display. With our FBI connections, the government might pay. He could have a steady income as he learned about our century. He could feel like he was doing something important and getting paid. We'd need to develop a persona or public presence so people would have confidence in him when they meet, even one on one. He'd also need a backstory. No idea what that might be at this point."

"In a way, this reminds me of Isaac Asimov's *Foundation* series. Remember when we read it in junior high? Great reading. In it there was this guy…"

"Harry Seldon."

"Right. He developed this idea of psychohistory that allowed him to use specialized mathematics to predict the future. He looked hundreds of years into the future."

"Seldon also insisted that the population had to remain in ignorance of his analyses because the group might otherwise change its behavior."

"Sort of like the world knowing greenhouse gases were destroying the planet and that compelled them do something serious to stop it."

I had to laugh. "You're so cynical at times, Miguel. Uncle His is negative on cynics, just so you know. Be positive. Anything we'd do with Luther would be very short term in comparison. Advising police on what to look for in a murder case, or who might win the next race for mayor."

"I like this. Make it so."

I gave him a Vulcan salute that may have looked more like a middle finger, based on his expression. Miguel was right. We didn't need someone else with inexplicable talents to suddenly appear in our midst.

...

"I think wire rim glasses will give you more of a nerd look which might help with your new 'augur' persona."

Luther looked at me like I was delusional. "My eyes are good. I don't need glasses."

"It's not a question of need, it's to give you credibility."

"I also hate the 'augur' term. I had to look it up."

"We could alternate with 'clairvoyant' if you like that term better. Uncle His has this talent, at least short term and he's often accurate but not a hundred percent."

"Extrasensory perception," Miguel read from a dictionary. "Or here's a winner: 'adumbrate.' I guess that would translate to 'adumbrater.' Sounds like a cooking term: Let me adumbrate the carrots."

"Enough!" Luther said to the two of us. We were all sitting just outside my bedroom. "I like the idea of being able to make money to carry my weight but claiming I have some weird insights, and worse, using pretentious words, is just too much."

I smiled at him hoping it would make him more cooperative. "Put the glasses back on, please. I'm guessing maybe *'augur'* is sounding better, considering the alternatives. Maybe we can get someone outside our group to use the term."

He put the glasses back on. I picked up a brush and combed his hair. "Maybe a part since it's long enough. You should look serious enough to have credibility when the right people want to meet you."

"All right," Luther said. "Do your worst."

"I actually think the glasses make you look even more sexy." Miguel licked his lips.

"Maybe we could take a break for an hour and you can show me what you mean."

"Guys. No. No. We are developing a business plan for our twenty-sixth century visitor. Sex later."

I sat on the nearby sofa, leaned back and examined my handiwork. "I think this's a good look. I'm also thinking we start small. Maybe some letters to the editor where you disagree with some other letter writer or editorial and state what's going to happen. Make it exact, like the percentage of victory in an election. Best if you predict an upset by the right number. Maybe changes in crime trends, or even profile the type of person they should be looking for in a major crime since we already know what the guilty party looks like, his name. Actually, focusing on crime might be the way to go. Get some attention locally without being high profile. Maybe another letter writer refers to you as an *augur*. Then another couple of letters that show it isn't a fluke. Then we approach our FBI friends about making use of your talents. Agree to a trial run."

"Great plan," Luther said.

"I *urgur*," Miguel said with a smirk. "So can we go cuddle now?" My best friend stood—clearly tired of talking—took Luther's hand and pulled him into my room. "You don't mind, do you? I'll change the sheets."

...

There were now six new security guards carrying semi-automatic rifles at the school, all looking like the bad guys in a gritty war movie, Army fatigues, unshaven, almost snarling, dark eyes that examined you as you passed by. The two who ran away during the attack were fired. The main entrance to the school now had thick steel doors with no windows and seven metal posts, spaced three feet apart, and set in concrete arched around the front door, and repeated inside just in case a tank managed overcome the first obstacles. I assumed it was to make us feel safe but it just reminded us of what happened.

We walked into school three abreast. People turned and watched, like we were some kind of freak show. Miguel, Haldir and I smiled and said hello. On this first day back, the air smelled like paint and disinfectant, everything was spotless. Signs offered grief counseling. Some scattered applause as we got deeper into the hallways. We waved.

Some guy yelled, "Haldir! District Champs!" People laughed and started coming up to us. Haldir got lots of attention which was nice. He felt comfortable here and wanted to fit in, hungry for community.

"Thanks, man," said a guy in the hallway who was from my class where I torched the terrorist. He squeezed my shoulder.

"You bet," I replied, realizing how inane that sounded.

The big question hanging in this room and everywhere—how did I and Haldir do what we did—just remained unasked. Students were still shaken by what happened, happy to have survived, not wanting to create problems, perhaps not ready to hear the answer. Homework assignments and tests can make you focus. Haldir was as popular as before, lots of high fives, something he now did with relish, and back slaps. Please don't let him turn into some weird eighth grader, I hoped. Yet for the most part he was humble, respectful and wicked smart.

No explanations had yet been given to the media. The FBI was handling the case and declined comment as they supposedly proceeded with their investigation. Fortunately, some details did come out, the names of the terrorists, where they were from, how they might have been radicalized—lots of people had opinions—how they related to other such groups. This fed the need for details and distracted from how the student heroes managed to do what they did. We'd been instructed to demure, I liked that word, to demure shyly and say we were not allowed talk about the attack under orders from the FBI.

Miguel and I had Mr. G's Modern Political Theory. No red baseball cap on him today. The door was new and a lot heavier, perhaps an upgrade. The shot up ceiling, the bloody floor, had been replaced. It smelled fresh, almost floral. He got up from his desk when he saw me enter and wrapped his arms around me.

"Thanks again for saving my life." He sounded a bit weepy and I felt embarrassed for this teacher who usually liked to argue. When he let go, the class was staring at us, breaking into applause and a few whistles. I felt my face burn. Putting an arm around Miguel's shoulders to share the glory, I tried to smile and not have some kind of breakdown myself. That had been one scary day in this classroom.

"Mr. G!" I said in a loud voice to quiet the noise, "THANK YOU for standing up for us!" Now students were applauding him. I liked that better and joined them in appreciation.

29.

I teleped Uncle His as soon as I got the registered letter from a lawyer at the *San Francisco Mirror.*

"Are you open to talk? I just got this letter..."

"I got one too," he replied before I could say more. *"Reporter Veronica Stong is asking if we want to comment on the attached article or just be listed as saying we refused."*

"Since my parents and the FBI are also on the letter, maybe we all get together for a strategy session."

An hour later we were in the living room of my parents, with Haldir, Uncle His, Daruk and the two FBI agents on speakerphone. Everyone had a copy of the article.

The room was quiet, only a couple of expletives amidst the grumbles as we reviewed the lengthy article, its proposed headlines and dozens of photos. In several places it indicated that extensive efforts were taken to obtain comments from all of us. Messages were left, it stated, and no calls ever returned. It was done in a way to suggest we were trying to avoid comment. Which was true but avoiding an obnoxious self-righteous, preening reporter offering bribes to get students to steal legally protected documents, seemingly indifferent to the consequences, was quite different to avoiding reaction to an article

"May I start?" Agent Williams asked on the speakerphone.

"Please," I replied, not sure who was in charge of the call.

"Our Indiana Jones wanabe anthropologist, Wilkins Vardan, has trashed his non-disclosure agreement with the agency. He's in breach of the sworn statement."

Agent Gorgeous was quick to add: "Yes, but the story is so explosive he must have assumed that would keep us from taking him to court. The public's right to know and all that."

Uncle His growled, clearly upset, "Let us consider a statement that this anthropologist signed a report with both agents that tells a very different story, adding dramatic new elements. Which one is the lie? Did his ambition, his hunger for fame infect his thinking, much like the anthropologist who hired a team to invade Haldir's homeland? How might such craving for fame warp a man's mind as I think it did for the other anthropologist, Professor Arnold Whitacre and his grad assistant, Otto Heinrich? I state this as a possible counter to the article. This anthropologist is the sole source for the new material. He gave his word he would honor the report. Now he has broken that promise by adding elements designed to sensationalize what happened. I give little credence to liars."

Everyone was quiet, considering this kind of take no prisoners response.

"He does not disagree with the formal FBI report that said the various academics and military guards killed each other. Nor does it mention Agent Williams being shot and later healed by Haldir." I tossed this out hoping it might narrow our focus. "Beyond recounting what happened within the limits of what was agreed to, the main new thrust is outing Haldir as Fae, sheer sensationalism, and showing photos inside his home in the cave. As a gay teenager, exposing someone whether for animosity, sport, personal gain or any other reason without their consent is repugnant."

"Maybe they were trying to limit aspects of the story so we would not do something drastic," Daruk said, visibly trying to control his temper. "Perhaps we could take the reporter to the seventeenth century and let her try being self-important in my world. No mention of Darwin killing two with his bow or Haldir killing one military vet with his special powers and disabling another. His magical talents mention healing, which has already gone public at the school, nothing about his offensive powers."

"That's helpful but compared with the totality of the story, only a part. Although I do like the idea of her and Vardan going on a one-way trip through time." I exhaled in frustration and rubbed my eyes. Damn this was complicated. The article tied what happened in the Russian Wilderness directly to Haldir and the school. Haldir and the child were not just orphans, they were a new race of humans, the legendary Fae. People would go crazy for it.

"You...killed...two men." My mother's voice was a broken whisper as she stared at me. She wasn't asking a question. She'd accepted it as true.

"If he had not," Uncle His responded, his tone that of a wise man, but with an edge, "your son would have been returned to you in a body bag. Both men were armed—one with an AR15, the other with an automatic pistol—and had murdered or ordered the murder of five of Haldir's family members and were preparing to shoot your son. He saved Daruk and the baby. In my estimation, that makes him a hero. Please be proud of him. I am."

I felt a bit overwhelmed by his words. Mom looked distressed, eyes wide, twisting her hands in her lap. My dad put his arm around her, kissing her cheek. He looked at me, smiled and nodded. He was proud.

I went to her and down on my knees, taking her hands in mine. "Mom, I'm sorry I couldn't tell you. It was self-defense. Please believe me!" I put my head down on her lap. She ran fingers through my hair. I could tell she was crying. There was a limit on how much she could handle. Or any of us.

"I concur with what Katnu stated," Agent Williams said over the phone. "The evidence proved self-defense. The two academics and guards were little more than glory-seeking thugs and mercenaries. Daruk and Darwin came across them by happenstance, saved two lives and dispensed justice. Bravo to them both. If that was all the anthropologist suggested, no real problem. But he's added the finding of a new human species. If he can prove this, he'll become a star academic with publishing, monetary and public speaking opportunities."

"He gets rich and Haldir becomes a target," I added, pissed.

"If I may add this about what Darwin did," Agent Tomas said. "He took out a military trained security guard who had just murdered three people. Imagine a seventeen-year-old armed with a bow and arrow stopping a trained killer with a semi-automatic rifle. Extraordinary. Be proud of your son. I admire him. He saved lives. Believe it."

"Why is my private life, my home, who I am being shared with the public?" Haldir asked, looking bewildered. Newspapers and any type of media were new to him, unlike most of my world. "Am I a freak?"

"You are a unique and marvelous human being," Uncle His responded. "I am proud to call you friend."

"Agreed. Haldir is my brother," Daruk said. "If we follow Katnu's advice, that might limit what new information is made public."

Uncle His steepled his fingers in front of his chin. "One helpful thing is the location. We never gave any coordinates to the FBI or Mr. Vardan. We picked them up and took them back. They landed on a mountain top. There are scores of those in the Russian Wilderness. We covered vast distances in minutes, faster than any aircraft on this planet. We also left no footprints. It's unlikely even trained scouts could find the spot."

"They don't know about the second Fae home twenty miles away from where we camped." I was beginning to sense a plan. "Maybe we limit the scope of the story to the existence of the cave where they lived. They had to have lived somewhere. Indicate the professor made up the Fae part or go further and say we won't confirm or condone idle speculation where there appears to be a financial motive."

"Should I be ashamed of what I am?" Haldir asked. "What is wrong with being Fae?"

"Oh, sweetie, there is nothing wrong with you or your heritage," Agent Williams responded. "You are unique, you and the baby, perhaps in the world. Your people are legendary, the stuff of myths, books, film. Verification of what he says in the proposed news article would create a media circus around you both. That can't be easy to manage. Beyond the media tsunami, desperate people will want you to save family members. That includes underworld thugs, even autocrats with armies at their command. So we need to be careful. But you are an amazing young man."

"All true," I added, looking at my new friend, offering a smile, leaning back from my mom, reaching for his hand, wrapping our fingers together. "It deals with your mythical lineage, ability to heal beyond modern medicine, and then links it to me setting two gunmen on fire at the school and how all that went down."

My dad cleared his throat. "I have an idea. What if you released the official FBI report with the professor's name and signature? It's lengthy, has the weight and tone of an official police document and it would limit sensationalism, given its legalese and dry descriptions even of the dead. Maybe couched as a 'this is what happened' statement. Maybe say the FBI has no comment on idle, unverified, provocative speculation that could harm two children. I'm not sure about giving credence to the photos inside his cave. They're outrageous and may spur people to go looking for it."

"The report is twenty-two pages long," I added. "I like that idea. It kind of dares the reporter to go forward. She wants fame and glory, damn the impact on her targets. I don't think the public has a limitless right to know on this kind of issue. Is there some public benefit I'm not aware of? The editor and the publisher would need to weigh a sensational splash against condemnation and lawsuits."

"Perhaps criticism within her journalist community, Dad said."

He had a point although I figured journalists would hang

together given the state of that mostly noble and threatened profession.

"Vardan is also in breach of his contract with the agency as an on-call expert," Agent Tomas added. "So that's another option."

"If that's the consensus, and I agree with it," Agent Williams stated, "let me discuss it with the Director of the FBI. If it's a go, we'll put it out as our official response. If it takes more than a few hours for approval, we'll let the reporter know a statement is in the works. I doubt she'll risk publishing knowing something official was on its way."

"I will talk with President O'Connor as well," Uncle His added.

• • •

The response was delivered to the reporter by messenger three hours later. After a talk with Uncle His, the president agreed with the plan. She wasn't thrilled with this development, apparently using language rarely uttered in front of witnesses by a government leader.

We waited to hear back but nothing came. When and what would they print? We needed to get involved in something new.

"Haldir, could we have a session with the medallions and knives?" Daruk asked as we had lunch with Uncle His in the cabin. A good idea to keep us occupied.

"Yes, let us," Haldir said. "Yet first who is this Tinkerbell you mentioned when we met?" We were sitting on the sofa and chairs in front of a low table.

"Oh, dear God. Yes, *Tinkerbell.*" Where to start? "You've seen a few cartoons with my brothers. A really famous movie and cartoon producer, Walt Disney, came up with a wonderful creation, Mickey Mouse." I was scrolling through my phone as we talked. I showed him the photo.

"Oh, yes, I saw a show with him on your television with your brothers. Highly amusing, a rat who can talk and sing and dance."

"Here it is. This is a picture of Tinkerbell. You see she's a winged creature, called a fairy." It was a classic picture, her in the air, holding a wand, her translucent wings flapping.

"I am a fairy. Let me see." I handed him my phone. He moved it closer to his face and then further away, tilted it left then right, up and down. He seemed perplexed as he handed it back.

Then he snorted and convulsed in laughter. I'd never seen him do anything like this, rolling back in his chair, his legs lifting to his chest, almost out of control. There were tears in his eyes. We all watched him, giggling ourselves. It was wonderful, he was a thing of beauty and happiness. Slowly, he calmed, his feet back on the floor, fingers rubbing the tears from his eyes.

"*I knew her sister well.*" He seemed so serious.

Our expressions radiated confusion as we glanced around. What? He tittered at first then guffawed, even more animated than before. "*Gotcha!*" he bellowed as his howling rolled.

Where did he learn this? It had to be my brothers. We giggled with him.

He reached into a canvas bag and lifted out four medallions, all ancient-looking with raised designs on the front. Even the muscular bronze chains were ornate.

"These are different from the medallions I gave you before. Those are for observing the world around you. These are for battle."

Haldir's had a plant motif with some kind of creature at the center. I leaned over to examine it as he held it out.

"What is it?"

"It is a male sable, originally from Persia, now Iran. It is a forest creature, about two feet long, luxurious dark brown fur, black on the legs, yellow at the throat. A ferocious fighter." He hung it around his neck before handing us each our own.

All of them were about three inches in diameter and heavy, lying surprisingly flat. Mine had what looked like a crow in the center, surrounded by leaves in a tree. Daruk's had a snake head, fangs out. Uncle His had what might be a falcon. All looked medieval or earlier and well worn. Likely worth a fortune.

"How old are these?" I asked.

"All go back hundreds of generations, handed down, father to son, mother to daughter. Maybe two or three thousand years. All powerful if we can connect each to your consciousness. Telepathy is necessary to link your mind with the power and personality of each medallion."

"Personality?" Daruk asked.

"Yes, each has its own psyche, its own quirks as you might say. If you make it part of you, if you link with it, the medallion, the force within it, can be very useful, each in a different way depending on your disposition, your needs and what it is willing to give. It can let you see what has happened in a particular space, a kind of history. It can also give you options when you might need help in a struggle. It will not happen all at once. You must work with it once you bind with it. You need to develop a relationship." He pointed to the front side of my medallion.

"It has intelligence embedded inside, like an AI device?" This was amazing.

"Yes, Darwin, it has been imbued with mental capacity but far beyond current levels of artificial intelligence. Please rub the face with your thumb, in a circle, focus your mind on the creature looking back. Repeat mentally, *'Spiorad na beanna, ceangail liom.'* Picture the face as you speak until you feel a connection. It might take a few seconds or several minutes. Or it possibly might not work at all. With this group, with your telepathic powers, I am confident it will succeed."

Katu said, "I believe you're saying, *'Spirit of the crow, connect with me.'* Or something close to that."

"Yes, very close. Katnu, you would substitute the word, falcon. *'Spiorad an fhabhcún ceangail liom.'* Daruk you would use the term for snake, *'Spiorad na nathrach ceangail liom.'* In this case the creature on the front is a forest cobra, also called a black cobra."

"I am not familiar with it," Daruk responded.

"It is known mostly in Africa, where my people first encountered it. It is the largest cobra species in the world, sometimes reaching ten feet, also dangerous due to its agressive behavior and potent venom."

"A perfect fit," I teased.

For the next hour, we worked on making our connection. Uncle His succeeded in minutes. Daruk took slightly longer. I felt something like a tickle in my brain, a feeling I wanted to touch, like scratching an itch but couldn't. Then I heard its caw, loud, harsh and unmistakeable, all in my head apparently since no one else reacted. It seemed like I was talking with it, understanding it. It asked questions and I did my best to answer. It seemed disappointed I was not Fae but promised to work with me when I needed it. It was a Fae creation, after all, and had certain obligations.

30.

My phone vibrated with a text. I pulled it from my pocket when my teacher, Ms. Stanio, turned to the whiteboard to draw an equation.

Katnu: *A black van is waiting outside. Darling is about to pull you and Haldir out of class. The Mirror has published its story.*

Darwin: Got It.

This had to be bad. I put my phone away and tried to focus on what she was saying.

Calculus was not my favorite subject in the best of times. It wasn't hard, just boring. And as a first period class on Tuesday, I wanted some coffee. Where did he get a black van?

Minutes later, the door opened and Principal Darling entered, walking to the instructor and whispering in her ear. Ms. Stanio pointed at me, gesturing me to follow the principal. I rose with my books and pack and quietly followed Mr. Darling from the room. Haldir was standing in the hallway with one of the school guards who looked like a cast member of *Hacksaw Ridge* or some other gritty war film. These guys would make terrorists squirm.

The four of us walked out into the parking lot. A black van

idled nearby, the window down with Daruk leaning out and watching us. The side door slid open; Uncle His was squatting inside.

"Good luck, Darwin, Haldir," Mr. Darling said. "Hopefully this won't create a sensation. Come back to us when you can. We can arrange online courses if need be." He shook each of our hands while we sat cross-legged on the metal floor. The van only had front seats, the back was open.

"Thank you, sir," I said. "We appreciate everything you've done."

The door slid closed with a clank and we began to exit the lot.

"Daruk, I didn't know you had a driver's license or even knew how to drive."

"I don't," he said, irritatingly cocky. "I don't live in this world, remember?"

I looked around the van. The inside walls were thick, maybe for sound or bullets, so were the doors. Did we need this kind of protection? I spotted a stack of blankets and pulled over several for the three of us to sit on.

"Here are copies of the newspaper," Katnu said, handing us each a copy.

Murder of 10 in Northern California Linked to Terror Attack at Hartman High. Two students Involved in Each.

Such a nice sensationalist, muckraking piece of journalism with insinuation in the headline that we did the killing. There were photos of bodies, slightly opaque, and shots inside the cave. You could see Haldir in two shots, slightly fuzzy on the face. Also shots of the statuary in full color, with the article suggesting it was a temple. There was also a shot of me with my bow, my face slightly obscured but still recognizable. It indicated that the family of the unnamed child and baby had been murdered by alleged treasure-seeking adventurers. Our anthropologist friend, Mr. Vardan, was quoted to this effect. Later on in the lengthy article, shots of Haldir and myself at the school, me setting a man on fire, Haldir lifting a gunman off the floor. A photo of my Fae friend healing Mr. Darling with a slight green haze over them. It did not say he was Fae but said there was no explanation as to how we did what we did. Since our names had been used before in coverage at the school, they were listed again, apparently assuming my parents gave permission this time which they had not. The implication that the two of us at the murder site in the mountains were the same guys identified as students at Hartman. So subtle. An unnamed source, likely Vardan, wonders if some of those murdered in the Russian Wilderness were an advanced race of homo sapiens. Nothing sensational there.

As we rode, I noticed we weren't headed to the cabin in Buena Vista Park or to my home. We pulled off onto Roosevelt Way and turned down a street I didn't recognize, then a hard left into the short driveway of an old Victorian home. A garage door opened. The door closed behind us and there was a hum. Slowly we began descending below ground.

"Four minutes," Daruk announced.

"Four minutes until what?" I asked, getting up on my knees and leaning over the seat back in front.

"Until we reach the bottom. Sixty-six feet down."

The lighting was dim. All I could see was a gray wall two feet in front of the van window. Finally, with a slight clunk, we reached the bottom. The van was turned on a circular rotation device. A door slid open ahead of us, lights turned on in a tunnel. Daruk put the van in gear and we drove several hundred feet before coming to a stop.

"We're home," Uncle His announced, sliding open the side door. I was too stunned to even speak. He walked to a nearby and familiar-looking elevator. Inside, it showed we were stopped at a middle level I'd never been on before, the ground floor entrance to the Passageway far below. We rode up to the top floor of the BV cabin. "How about a kale and peach protein smoothy?" He went to the sink and started preparing the drink.

"Please," said Haldir. He knew I loved them.

I nodded, still gathering my wits. "Would anyone like to explain what just happened?"

"Yes, Darwin, delighted to tell you more about our world." He waited until he added juice and the protein powder, hit the blender switch and poured four glasses.

He moved to the sofa and sat, and we gathered around him, enjoying our drinks.

"I decided about fifty years ago to add a secret entry and bought the house you saw. We brought in engineers from the twenty-sixth century who did the design and actual work. To any city engineer, this whole area appears to be solid rock because it is and thus not attractive for any subways or other uses. The existence of the tunnel is hidden electronically in the unlikely event someone goes looking for it. The van is reasonably bullet proof, not that we would need that capacity, but I like to be prepared. I rarely use it, preferring our aircraft, public transportation or walking."

"Is this because of the media descending on the school or my parents' house?"

"Principal Darling texted me after he talked to your mother., Television news crews are at the school and in front of the house. We should stay out of sight until we can gauge reaction. Your parents and the boys are home with them now along with the baby. We have four security guards at their site and other special protections. They're safe from even the most predatory reporters or archeologists."

"Thank you," I said. Were we all going to be prisoners?

"Two lawyers who work with me on occasion will be here soon for an early lunch. President O'Connor has been given a copy of the news story and her people are analyzing it for response."

...

Listening to the lawyers argue was instructive. Clearly this was a profession I did not want to enter. The grilled cheese and tomato sandwiches were tasty. As my attention drifted to my recent adventures, I wondered what I would do as a career. My parents now knew about my new world of excitement, multiple Earths.

Was that a career? Guardian of an earth no one knew existed? Would I live to be old, like Uncle His, and outlive my parents and brothers? I found that depressing.

"Do you agree, Darwin?"

"Darwin!"

I jumped. "What?"

"Are you comfortable with this plan?" asked a silver-haired attorney, Matthew something, a distinguished looking man in his fifties wearing a pinstriped suit. Not an outfit I saw much of nor did I want to.

"Sorry. Could you restate the plan?"

"We'll seek to finalize Haldir's and the baby's adoption by your parents," Matthew said in a deep resonant voice that would captivate jurors. "Our understanding is, it's ready thanks to some good work by members of the president's staff and only needs signatures from your parents, the California Department of Social Services and then registration. That guarantees them legal protection and puts your parents in control. We can do that this afternoon."

"Second," said the other attorney, no idea his name, younger, in a dark sports coat, a blue stripped shirt, no tie and three buttons open showing nice cleavage. Maybe in his thirties with a nice smile and other parts certain to connect with jurors. "Your parents are sending a registered letter demanding a retraction, claiming deception, use of their son's name as a minor without their permission, causing harm to him, and threatening suit. The school district will file a formal complaint with the police about the reporter seeking to bribe students to break the law and pull protected files. The principal says he has the names of the students, I think there are three, all of them willing to state what happened. All had complained to Mr. Darling about being threatened by the pushy reporter."

"Quite a plan," I said. "Will the FBI seek a retraction?"

"Not a retraction but other important steps. Perhaps go after Mr. Vardan for breach of his signed FBI statement on the Russian Wilderness case and interfering in an active case, meaning what happened with the school. Also his basic employment contract. It would likely substantiate motivation—the fame, glory and money angle. We'll file for any correspondence with potential publishers or others. This'll lay out the case in follow-up stories that he had a financial reason to lie." The younger guy looked right at me with his blue eyes and earnest expression. Female jurors would love him. "We move on multiple fronts to confuse, scare and discredit. We also think it may compel some newspapers to editorially criticize what the *Mirror* has done."

Uncle His patted my knee. "One of the remaining issues is the role you and Haldir want to play. Do you want to avoid the press, perhaps seeking an injunction from contact, likely filed by your parents? Or maybe you want to speak out, offer a powerful denial in a press release which might also include some of these other steps?"

"I don't want to do any interviews. I'm not that good on my feet."

"You are better than you think," Daruk reassured me.

Haldir listened intently as we talked. His telep receptor was closed, neither reaching out nor accepting calls. He shook his head.

· · ·

The adoption papers got finalized without incident, likely setting a speed record. Reporters trailed after my parents as they left their house and were driven to City Hall by two security guards. Reporters shouted questions, my father told me later, and they ignored them. The Social Services rep was an older woman, white hair and pearls, my mom said, grandma type-casting, likely intentional, and was epic in getting it done, cutting any red tape, pushing every button until it was final. Her name was Constance Hope. Thank you, President O'Connor.

Haldir Darwin McQuaid and Diarmuid Daruk McQuaid today legally became my brothers.

My mother called after it was over and said we had to watch the local news tonight. Then she giggled, refusing to say more.

The school formally filed a complaint with the police about

the reporter attempting to entice three students to break the law. Police agreed to investigate. The school issued a press release on the action, making it likely to be reported in any follow up story.

The FBI filed a breach of contract suit in federal district court in Washington, D.C., on violating both Mr. Vardan's work contract and what he signed in the Russian Wilderness. He'll need a lawyer.

The four of us sat around the television for the 5:30 pm newscast on Channel 4. "What did she do?" Uncle His asked.

"She won't tell me, neither will my dad. I hope it's good."

"Reporter slammed by angry Mom in confrontation at City Hall," read the newscaster as a teaser as the news logo flashed.

"The author of a sensational story in the San Francisco *Mirror* this morning got roasted by the mother of one of boys mentioned in an article which linked them to the murder of ten people in the Russian Wilderness last month and the terrorist shooting at Beckman High School. Mrs. McQuaid of San Francisco is the mother of Darwin McQuaid, a senior at Bechman High who is credited with subduing three of the terrorists, saving countless lives and almost died from the wounds he received in the process. She was finalizing her adoption of a young man and baby found in the Russian Wilderness after adventurers murdered their family. Take a look. This is Mrs. McQuaid, *Mirror* Reporter Veronica Stong, and Constance Hope, a worker in Social Services who was helping with the adoption.

Next scene: The back of a woman's head shouting questions to two women on opposite sides of a counter filling in paperwork.

"Mrs. McQuaid! Mrs. McQuaid! It's been said your new sons are not human, is that true?"

Woman swings around to face her, jaw set, eyes flashing. Gray-haired woman comes around the counter and joins her.

"How dare you! How dare you hurl ridiculous accusations at my children! You should be ashamed! You base your story on the word of a man the FBI has debunked as a liar! You tried to entice children to break the law! Yet you continue to spout this nonsense instead of retracting it!"

Gray-haired woman in pearls, waving her finger:

"You wanted students to commit a crime hoping you might find a story. You didn't give a damn if they got hurt! Shame on you! Shame! I know a police complaint has been filed against you by the principal. You should be put in jail! You dishonor the work of honest reporters and try and hurt children."

We all applauded as we watched. The camera caught the reporter's reaction. She looked shocked, then furious, almost incandescent, as both women crowded around her. Mama Bear and Grandma Bear were not to be trifled with.

"That may help change the narrative in the short run," Uncle His said, watching with us. "Yet the story is still out there and questions remain which are not easily answered. This is a skirmish in a war. We are dealing with a reporter without ethical standards and judging from her expression, may not be rational in how she responds."

Haldir offered no reaction to the news story.

When we congratulated him on now being legally a McQuaid, we all stood, applauded and took turns giving him a hug. He smiled sweetly, looking shy and squeezed me back hard, giggles surfaced softly at first before morphing into full throated glee. Seeing him happy was a treasure.

My parents made a video call with him, my mom holding Diarmuid. My friend was beaming, his lips spread wide in a constant grin.

I started making dinner. It was my turn. Scrambled eggs and toast with jam was about the best I could manage. Daruk set the table.

All our cell phones binged. We had texts.

They were from the lawyers.

Copies of the original *Mirror* story, naming Haldir and the baby as Fae, were showing up in journalists' email boxes around the country.

"Ms. Stong is lashing out with everything she has," Uncle His stated as we read the text. "She will not go down without a fight and is willing to take hostages down with her."

"But she will go down," I added, my teeth grinding. "Nobody is going to hurt Haldir. He's suffered enough!"

31.

s a distraction from all that was going on, Daruk and I
practiced with our Fae medallions. With very little effort, I
could contact the essence of the crow who lived or existed
in my bronze piece of art. That Essence seemed like a good way
to describe it because it was elegant, thick but not huge, created
at some point by a talented Bronze Age artisan and then imbued
with what I'd call magic but perhaps just downloaded with the
crow spirit using that strange appendage in the Fae brain. My
crow referred to himself simply as *Crow*. That simplified things.
After some discussion about what I was—because a previous owner had been a Fae prince and I was far less glamorous,
and so its disappointment was obvious—Crow simply called
me *Human,* squawking in a way that the H was silent. *U-man.* It
was pleased to have some action again and informed me that I
should release it from time to time, if I wanted it to stay cooperative, to let its spirit soar and improve its mood. It gave me
instructions. I went out of the cabin and sat on a rock outcrop
in Buena Vista Park.

I uttered the words he suggested, then whispered *"Soar, Crow!"*

There was a sudden pushback of the medallion into my chest. I heard a loud *"Caw"* overhead and looked up. There was the biggest crow I'd ever seen. Its wings were flapping as it gained altitude. It was letting the world know it was back with rich sub-song, hoarse coos, caws, rattles and clicks. A hundred feet above me, it stretched out its wings. From tip to tip, it might have been four feet, maybe five. It sounded like the crow was connecting to me mentally even while it carried on a loud conversation with the forest through his beak. It startled a dozen other crows in a near-by tree which took off in the opposite direction. Crow flipped around and easily caught up, diving through and around the mur-der, and eventually they followed. Murder—such a strange word to describe a group of birds.

Daruk wandered out and sat next to me on the rocks. He was working on his medallion entity. He had a black cobra, a creature I did not want to meet. "This snake growls," my lover announced. "Now it is shrieking into my head. I don't understand what it is saying."

"I thought snakes hissed."

"Not this one. It is like the sound of a fast-approaching storm, maybe even a train." He held the medallion closer to his face, studying it, perhaps analyzing the noise.

"Yeeaaaa!" Daruk yelled, jumping up, his arms flung overhead, as his new pet materialized from the medallion. It twisted around and lifted up high, making a terrible shriek.

I jumped and moved away. "What the fuck, Daruk!" It must have been ten feet long and thicker than my bicep, black pupils surrounded by gold, a long tongue lashing out.

Daruk stepped down from the rock pile, never intimidated, and cowboy-walked over to the snake, two toughs ready to fight, their heads just inches apart. It sounded like they were both hiss-ing. The standoff went on for over a minute while I held my breath. Then the snake nodded, pulled in its tongue, and wrapped around Daruk's leg. My boyfriend had won.

I jumped but did not shriek as Crow landed on my shoulder, claws pressing tight but the talons held back, protecting my skin, all the while leaning forward, eyeing the snake. It made a sound like: *"Oh pleeeaase!"* But it couldn't have, could it? The snake turned its head and the two mythical creatures stared at each other before disappearing in a flash. Back into the medallions, I assumed. I hoped.

Daruk put his arm over my shoulder, ready to move on, and I returned the favor, an easy ritual. "Might I interest you in some special exercise to keep your heart pumping?"

"I was just thinking the same thing."

• • •

When we emerged from our room, Uncle His was reading a book and Haldir was sitting in an overstuffed chair with a dark brown hairy bundle in his lap. It lifted its head, exposing a yellow throat, and my friend rubbed its ears resulting in a contented cooing sound.

As I reached out to pet him, the creature barred long white fangs and hissed. Haldir grasped and turned its head to him and some message was passed between them. The sable being looked back at me and turned its head, offering its neck. Haldir nodded and I reached down and rubbed the most luxurious fur I'd ever encountered.

"Is this your friend from the medallion?"

"Yes," he said, lifting it up and running his cheek against the side of the animal. "I call him Oberon, the fairy king in Shakespeare's *A Midsummer Night's Dream.*"

"You know about Shakespeare?"

"Some of my medieval relatives were friends with him and inspired the play. It is in our own literature. I chose the name because I like the sound and the talents of this warm, silky creature are amazing. It can be a ferocious, devious fighter and it feels so good."

I knelt down by his chair, the sable coming over and climbing on me, wrapping around my neck, then down into my lap. "You get a divine furball, I got a massive crow and Daruk got a snake as thick as a fire hose. Is there something you aren't telling us?"

"All will serve you well. Each spirit has special talents that will link to you, offering protection. As long as you wear your medallion or have it near, the phantasm will stop any harm coming to you. Oberon has been with me since I was a baby, a gift from my parents, handed down from my great-great grandfather."

"May I ask a difficult question?"

"Anything."

"Why didn't the medallions worn by the Fae in the Russian Wilderness protect them?'

Haldir lowered his eyes and was quiet. Had I upset him? Then he looked back at me, placing a hand on my shoulder. "Ask any questions. I am not a fragile flower. We had never experienced weapons like what they carried. Also, the leader of the group sought to assure us of their peaceful intentions, that they were scientists seeking answers. It did not seem likely they would commit violence. We have lived or had lived in the mountains for centuries without human interaction, forgetting the evil that darkens the hearts of so many. I will not again be so easily fooled."

The sable rubbed against my cheek as I watched my brother. He smiled. "Your heart is pure, the same with Daruk and Katnu. Your parents and brothers are also exceptional, as are Miguel and Luther. Beyond that, I will always be cautious."

32.

The *Mirror* carried the story the next day with a disclaimer in the first paragraph, pretending they were printing this as a public service even as they investigated the veracity of the claims. I guess they figured they could have it both ways.

Haldir got a call from a friend on the basketball team who told him his teammates were calling, emailing and writing the paper to complain about sensationalist, inaccurate journalism. They were also recruiting friends and parents. The school's Booster Club, thrilled to finally have its first championship in any sport ever, were also involved. Some were businessmen and women who threatened to stop advertising or to never start. The group, or maybe team members, started sending in sham letters supporting the story, identifying as the Society of Fae, the Tinkerbell Association and the Elvis Club. Haldir had no idea who Elvis was. We played *Hound Dog* as a sample of Elvis Presley's talent, and he fled the room.

Other publications were quiet. One local television news program carried excerpts from the *Mirror*, attributing the content to them as if that might absolve them of any obligation to verify, using shocking quotes as teasers followed by "Could this be true? Details at six." Sometimes television had no shame. But they also carried stories about my parents' complaint and threatened lawsuit, the police investigation of students being recruited to break the law and the FBI breach of contract lawsuits. I was hoping people would read more into it than the titillating headlines. There were no more reporters in front of our home which was a relief. Darling phoned my parents to say reporters had left the front of the school. The FBI had still not explained what happened at the school invasion but it was hopefully slipping into the category of old news. Reports of another flying saucer sighting seemed of greater interest. How many times could Uncle His pull this off?

Miguel texted that students had seen some stories but mostly didn't care, with a few mutual friends asking him how they were doing. Principal Darling suggested we stay home for a few more days to let interest cool. He also announced that all the lights in the school had been changed to allow Haldir to comfortably be in any classroom, study hall, gym, bathroom, hallway, storage closets, and outside lights should he be there in the evening or when skies go dark early during daylight savings time, without any harm or discomfort to his eyes. Haldir said he would gladly retire his designer dark glasses. Of course that meant his exceptionally large eyes could be seen by anyone.

"If I go back to school without my glasses, I would like to also not hide my ears." Haldir made the statement at dinner the first night we all got back together. He had started loosening his hair when home, letting his elfin ears stick out. Rubbing an ear with one hand as he finished his meal, he said, "I am not ashamed of who I am or what I am."

"Nor should you be," Mom said.

"My ears and scalp get sore having my hair pulled so tight. The carved bone barrette I have from my mountain home is perhaps too effective. It feels like hiding my ears is punishment."

"You're a spectacular young man," my dad told him. "I wish I had ears as small and perfect as yours. My father used to tease me that mine came from an elephant." We all laughed.

"I read that ears are like fingerprints," I added, "unique in shape and position on each person." I wanted to encourage him to be himself even if there were risks. "Ears come in all shapes—square, pointed, narrow or sticking out. So your ears aren't that unusual. If you want to wear your hair down, do it. Be proud of who you are, a unique man. A beautiful man."

My brothers applauded. My parents grinned.

Haldir smiled in his boyish way. "Thank you. You are all very kind, much like the people that birthed and raised me. I have been surprised that the basic goodness of this family, and Daruk, and Katnu and Miguel, are not universal traits. So many, when I watch your newscasts, are frightened by differences that are part of human variation. Many seem obsessed with skin color, the shape of eyes, length and style of hair, sexuality, even religions. Perhaps many would be frightened by me. Does that mean I am a freak? Someone to fear or hate? It seems to me that someone's honesty, willingness to help others, generosity of spirit are far more important."

We sat, staring at him. This fourteen-year-old knew what really made for a better world. "Beautifully said," Mom responded. "Spot on. We're so proud to have you part of our family."

My dad called Mr. Darling on Wednesday and let him know Haldir and I were returning to school Monday and mentioned no dark glasses and his hair loose, so be prepared. The principal said he'd notify staff at the regular Friday meeting. He didn't foresee any serious problems. "Haldir is popular and Darwin, well, everyone's pretty much in awe." Nice to hear. In less than a year I'd gone from being an easy target for bullies to someone they didn't want to mess with. After just a few months, Haldir was now a hero and not a freak. Yet, so many issues were still out there.

• • •

The five of us wandering the pathways through Buena Vista Park each Saturday morning and then into the Haight for lattes or ice cream had become a fun routine.

Miguel, Luther and Daruk sometimes ganged up on me, tickling until I yelled, "Uncle!"

Daruk whispered in my ear. "You know they are following us, right?"

"You mean Vardan and Veronica, the reporter? Yeah."

"What?" Miguel said in too loud a voice and looked behind us.

I grabbed him and jumped on his back. While he squirmed and twisted to buck me off, I whispered: "Ignore them. Pretend they aren't there. Let's see what they're up to."

As we walked down the back side of the park, I remembered five bullies chasing me up the hill when Daruk stepped between us.

"This is where we met," he teleped me. I put my arm around his waist, and he did likewise with me.

Haldir started practicing his bird calls, drawing the squawking appreciation of the wild parrots that lived in the urban forest. A dozen of the cherry headed conures landed in a small tree in front of us, squawking, screeching, looking at our friend. Haldir signaled us to stay back and he moved forward. He made some odd sounds, and five birds flew to him, landing on his outstretched arms. He talked and they responded or at least that's what it seemed like.

"Can you understand them?" Miguel asked.

"Most of it," Haldir replied as one bird stepped to his shoulder and rubbed the back of his head against Haldir's neck. "They can also mostly understand me." More squawks. "Yes, they want blueberries from the fruit stand on Haight Street." He giggled, a boy having fun, walking ahead of us as we exited the park and down the street. People stared and took photos as this bird man strolled two blocks to the market, birds on him and circling above.

As he reached the store he uttered a squawking sound and the birds flew off him and into the fire escapes above. He bought several baskets of blueberries and strawberries, the birds above suddenly quiet, watching his every move. We accompanied him to a vacant lot covered in grass. He dropped down cross-legged, scattered the fruit around him, bird-talked and was surrounded by the conures. He was laughing and we took photos.

One bird stopped eating and shrieked, glaring at a row of trees behind him.

Haldir turned and slowly pulled out his knife. "There is a hawk that preys on this *pandemonium*. That is what you can call a group like this. I like the term. They are noisy, chaotic and manic." Facing the tree, he stared at the hawk, pointed the knife and whispered something we couldn't hear, a mantra, then louder. *"Thosaigh!"* I thought he said. Begone. The branch the raptor was on erupted in flame and the bird flew away at hyper speed much to the squawking delight of the parrots. "He knows I am their protector and will not likely be back."

Haldir said his goodbyes to the pandemonium as we returned to the main street.

"Lattes!" Daruk yelled and we headed to a nearby coffee shop. I thought I saw our two stalkers walk past us across the street, their heads turned as if they were looking at merchandise. We went into Grinder, an odd and yet not odd name for a coffee house. Daruk ordered lattes for us all.

Three police cars raced past us, sirens blaring, as we exited and walked up the street toward Ashbury. I loved the hippie history of this neighborhood, the smell of marijuana always thick in the air even when it was illegal, the old Victorian buildings colorful and proud. Two blocks ahead, a half dozen cop cars, a fire engine and two ambulances blocked the street. A police officer was waving traffic down a side street. It looked like it was an incident at a bank.

A gunshot. Then several from inside the business. A child screamed, "Mommy!"

A black uniformed police sergeant yelled into a bullhorn, "You're surrounded. Let everyone inside go, then come out with your hands up!" He was a handsome man, early thirties, impressive build and a tough guy stance.

"We start shooting hostages, until you move away." The male voice sounded stressed and a bit slurred.

Haldir closed his eyes. "A woman is bleeding out," he stated loudly. "Two of the men are high, maybe fentanyl. We must save her. I sense five gunmen."

"Get back. boy!" the sergeant commanded with a gesture at us, directing police in different directions and talking into his headset.

"There is no time!" Haldir announced, his forehead scrunched and his lips tight. "She only has minutes to live." Haldir stepped forward, lifted his knife, whispered something, spread his arms dramatically and two police cruisers blocking our way were pulled aside like bumper cars in a kiddie playground. He swaggered toward the bank as police looked on, jaws open *"What the fuck!"* somebody shouted.

We followed—ignoring police shouting "Get back!" The three of us moving toward the bank, like Gary Cooper in the fabulous old western, *High Noon,* with two deputies backing him up, or better, Dwane Johnson—the Rock—his teenage sons, if he had kids, marching in step, eyes forward into battle.

Haldir flicked the knife blade and the glass front of the building shattered, covering the sidewalk in thousands of pieces of glass shining like diamonds in the sunlight. We continued our march.

A man inside screamed, "GO BACK!" holding an automatic rifle to an old man's head. He lowered his weapon and fired at us. Haldir waved his knife and the bullets exploded in harmless puffs.

Haldir teleped *"I must get to the woman or she will die. Please eliminate the criminals."*

"*Soar, Crow!*" I whispered and the world's largest Corvus bolted from my chest, like a black rocket from hell straight to the man. The gunman screamed, the rifle falling aside as the bird ripped his face, lacerating an eye. He collapsed, covering his head, crying, yelling for help.

"*Run!*" I yelled at the prisoner.

Crow looked at me, the gunman's nose in his beak. I nodded. With a triumphant *caw* he flew back, disappearing in a black swirling cloud as he hit my chest, *"Fun"* the last thought he sent to me.

The police were in shock, just the flashing lights. A few more, *"What the fucks?"* from myriad throats.

Haldir ran to the woman and the crying little girl, kneeling beside them. He touched the girl's forehead and she calmed. "I will heal your mother," he promised. He ripped open the woman's blouse and placed his knife over the wound in her gut, chanting, as the bleeding slowed. We could hear his thoughts. He concentrated on extracting the bullet, sanitizing the wound, healing ripped flesh deep in her gut.

Two more gunmen were visible. One behind the counter held a pistol leveled on a half dozen bank employees. One hostage I recognized from school, a senior named Bravill who I knew had a part time weekend job. I had no idea it was here.

"Darwin?" he cried out, looking stunned.

"Him!" I heard Daruk order pointing to the criminal. The giant cobra flew from my lover's chest, black swirling dust, and materialized around the neck of the gunman. The guy screamed, dropping his gun, trying to pull off the giant black snake. "Run!" Daruk ordered. And they did, yelling, tripping, crying all the way to safety. Bravill stopped and touched my shoulder, *"Thanks, man!"* and ran after the others. The snake tightened around the man's neck. Within a minute he was unconscious and it flew back to Daruk, dissolving in the air, a black cloud.

A third man stepped out of a back office, a satchel over his shoulder, rifle pointed forward, his mask askew, looking a bit deranged.

I pointed my arm in his direction, *"Fire!"* and he exploded in flames, dropping to the floor, rolling around to put out the inferno. I was getting better at this.

Another man emerged from the giant safe in the back, so big it looked like a stage prop. He was balding, wearing a Covid mask, opening his jacket to show a bomb.

"Surrender!" I yelled as Daruk stepped in front of me. He wanted this one.

"Any closer I'll set off the bomb!" Seemed a strange threat given the bomb was attached to him.

Daruk closed his eyes. I knew what he was going to do. He waved an arm. With surprising speed, the metal door swung closed, knocking the man back inside. There was an explosion inside the vault.

I turned to Daruk and we embraced as several police and an ambulance crew raced inside.

"Medics, two women, stooped beside Haldir with their equipment. As he stood, holding the child, he hollered, *"All clear!"* Where did he learn that phrase? My brothers and television.

The lead cop came up to him and Haldir handed over the child who put its arms around the policeman's neck.

We started back outside. Half a dozen television cameras and numerous phones were aimed at us.

"Smile guys," Daruk said. Haldir was in the middle, we put our arms around him and grinned, stepping back into the street.

"Are you nuts?" another cop shouted as he ran up to us. "You interfered with a police operation!" He had captain's bars on his dark blue shirt collar. "You and all the hostages could have been killed!"

"Nobody died except the guy in the vault," I responded feeling a bit indignant. "All the hostages are safe. If we hadn't stepped in, the woman would have bled to death. Ask the medics. I suspect she and her family are pleased. You're welcome."

"I need your names."

Miguel and Luther slammed into us.

. . .

Students came up to Haldir as soon as we entered school on Monday. "So good to see you again," was the mantra. "State champs!" others said, hoping it would happen if the independent schools organized throughout California, uniting the separate districts.

There was no way they hadn't seen the story, all over the front page of the two local newspapers, lead report on all the newscasts, radio and television. Three girls and a couple of guys gave him a hug. Others stood back, watching him, watching me. Miguel stayed close to me, letting people focus on Haldir. He was the real hero.

His hair hung to his shoulders, his ears stuck out. A couple of students looked at him in visible curiosity but no one said anything. For the first time, I looked closely at other student's ears. Big, small, pointy, but not as much as his. No designer dark glasses. His big green eyes were fully visible, no longer hidden. I thought he was beautiful.

Throughout the day, I kept thinking about last night at the police station. We'd been kept for hours. Through teleping we decided to be vague in any statements. Media, police, hostages and anyone else saw what they saw. We didn't have to explain it. We'd saved lives in our very unconventional intervention.

We were separated and different police officers interrogated us, unaware that we could share what one was told to all of us. They were frustrated.

Police body cam footage was shown to us. "What do you see happening?"

"A bad guy getting justice, hostages being freed," was our common refrain.

"And what was this thing that came out of your chest?"

"What thing?"

"The crow, the giant snake!"

"Is that what you see in the video?"

The policeman looked exasperated.

"Look," I said finally, "we knew we could save lives faster than you could. No disrespect. The mother's blood was seeping out and her life fading in front of her child. So we did what we did. She's alive. The little girl has her mama. Hostages are alive. The ambulance crew confirms what Haldir did to save the mother. Be pleased. Results matter."

Some police were resentful that we interrupted their operation, but most were curious, some awed, some complimentary. My parents, my brothers, Miguel and his dad, Uncle His, all joined us at the station. Lots of hugs and tears. My mother was particularly adamant that they end the interrogation.

A young Asian woman officer introduced herself as the hour got late and we assumed we were about done. "I'm Connie Chong, the police department spokesperson. A large contingent of media are in the pressroom anxious to talk to you if you're agreeable. I know you didn't divulge much. I'm sure you had your reasons. Police are frustrated. But I think you're all superheroes."

"Boys," my mother said to us in response to her, "If you stonewalled police on what you did and how you did it, that was in private and followed a set of written procedures. Reporters have no such rules. If you stonewall them, they may write that you're hiding something, maybe something shameful. And it will be very public. So be aware."

"Thank you, Mrs. McQuaid. I believe honesty is important." Haldir wiped his hands over his face as he reflected. "There are risks to speaking and risks to silence. I am not ashamed of who and what I am nor what we did to save lives." He looked at the door leading into the press room and at our faces. "Let's do it," he said in a soft voice.

"Okay," I responded. He should be proud of who and what he is. Just like the LGBTQ+ family.

Daruk nodded in agreement. "Brothers stick together."

With Haldir grinning, we walked into the media room, shoulder to shoulder, our new friend in the middle with what sounded like a Fae battle song teleping through our heads.

A podium was set up, a dozen or more television cameras, photographers, reporters. Questions came immediately, a cacophony, impossible to make sense in the jumble of words.

"Are you Fae?" a woman's voice sliced through the air. It was her.

Haldir placed his hands on either side of the podium. We stood tight on each side of him while he remained silent, waiting for the noise to stop. A few reporters started calling for quiet. Finally, he nodded and smiled.

"Thank you. My name is Haldir. Haldir McQuaid. These are my friends and brothers, Darwin and Daruk." We both did a Queen Elizabeth hand wave at all the rapt faces staring at us in the room.

"To answer the last question: Yes. *I am Fae.*"

ACKNOWLEDGEMENTS

Special thanks to my longtime editor and friend, always an inspiration, Katherine V. Forrest, author of the acclaimed Kate Delafield mystery series.

Appreciation to my husband Greg, always offering an honest view and encouragement. Writers need that.

And to my readers. I am grateful.

FEEDBACK

Thank you for reading Passageway 2. You can find my upcoming works by following me on Amazon.

If you liked this novel or any of my books, please consider leaving a review on Amazon, Goodreads or any other book platform. How about posting your thoughts on social media? Independent authors need and appreciate your support.

Thanks.

I can be reached through my web site:

www.stevenacoulter.com

Please consider subscribing to my newsletter at my website.

About the Author

Steve writes (mostly) science fiction with lots of action, nasty bad guys and reluctant heroes (sometimes) exploring issues of consequence but (always) with a touch of romance.

His work is enriched by his varied careers—soldier, teacher, journalist, state legislator and library commissioner. He has a BA and MA in Journalism and was a Lambda Literary Fellow in 2008 and 2013, later spending two years on the Board. He lives in San Francisco with his husband, Greg. They favor bittersweet chocolate.

Other Books By This Author:

CHRONICLES OF SPARTAK: RISING SON
Science Fiction/LGBTQ Fiction/Romance

Weaves sci-fi, fantasy, and a hunky hero in a future eerily extrapolated from today's political reality.

The ruling elite see Spartak as a trophy; the people see him as their best hope. By the year 2115, twelve families control all wealth in America, the middle class is myth, democracy a con game and the Supreme Court has just legalized a new entertainment option for the bored elite. Spartak Jones is kidnapped and forced to become the first legal slave since the civil war, a souvenir birthday present for the eldest son of the richest family. Handsome, seductive and athletic, he is not shy about using his talents to survive and protect those he loves.

When a war erupts within the ruling class, he proves to be a lethal warrior, fearless, resourceful and photogenic. His swashbuckling exploits awaken a long dormant liberal underground hungry to restore democracy. In a world both familiar and horribly twisted, Spartak becomes a symbol of hope, a flesh and blood icon for an America that used to be and might be again, if he can survive.

REVIEWS

"Brilliantly written…creating superheroes of substance!" **Grady Harp, Amazon, Top 100 Reviewer**

"If you love The Hunger Games, and you want a bit more of a gritty and adult feel, you may love Rising Son." **Queer SciFi.**

"A multitalented, bisexual, teenage slave becomes a symbol of freedom in this debut sci-fi saga… with energetic action scenes and sharply drawn characters, and the result is a vigorous tale." **Kirkus Reviews**

"Straight up Ayn Rand stuff…Holy Shit!…So shockingly different from the literary icon for searching youth…Holden Caulfield of Catcher in the Rye." **Jack Saunders, author of Baseball Comes Out: A Revolutionary Novel**

"Highly imaginative and creative, action packed, with a fascinating young protagonist who combines the physical and moral attributes of both Spiderman and Superman in his remarkable body and psyche." **Katherine V. Forrest, author of the Kate Delafield mystery series**

"The treacherous world of 22nd century San Francisco as imagined by Steve Coulter would be a challenge to anyone but to 16-year-old Spartak Jones it becomes the stone on which he hones his athletic skills and his bravery. Coulter's writing can make us feel both at home and uneasy at the same time as he skillfully reveals a future we must fight against at all costs." **Jewelle Gomez, author of The Gilda Stories**

"Totally absorbing. I stopped everything else and read the book to completion in one setting." **Amos Lassen, blogger**

THE CHRONICLES OF SPARTAK: FREEDOM'S HOPE (BOOK 2)

Science Fiction/LGBTQ Fiction/Romance

Fighting to restore the America of legend, Spartak Jones becomes one.

By 2116, the war between the ruling elites is now full frontal and the seventeen-year-old has become its celebrity warrior and icon for an America that used to be.

Is he a pawn or hero? How much evil is acceptable if you believe your cause is just? Love may be his greatest weapon.

From the Space Elevator, 22,000 miles above the earth, Spartak and Zinc McClain launch an audacious scheme to thwart a religious war and a military coup.

Fast-paced, disturbing, heretical, uplifting, and ultimately romantic, the novel weaves science fiction, fantasy, politics and a strapping hero telling his own story.

COPPERHEAD

Action Adventure/LGBTQ Fiction/Romance

Student. Singer. Lover. *Spy.*

When his family is torn apart, a college freshman uses his charm and looks to infiltrate the world of the rich and powerful, risking his life for a greater cause.

Abel Torres knew hardship growing up but with his high-octane singing voice the young man dreams of a bright future with a scholarship to San Francisco State.

A mentor at the university, knowing his desperation, makes an unusual introduction and soon the handsome 19-year-old is performing at a swank party, charming California's political and social elites. The wealthy host offers to connect him to rich gay men who would pay handsomely for his attention. Battling his conscience and pride, he accepts the offer. Complicating his life, he begins dating a sassy waiter who just might be the love he is seeking. The FBI approaches him after he begins seeing a gay

Congressman, asking him to work undercover to help bring down a terrorist plot on U.S. soil.

As Abel faces even greater dangers, can he juggle his various identities as a student, singer, lover and spy? Or will he lose everyone he loves if they discover just how far he's gone to save them?

REVIEWS

"We all need heroes to personify our dreams and inspire our lives. Abel Torres, son of a Black mother and an illegal immigrant father, is just such a hero. In confronting the challenges and mores and judgments of American culture, and his many personal crises of conscience, he reaches for the ultimate American dream, emerging as a hero to us and best of all, to himself. Courage, conscience, honor, patriotism, not to mention an Andrea Bocelli-like singing voice, it all comes together in this highly entertaining and uplifting story. Bravo!" **Katherine V. Forrest, author of the Kate Delafield mystery series**

"Abel Torres, Copperhead, takes us on a journey as he goes from being a young gay man with a magnificent voice to an American hero. I wish it had a Soundtrack. This is Steve Coulter's third book set in the SF Bay Area, which makes it a fun read for a native San Franciscan…" **Amazon reader**

"This is a great read, hard to put down, keeping me up late. Lots of action and adventure and of course, a bit of romance making for a very entertaining escape. Copperhead, or actually Abel Torres, is a compassionate and outstanding singer…and sexy to say the least…" **Amazon reader**

"Action-packed, sensational, and expertly told narrative… brings top-level entertainment…Fans of LGBTQ action will love this large, well-woven plot that includes passionate love and sex, espionage, the FBI, terrorism, music, the media, and politics." **Foluso Falaye, San Francisco Book Review**

COPPERHEAD 2
Action Adventure/LGBTQ Fiction/Romance

Hero. Heartthrob. Hustler. **Prey.**

Abel Torres is now one of the most famous young men in America, a national hero, a sophomore at San Francisco State on the edge of superstardom. At the same time, white supremacists seethe over his role in the death of their fellow conspirators, ruining dreams of a civil war.

As he prepares for the opening of *Les Miz,* a reporter quotes anonymous sources claiming he worked as a prostitute with dozens of wealthy men, not just the infamous congressman. Has he been betrayed? This could ruin his image and tank his career. His family would be disgraced. Prince Ali could be implicated, his uncle powerful and ruthless. Could Dirksen be arrested?

The pressure and rising violence begins to unravel the mental health of his boyfriend, Zachary. Abel signs a major record contract just as militia groups close in.

As always, his voice soars.

PASSAGEWAY
Science Fiction/Young Adult/LBGTQ+ Fiction

Chosen by mystical warriors to protect a parallel Earth from a catastrophic future, a young man must push his mental and physical abilities to the limits if he is to help save mankind.

As seventeen-year-old Darwin McQuaid flees from high-school bullies, the teen is taken aback when he is saved by an enigmatic stranger; an indigenous teenage warrior who was born 500 years in the past.

Strong and powerful, Daruk possesses an intelligence that exceeds his rugged youthful appearance, and Darwin is drawn to learn more about the magnetic young man. And, surprisingly, the high-school student learns that the mysterious warrior has a connection to an old family friend—an elderly indigenous shaman called Uncle His.

As the attraction intensifies between Darwin and Daruk, the warrior reveals a secret known only to a few—that he and Uncle His are Guardians of the Passageway and they are destined to protect the crossroads of three parallel universes, three Earths, each 500 years apart. And now Darwin, with his own planet past the point of saving, must join them in their mission to protect another version of Earth from the same tragic fate.

Discovering worlds he never knew existed, along with an untapped power within himself, can the highschooler become the warrior needed to defend this ancient world from corrupt invaders? Or will the death and danger of a more primitive time prove to be too much for this 21st century teen?